AF612165

Italicae Historiae Collection

Petra Rubea

Stezzano-BG-IT
www.wlmedizioni.com
wlmedizioni@tiscali.it
info@wlmedizioni.com

First edition: March 2015
Second edition: November 2020
ISBN 9788897382492
Second edition eBook ePub: February 2021

First edition English Version: March 2023
ISBN 9788835450542 Book
ISBN 9788835450535 e-Book
Translation by Dena Marzullo

Cover: photographic layout by Pio Bianchini, private collection
Cover graphic: agatti.com

The events narrated in this novel, while referring to historic documentation, are for the most part a product of the imagination of the author. The places and names of some of the characters that actually existed have been recreated with the utmost care possible and adapted, when necessary, in order to better the story.

PREFACE

Availing oneself to books that narrate the events which, in late Medieval times, have established the history of the ancient region of Montefeltro and drawn inspiration from the works of various writers from the past, such as Orazio Olivieri, Antonio Maria Zucchi Travagli, Giambattista Marini, Luigi Tonini, up to the more recent works of Francesco Vittorio Lombardi and others, including those composed and published by this writer, the author has undertaken the endeavor of writing this engaging and readable "novel", which for the most part was reconstructed with imaginative fragments of local history based on real events, whose intention is to breathe life into the collective imagination some of the aspects of daily life which, at the turn of the 13th century, have accompanied/conditioned the people who lived in that part of the Feretrano territory, including the area between the left slope of the Foglia River and the river basin of the Marecchia.

It is true, the story has been freely adapted and dramatized from historical events, that is to say romanticized and, therefore, free from all limits of documentary or bibliographical quotes, but the constant and frequent reference to tangible facts and to real people, allows our kind reader to become immersed, as if under a spell, in that particular epochal dimension which, with the difficulties and atrocities of every kind, have characterized this thematic ambit of feudal particularism.

Pio Bianchini, a serious and convincing writer, is already the author of another compelling novel, "La leggenda di Cá Battaglia". *Gifted with an indisputable and innate literary command, he has brought to life two amazing works which, rich in detail, at times moving and in other cases exhilarating, delivers with astonishing and clear truth, some of the implications of the tormented existence of those populations who lived in that era, and who struggled for the most part from deprivation and tyranny, in a distant and nearly forgotten epoch, in an area of that mythical Feretrano territory with a wealth of history and of ferocious vicissitudes among bordering and dominating rival families and, consequently, also fascinating and realistic legends like the account in his previous work, as well as this intriguing and praiseworthy second volume.*

Mercatino Conca, 10 August 2014
Luciano Alberelli

BIBLIOGRAPHY AND SOURCES

1. **Alberelli L.** *Castelli scomparsi nella Valconca del Montefeltro,* Rimini 2008.

2. **Alberelli L.** *Memorie sull'antico castello di Monte Grimano e sue pertinenze, written by Francesco Massajoli in the 19th century,* trascr. by L. Alberelli, Rimini 1996.

3. **Alberelli L.** *Mercatino Conca, note di storia locale,* Rimini 1991.

4. **Alberelli L.** *Origini e memorie della famiglia Sensoli di Mercatino Conca e dei suoi diretti discendenti Bianchini Massoni, Ricci and Bianchini,* Rimini 2013.

5. **Brigliadori E. – Pasquini A.** *Religiosità in Valconca, vicende e figure,* Cinisello Balsamo 2000.

6. **Cecini N.** *Appunti sulla cultura locale dal XIII al XX secolo,* in "Il Montefeltro",vol. I (Ambiente, storia, arte nelle valli del Foglia e del Conca - *Environment, history, art in the valleys of the Foglia and of the Conca*) a c. by G. Allegretti and F. V. Lombardi, Villa Verucchio 1995.

7. **Curradi C.** *Pievi del territorio riminese nei documenti fino al Mille,* Rimini 1984.

8. **Delfico M.** *Memorie storiche della Repubblica di S. Marino,* IV edition, 3 parts in one volume, Naples 1865.

9. **Fasoli G.** *Castelli e vie di comunicazione,* in "Natura e cultura della Valle del Conca", a c. by P. Meldini, P. G. Pasini and S. Pivato, Rimini 1982.

10. **Franceschini G.** *I Malatesta,* Varese 1973.

11. **Franceschini G.** *I Montefeltro,* Varese 1970.

12. **Lombardi F.V.** *Dal castello di Conca al municipio romano, Forum Julii Concubiensium,* Rimini 2014.

13. **Lombardi F. V.** *Gli idronimi desinenti –a dall'Agro Gallico alla Pentapoli: preesistenze, persistenze, desistenze,* in "Studia Pi-

cena", 2013.

14. **Lombardi F. V.** *Il millenario castello di Pietrarubbia ed i suoi conti,* in W. Monacchi, "S. Silvestro di Pietrarubbia", Pesaro 1991.

15. **Lombardi F.V.** *Mille anni di medioevo,* in "Il Montefeltro", vol II, (Ambiente, storia, arte nell'alta Valmarecchia - Environment, history, art in the higher Valmarecchia), a c. di G. Allegretti e F.V. Lombardi. Villa Verucchio 1999.

16. **Lombardi F.V.** *Territorio e istituzioni in età medievale,* in "Il Montefeltro", vol. I (Ambiente, storia, arte nelle alte valli del Foglia e del Conca - *Environment, history, art in the valleys of the Foglia and of the Conca*), a c. by G. Allegretti and F.V. Lombardi, Villa Verucchio 1995.

17. **Lombardi F. V. – Monacchi W.** *Il castello di Monteboaggine nel Montefeltro,* Urbania 2001.

18. **Marini G. B.** *Saggio di ragioni della città di San Leo detta già Monteferetro,* Pesaro 1758.

19. **Olivieri O.** *Monimenta feretrana ab exordio religionis christianae usque ad annum MDCXLIV,* (1644), ed. critica e trad. a c. by I Pascucci, San Leo 1981.

20. **Pari S.** *La signoria di Malatesta da Verucchio,* in "Centro Studi Malatestiani", Storia delle signorie dei Malatesti, I, Rimini 1998.

21. **Tonini L.** *Della storia civile e sacra riminese,* 6 parts in 9 volumes, Rimini 1848-1888, t. III (Rimini in the 13th century), 1862.

22. **Zucchi Travagli A.M.** *Animadversioni sull'Apologetico feretrano e sul Saggio di ragioni per la città di S. Leo dell'arciprete Giambattista Marini,* Urbino 1763.

CHARACTERS

PIETRARUBBIA
(ancient name Petra Rubea)

Family of the Counts of Pietrarubbia
Corrado, Count of Pietrarubbia
Costanza, wife of Corrado
Taddeo, Count of Pietrarubbia
Agnesina, wife of Taddeo
Giovanna (also known as Giovannina), sister of the Counts
Filippuccio (also known as the Bastard), half-brother to the Counts
Roberto, son of Corrado

Gostolo family
Gostolo, head of the family
Carola, wife of Gostolo
Agnolo, first-born son of Gostolo
Maffiolo, first-born son of Agnolo
Gabriolo, second-born son of Agnolo
Gostolo (also known as Gostolino) third-born son of Agnolo

Gasparini family
Bastiano, younger brother of Gasparino and older brother of Zanino
Mafalda, wife of Bastiano
Martino, first-born son of Bastiano and Mafalda
Zanino, younger brother of Gasparino and Bastiano

Other characters

Fraudolente, *famiglio* of the Counts

Alvisio, archer and *famiglio* of the Counts

Tosco, executioner and right-hand man of Pietrarubbia

Anselmo, servant

Domino Baldassarre, presbyter of Pietrarubbia

MOUNT SAN LORENZO and COMBARBIO

Bonzio family

Marino of the Faggiola, father of Bonzio

Bonzio, head of the family, vassal to the Counts of Pietrarubbia

Maddalena, wife of Bonzio

Rosa, first-born daughter

Maria, second-born daughter

Ada, third-born daughter

Isotta, fourth-born daughter

Bruna, fifth-born daughter

Bertino delle Ville of Combarbio

Donato, father of Bertino

Bertino, head of the family

Lucia, daughter, servant at San Lorenzo

Mina, daughter and wife of Brizio of Sant' Arduino

Other characters

Gasparino, *famiglio* of Bonzio

Domino Santi, senior presbyter of Combarbio

Domino Ubertino, second presbyter of Combarbio

Giacinto, cleric of Combarbio

Dionigi, child of the Pieve of Combarbio

PIEGA

Family degli Olivieri of Piega
Bartolino degli Olivieri, head of the family, Lord of Piega
Geltrude, wife of Bartolino
Oliviero, first-born son
Antonio, second-born son
Agnese, sister to Geltrude and mother of Tignaccio
Tignaccio, son of Agnese

Other characters
Domino Maliocco, presbyter of Piega
Lapo, right-hand man to degli Olivieri
Tessa, midwife

SECCHIANO

Galasso da Secchiano family
Galasso, head of the family, Count of Secchiano and chief magistrate of Cesena
Guidobono, first-born son of Galasso
Bonconte, second-born son
Cavalca, younger son

Uguccioni family
Uguccioni, head of the family
Alina, wife of Uguccioni
Magnino, first-born son
Cecco, son
Renzo, son
Carlino, son, shepherd

Other characters
Domino Giovanni, presbyter of Secchiano

Paolino, right-hand man of Galasso
Gano, cleric of the parish church of Secchiano
Petro, notary

CESENA AND MONTESCUDO

Malatesta da Verucchio, Lord of Rimini
Gaboardo Gaboardi da Macerata Feltria, ally to Malatesta da Verucchio

OTHER CHARACTERS

Raniero, blacksmith
Albina, wife of Raniero
Domino Gaddo, presbyter of Sant'Arduino
Brizio of Sant'Arduino, husband of Mina of Combarbio

To my father

PIO BIANCHINI

PETRA RUBEA

Forlì

Cesena

Rimini

Secchiano

Piega

Montescudo

Pietrarubbia

Macerata Feltria

Urbino

Some places disputed in the thirteenth century between the noble families of Montefeltro and Malatesti, who will see in the following centuries consolidate their domains with each other with the Duchy of Urbino and the other with the Lordship of Rimini

Character's itineraries of the novel

THE MONTEFELTROS

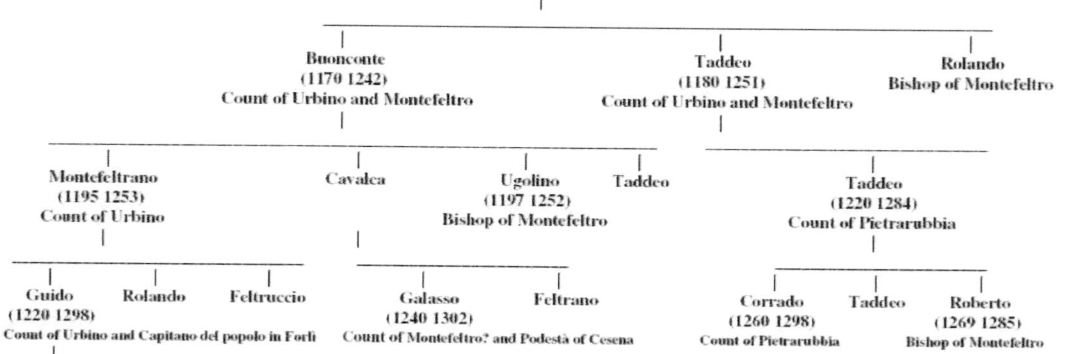

Montefeltro: ancient name of a diocese between the Marches, Romagna and Umbria.
Count's titles listed above do not always correspond to an official investiture, but often to a de facto position.
The first investiture as Counts of Urbino was by the Emperor Frederick II of Swabia for merits on the battlefield.

The Pietrarubbias

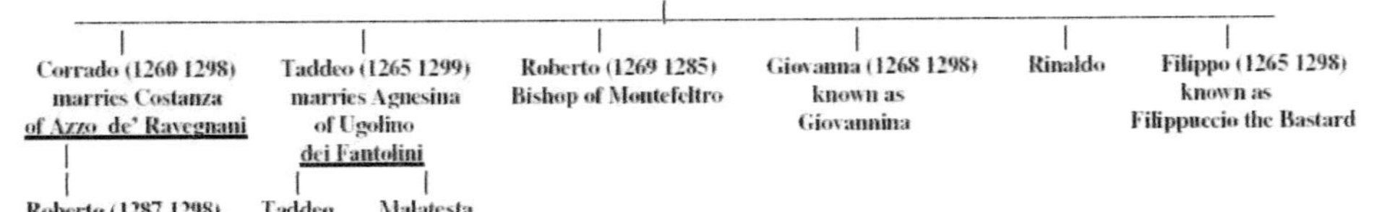

Princeps probitas iusti

THE MIDDLE AGES

Long ago, there was a castle that dominated a valley. Situated on the summit of Mount San Lorenzo along the right riverbank of the Conca torrent, it faced the Montegrimano village near the border separating the Romagna and Marches regions. On the trail leading to the river's mouth, there was a place of worship whose legend recounts an ancient parish church.

At the turn of the 13th century, the old castle was held together by a vassal of the Counts of Pietrarubbia, a minor branch of the Montefeltro family.

The human life span in that era was brief and very difficult, particularly for those who did not have the good fortune to be born into nobility and wealth. The poor had nothing to eat, and were bound to a house and a piece of land that did not belong to them, forced to share the fruits of their labor with their rulers. Disease, starvation, war, poor hygiene, hunger, cold, obscure medical care and ignorance generated an incredible number of victims. Infant mortality was common and many women died during childbirth.

Nobility and clergy, often times corrupt, lived a different reality, enjoying the comforts and luxury that were denied the servants. Well nourished, the wealthy did not work, and were often stronger and taller in stature, well-groomed and happy, living a longer life compared to those who suffered starvation and were brutalized by generations of fatigue working the fields.

As we know, the Middle Ages were a barbaric and dark period of history, however those who lived or survived that period experienced the same sentiments and emotions of today's human race: love and hate; joy and sufferance; laughter and tears.

FRAUDOLENTE

In Sant'Angelo in Vado, just before sunrise on 20 July 1262, a swaddled infant was abandoned on the porch in front of St. Michael's church. Pitch black, he was a beautiful baby who, desperate from hunger, was found screaming at the top of his lungs. Needing a nursemaid, he was given to a girl who had recently delivered a son who tragically died shortly after birth. So she passed down this unusual name to the infant: Fraudolente.

Raised by the clergy, the boy lived his childhood within the old rectory. He was lively, healthy, intelligent and astute. The old parish priest, a small man with strong inner strength, was a true presbyter, virtuous and seriously consecrated to chastity. He loved Fraudolente like a son.

The unfavorable episode that upset the life of the boy happened at the beginning of the summer of 1274.

On the occasion of religious ceremonies, Martina used to drag herself around the churchyard, limping with difficulty, to ask for a handout.

The girl was an unfortunate orphan, homeless and without family, born with a slight hunchback and one leg shorter than the other. Small and sickly with a violent cough, she would shake her disheveled, sparse and reddish hair while contorting her pale and emaciated face into a horrible and nearly terrifying grimace, thanking her pittance with a timid and hideous toothless sneer. No one knew how she was able to survive the last freezing winter, her only refuge in the ruins of an old damp pigsty, curled up in the straw in patched and filthy clothing.

Behind the church at the cemetery, there was a small vegetable garden and a well. This is where Domino Giuliano found her, under a fig tree curled up on a patch of lawn in a mass of fetid rags. The beggar girl, who appeared to be moronically contemplating the sky, was moaning ecstatical-ly and smiling while the boy frenetically touched the poor beggar's devastated body.

The priest was horrified and speechless with surprise and shock. He let out a high-pitched scream.

«Evil wretches! What are you doing?»

It took a few seconds for Fraudolente to squirm his way out of Martina's embraces, leaving her on the ground, victim to her own frenzy.

Domino Giuliano took a deep sigh of relief, knowing that he had arrived just in time.

Caught in the lewd and despicable act left the boy terrified. The priest said nothing more, ignoring the sinful creature that lay on the ground, and dragged Fraudolente by his ear to the well. Leaning against the trough was the strong and sinewy branch from a willow tree used to herd the animals from the courtyard. The Domino grasped the whiplike twig, swinging till it whistled through the air. He then led the sinner into the canonical cell.

«Undress!» he ordered. With eyes lowered and a shaking mouth while holding back tears of fear, Fraudolente obeyed.

«Kneel!»

The boy, resigned to his fate, lowered himself onto the faldstool.

Domino Giuliano flagellated him with rage, releasing repressed delusion and frustration with each flogging. How could this ungrateful boy betray his trust?

Fraudolente did not beg for mercy, shout or weep. In the end, devastated by the pain and humiliation, he fainted and slid to the stone floor.

The presbyter left, closing the door and abandoned Fraudolente on the ground naked and bleeding. He went searching for Martina in the orchard, but the poor girl had run away. He then went looking for her at the old pigsty.

But she had fled.

1285

Alvisio and Fraudolente were like brothers, companions in revelry and looting.

Skilled at hiding in order to attack from behind, on those few occasions in which he found himself face to face with the enemy, Fraudolente, swift and steady, was never subject to defeat.

Alvisio, on the other hand, appeared more placid, having become a soldier almost by accident. He was short and stout with two fair-colored wide set eyes separated by a button nose. Despite his appearance, he was hearty, but humble and cautious.

Like his friend, Alvisio was an abandoned infant. Found in a basket on the doorstep at Combarbio in swaddling clothes, ill and suffering from malnutrition, he survived starvation thanks to the charitable clergy.

Raised in the guaranteed abundance of the church, the two boys showed little inclination to religious life. Ill-suited to tonsures, their presbyters entrusted them as *famigli* to the Pietrarubbia Court. Fraudolente, who knew how to read and write, became Squire to Corrado, and Alvisio a simple archer.

Wives, as was often the case, were no longer in the graces of their lovers; consequently they frequently found that the illegitimate sons were more to their pleasure than their own legitimate brothers.

Filippuccio, Corrado's stepbrother, was the bastard son of the elder Taddeo of Pietrarubbia. About twenty years old, strong and healthy even if not particularly tall, he had inherited his father's looks and rebellious nature, and from his mother, her stature, brown hair and light colored eyes.

In 1283, Forlì and Cesena surrendered to the Guelph

troops, and the Ghibelline leader Guido of Montefeltro, cousin of the Pietrarubbias, was forced to take refuge in Urbino.

The relations between the Malatestis and the Pietrarubbias, both belonging to the victorious Guelphs due to ancient contrasts between the two bordering lineages, were turbulent.

At dusk on a day in October 1285, Filippuccio and Corrado, together with Giovani Bartolini, Raniero, Marino of Faggiola, Alvisio and Fraudolente awaited in the shadows.

After a long and rowdy day of feasting, they took position with their weapons under their cloaks in the lane behind the house of the Eremitanis of Cesena.

The man was walking quickly in the middle of the passage.

Marino was the first to come out of the shadows. He was the oldest, but the biggest and strongest, and the most feared among the group of assailants.

Malatesta stopped in his tracks and uncovered his head of disheveled red hair to show himself. The man standing in front of him was imposing. Anyone in his presence, even the most courageous and strongest warrior or thief would have run for his life.

Malatesta stared at him defiantly.

Marino bravely stared back in the eye of his enemy.

With a display of indifference, Malatesta set his hand on the mother-of-pearl handle of the baselard tied to his hip.

«What do you want? Let me pass!»

His tone was that of one used to commanding and of being obeyed.

The giant didn't move an inch. On the contrary, he sneered with a satisfied look on his face. It was an unusual pose.

Then Malatesta understood. Men waving daggers and long knives came forth out of the darkness.

Marino smiled, «Please, my Lord, go ahead!»

With a mocking bow, he took a step back. But the road was occupied by the others.

Turning and running would have meant his death. Out of the corner of his eye, he saw the door of the convent slightly open just beyond his enemies.

Unexpectedly, without giving them an instant to react, he pulled out his knife and pounced upon the smallest of his adversaries.

Unprepared, Filippuccio froze, astounded. The attack was impossible to avoid!

It wasn't Fraudolente's nature to play the hero, but this was his master's brother, and he was about to be stabbed. Without thinking twice, he threw himself between the man and the knife. The sharp blade went right through the surplice of mail, stabbing him in his side. The pain was blinding. He shouted out in fear of dying.

Filippuccio fell backwards.

The road filled with shouting, and the men hesitated for fear of harming their master. Malatesta remained coldblooded in the face of danger, glancing at the door to the convent that was still ajar. Taking everyone by surprise, in one single jump, he slipped into the narrow opening and tried to shut them out.

Marino pushed the door as hard as he could and was able to thrust it open. Malatesta ran to the cloister while all of the enemies, with the exception of Fraudolente, chased the prey.

In just a few seconds, the conspirators found themselves surrounded by several severe and menacing friars.

Unhesitatingly, Marino dropped his weapons. Without the comfort of Fraudolente, Alvisio did the same, followed by the others. Before surrendering, Filippuccio cursed blasphemy.

Leaning against a column, Fraudolente held his side tightly with a hand.

«Cowards...» he whispered before fainting.

The attackers of the *Magnifico Signor Malatesta de Verucolo* were captured and tried before Giacomo of Tolentino and Benedetto of Spoleti, local judges of the province.

After a serious lecture, they were condemned to an enormous pecuniary punishment and were ordered to reimburse their illustrious victim. Corrado paid for all of the expenses.

It wouldn't have been worth having the Pope and the Guelph party foster a diatribe between the allies.

In any case, there was a winner: Fraudolente. Having saved Filippuccio from certain death, he was celebrated by the Pietrarubbia people as a hero, and from that moment he became Corrado's most trusted man.

Marino, on the other hand, came out rather badly. Someone had slandered him, claiming that he had spent too many years at the service of the ancient family council, and was considered too old at sixty to carry on as a soldier.

In the cloister of the convent at Cesena, he was the first to lay down his weapons in front of the friars. He had surrendered in order to avoid executing a sacrilegious act on sacred ground, as well as his uncertainty of having to sooner or later answer to God. It was not actually a cowardly act, rather a hesitation on his part due to caution, experience and age.

Fraudolente did not forgive him. How could the favored elder of Count Corrado succumb like a child in the presence of his father?

Fraudolente was expecting the Count at the Court. The horses quivered snorts of vapor in the cold morning air. Corrado grabbed the reins and took off at a gallop. Under his cloak, he was wearing a leather tunic and held his sword.

«Where is your friend?»

«My Lord, Alvisio is coughing and spitting. If you wish, I will bring him to you.»

«Coughing and spitting? Or is he still drunk from last night?»

The Count scrutinized the servant from head to toe and

Fraudolente tried to hold his glare.

«My Lord...» he began by lowering his gaze.

«My Lord... I could give a damn!» Corrado interrupted, lowering his hood. «Let's go,» he ordered.

They climbed the ridge and took the road to Petra Fagnana. A cloud covered the peak of Carpegna, while the sun began to melt the ice on the cobblestones. Corrado preferred to travel on the grass along the road, and Fraudolente followed his lead.

He waited until the pasture of Monteboaggine to ride at his side. How can I tell him? It's now or never!

«My Lord, Marino is a coward!» he blurted out, not caring about the speech agreed upon with Filippuccio. «He is a coward and a traitor!» adding insult to injury.

Corrado stopped his horse on the frosty grass and uncovered his head to enjoy the first rays of the sun. Without uttering a word, he waited for Fraudolente to continue.

«It was his fault that your brother nearly died! He should be punished, or at the very least banished.»

«It's not for you to decide what happens to Marino, nor is it up to Filippo,» declared the Count.

Enough squabbling! The shepherds from Monteboaggine had dismissed the terms, and Antonio of Montecopiolo was waiting for him at the border to decide where to reposition them.

He went from scorn to indifference. «Let's get moving, my cousin expects me before lunch.»

They carried on, taking the road to Monteacuto.

Corrado invited him into the large hall of the castle. The Count was seated high up on an enormous chair like a throne. Marino was wearing his finest clothing.

«Marino, you have been a faithful servant for many years, in peace and in war. But the time has come for you to leave.»

Marino caught the Count's gaze and noted the sufferance of his decision.

«My Lord, you command, and I am your servant.»
He lowered his head and accepted the will of his master.
«You will return to your son in San Lorenzo.»
This is how he dismissed the Count.

JULY 1289

The troops of Corrado of Pietrarubbia were about to occupy Urbino.

Around the fire at the encampment, after gorging themselves on lamb watered down with sour wine, Fraudolente and Alvisio were playing dice for the next spoils of war.

As usual, Fraudolente won.

The blacksmith, Raniero, in his early twenties, lived with his wife Albina in a tiny hovel of a village.

There was no defense that could have sustained an attack by an enemy. Hidden on a summit covered by bushes, the village was eluded by raids. The other inhabitants, about twenty people, had fled to Urbino.

Raniero's father, who died during the freezing winter of 1287, had taught his son that the villas were safer than the city.

«Once inside the walls of the city, no one gets out! Here, on the other hand, you can always escape. And they should know that you are here...»

Having inherited his craft and workshop, Raniero began searching for a wife. He didn't go very far, just two doors down. Cousin Albina, tall, brunette and shapely, had doe eyes, and if truth be told, a protruding chin.

Raniero, with a profession, an in-house workshop and a small farm, was a good catch and Albina's father, with three unmarried daughters, was happy to give him her hand in marriage.

In just a couple of months, the bride was already expecting an heir.

Mindful of his father's advice, even with the threat of surrounding enemies, Raniero stayed in the village.

On that beautiful July morning, after having slept longer than usual, he was setting up for work. His was a difficult job. It normally took a few months to make a sword. For one as skilled as him though, it only required a month. And given the times, orders were abundant.

Suffocating from the heat of the forge, the young man stood at the threshold to get a breath of fresh air. He saw his wife at the farmyard drawing water from the well and lifted his hand in a wave.

The arrow arrived with a hiss, and pierced his dark apron.

Struck in the heart, Raniero fell backward in silence.

She screamed with all the breath in her body and ran across the courtyard. Her husband lay still, so she had to straddle over his body to get in. Kneeling, she shrieked his name and shook him in vain. There was nothing left to do. She hugged his head and covered it with kisses and began to sob desperately.

«There is my prey!»

The virile voice was crass and violent.

She had no time to react. Fraudolente entered the workshop, pulled her by her hair and forced her to stand up.

Albina tried, to no avail, to turn around and swing her arms behind her.

«Eh, so this is how it will be? You want to struggle?» sneered the unknown man and, with his free hand, brutally punched her in the back, taking her breath away.

Fraudolente looked around. Holding her by the hair, he shoved her toward the plank in front of the forge, pushing her onto it, crushing her face on the worn wood. He lifted the long skirt, stripped her underclothes and penetrated her.

Albina flailed desperately until she felt a thin sharp awl between her fingers. She grasped the handle with her right hand. It was useless to try to rebel. She was forced to endure helplessly.

At the door, Alvisio was waiting his turn. Damn! Last night his accomplice had won at dice, and the pact was that he would get the young thing first.

He could at least hurry up...

Pulling out, Fraudolente loosened his hold on Albina's head for a second. The girl rolled over onto her back, and with a surge, wounded him. The awl slashed the soldier's cheek who, recoiling with his face in his hands, cried out, «Damned bitch!»

Now Albina was standing up in front of her enemies.

With one hand, Alvisio grabbed her wrist to keep her from stabbing and with the other, he pulled out a knife. While looking at her in the eyes, he sank it into her abdomen over and over.

For an instant, Albina was able to stand. When she dropped with a groan next to her husband, Alvisio finished with a stab in her back, exclaiming, «Idiot! You made me kill her. I can't hump a dead girl!»

«You wouldn't have been able to anyway!» snarled Fraudolente. Then, in pain, he fell silent.

1293

It was sunrise on 8 October 1293 and the weather was mild. The dew shimmered by the still faint rays of sun on the lawn in front of the castle.

While they finished saddling his war horse, Taddeo checked that the knights under escort were ready.

After passing through the walls, they took the road toward the valley floor. There was no danger, at least at the beginning of the route. Who would have ever dared attack them? Beneath their heavy armor, they were nearly invulnerable and, above all, fearsome.

After wading through the Apsa, they reached the fork in the road and Taddeo stopped. The horse shied, struggling to a halt.

«Whoa! Tonight you won't feel much like pawing at the ground.»

The valley was dominated by the impressive castle. The early morning warm light illuminated it, almost like golden amber, similar to the rocks and the entire mountain.

«Let's go,» he sighed as he turned his back on Pietrarubbia. Who knew when, or if, he would ever see it again.

His son rode proud at his side.

They climbed back up the hill of Macerata, the ancient Pitinum. Waiting for them outside the gate of the castle were the nobleman Gaboardo and his faithful Amato, vested for battle.

The Gaboardi of Macerata, Guelphs allied with the Malatesti, had mediated to reach an agreement with Taddeo, and that would have been the day of the definitive alliance.

Count Corrado, elder brother to Taddeo and head of the family of Pietrarubbia, conquered Urbino in 1289, and at a great cost of men and resources, drove away all of the usurper Guelphs and summoned the exiled Ghibellines back to their homeland. Later, he was forced to abandon the city without actually concluding any benefit from his efforts. As a squire, a warlike expedition of that kind had implicated a fatal decrease in resources and prestige, with the necessary consequences of new agreements with strong powers.

Forced into an agreement with his bitter enemy, Taddeo was about to draw up an unfortunate and unfavorable pact with Malatesta against Count Corrado.

They rode back up Mount San Lorenzo, upon whose summit sat an ancient and dilapidated run down castle, a fortress on the valley of the Conca. It had belonged to Roberto of Pietrarubbia. After his death, it was ruled by Bonzio, vassal of Taddeo. The Count had bequested the castle with a few thousand acres of woods, high ground pasture and grain fields which were exposed to the north, and supplied barely enough for the survival of the castle and its people.

Riding horseback, even while wearing modest armor, Bonzio made a striking impression. He was waiting at the San Lorenzo Walls, ready to join the group. Taddeo wanted Bonzio with him on that important day, because even with his rough and crude appearance, he had an incredible ability, rather unusual among soldiers during those times: he knew how to read, write and do sums. He was the right man for drawing up the treaty.

«My trusted Bonzio!» greeted Taddeo. He wanted him to ride close by. It would have bestowed him an honor, as well as an excuse to feel safer.

They traveled along the edges of the muddy road until they were facing Montescudo. They rode down to the river and waded across. That would have been the most opportune moment for an ambush.

Fortunately, nothing happened.

Until then, they had traversed reasonably safe roads, all more or less, under the compliance of the Dominion of the Counts of Pietrarubbia or of their allies and trusted vassals.

Just before midday, they reached the Church of San Paolo,

unharmed.

Malatesta arrived shortly thereafter with a fierce band of knights. Seeing such movement of men and of animals, the few peasants on the streets closed themselves into their houses.

Apart from the knights, the village appeared uninhabited.

Born in 1212, Malatesta of Verucchio, in spite of his eighty years, was athletic, vigorous and fully active.

After some sideways glances and a few minimal gestures of greeting, the guards moved away, and divided according to their emblems. The contracting parties and witnesses stayed in the churchyard. Taddeo and Malatesta dismounted their horses, set down their shields and uncovered their heads.

Taddeo had short black hair, while his future ally had red hair and pale skin with proud and mean blue eyes. They moved to the dim light of the church, and the witnesses followed at an appropriate distance.

The young notary from Rimini, a little man dressed in grand style, but with a treacherous and subservient demeanor, rode among the knights, appearing even more feeble and dwarfish.

The men seated themselves on the benches, set facing each other for this solemn occasion. Taddeo was shocked. He couldn't believe that secular laypersons would be allowed to sit in a church for such a matter. Soon after, he realized that the sunlight from the alabaster window was shining directly into his eyes. This was no accident. In the unfortunate hypothesis of some kind of disturbance, he would be at a disadvantage. He consoled himself with the thought that Bonzio, behind him, was keeping his eye on the enemy in obscurity.

As all notaries who convene, the little man began to recite a long spiel in Latin.

The proud Malatesta looked into the eyes of Pietrarubbia, enjoying the moment as a victory. Taddeo, while having the guarantee of neutrality at the consecrated location, feared deceit and, feigning indifference, kept his eye on the dark areas of the church.

This was an official reconciliation, in which Taddeo would accept to reenter into the good graces of the Guelph Malatesta, granting him help against all of his enemies, *especially* against Count Corrado.

As collateral, he would leave his son as a guest, in reality a hostage, with the new ally.

It was known *that a source of peril would be blind faith* in a pact with the Malatesti.

«Ego Salamon filius olim Berardi de arimino imperiali auctoritate notarius hiis omnibus praesentibus rogatis, subscripsi et pubblicavi» the voice of the little notary shrilled in sealing the deal.

Taddeo couldn't relax until, having crossed the ford of the Conca, he was on back on land.

Bonzio breathed a sigh of relief. The worst was over.

The road, with hawthorn vines and clumps of bristle broom bush, randomly diffused by stone walls laboriously gathered by plow from the fields, flanked the valley of the Conca torrent with its continual rise and fall.

They passed through a miserable village of shanty hovels with straw roofing. Some of the quivering farmers, recognizing the Count, took off their hats and lowered their heads and eyes. The women and children, hearing the knights' arrival, ran into their houses.

Mud was everywhere, and the foul stench of pigstyes and animal feces were heavy in the air.

Taddeo, carrying on as if it were nothing and without deigning a glance at those poor people, continued on his way.

At the bottom of Mount San Lorenzo, the path, no longer on the valley floor, led up toward the ridge.

Darkness had already fallen and they needed to hurry.

At the summit, within the castle, preparations were in full swing.

Maddalena, Bonzio's wife, was a petite woman, prematurely gray, with sharp features and a thin nose. She had sprightly blue eyes that contrasted her physique which was consumed more by fatigue than years. She had had, even while in good health, a difficult and exhausting life. Running that big old broken-down hovel, even with the help of servants, was nothing less than grueling. The men wanted to eat and be looked after, and she, even as the proprietor, had to make haste, often times more than the help. She had seven children, two of which died shortly after birth, and a couple of miscarriages. A woman of strong temperament, she was able to overcome misfortune thanks to the love and support of Bonzio. The girls were reaching adulthood, and the eldest, at sixteen years old, was a bit beyond the age to marry.

In honor of the important guest, a piglet had been sacrificed which, generously seasoned and marinated in aromatized red wine, had been hours roasting over the spit. An intense and inviting aroma lingered throughout the premises, and the servants, aware that the only thing left of that succulent meal for them would be the savory perfume, suffered in silence. They could only hope to share some miserable leftovers to eat with the usual stale, old bread.

Only nobiles and the soldiers were allowed the luxury of satisfying their hunger.

A huge trunk of beechwood burned, crackling away in the fireplace of the castle's hall. The oak plank had been set with crockery and various mismatched earthenware.

Maddalena had filled the pitchers with mulled and boiled red wine, reminding the servants to keep them full during the meal.

The dogs' barking signaled the arrival of the men.

Taddeo, tired and hungry, couldn't wait to get out of his

iron armor and sit at the table in front of a delicious dinner.

Having reached the entrance to San Lorenzo, the Count greeted Gaboardo who, out of worry of darkness, hurried on with his men toward Macerata.

For fear of speaking out of turn, Bonzio remained silent for the entire journey.

It was known by all that the Pietrarubbias and the Gaboardi were not on good terms, even if the problem seemed to have been resolved with the recent stipulated agreement.

Once within the safety of the castle, Taddeo burst out, «I traveled the whole journey in fear of an ambush.»

Bonzio grabbed the reins of the Count's horse.

«My Lord, if we had fallen into a trap, the first to die would have been Gaboardo.»

Given the size and strength of Bonzio, who could have ever doubted him?

Dinner was ready, and a place at the table and the best food was reserved for Taddeo. The Count wasn't fond of overindulgence, and drank in moderation. His eyes fell upon the graceful shape of Bonzio's daughter, Rosa, whose job was to order the servants.

The Count raised his full tankard and made a toast, «Here's to male children!»

The irony did not go unnoticed by Bonzio.

«My Lord, I would also like to toast, even if all of mine are female children.»

«Ah yes, your beautiful girls... someone is already of marrying age, and you could soon become a grandfather.»

The fellow diners, soldiers accustomed to scoffing and vulgar jokes, sniggered discreetly. With Bonzio, there was no tempting fate, and nobody, with the exception of the Master, would have ever dared to openly mock him.

The vassal towered over everyone by a span. He was a mass of muscle and, at thirty-seven years old, was still a formidable warrior, with the appearance and physique of a young man of twenty.

After the soup of lard and spit-roasted pork, the daughter brought the cheese tort to the table, and the surly warrior transformed into a loving father.

«My Count, our Rosa will become the best of brides, and I will do my best to find a husband worthy of such a cook.»

Tasting the decadent treat, Taddeo nodded.

Back in the kitchen, Rosa saw her sister secretly guzzling some wine from the pitcher. She was horrified and stared with her light-colored eyes wide open.

«Are you crazy? What if mother sees you?»

«Leave me alone!»

After a long gulp, her empty stomach contorted, and Maria fought back the impulse to retch.

«Idiot, you'll end up vomiting!» shouted Rosa, holding back a lock of her blond hair from her forehead.

«Ugh, I'm better now. I just wanted to taste the wine,» grumbled Maria.

She couldn't stand it when Rosa acted like the older sister, but begged her anyway, «Don't tell mother...»

That night, Bonzio and Maddalena gave Taddeo their pallet in the big bedroom, the only one in the entire castle that could be defined as a bed.

They retreated to their daughters' room, and shared the straw mattress.

Bonzio, tired and worn out from the journey, in addition to the dinner feast, almost immediately began to snore like a boar being chased by a pack of bloodhounds. The girls had a long and busy day, and that deep dark rumbling, interrupted by sudden jolts like sharp grunts didn't seem to bother them in the least. Maddalena waited patiently for all the girls to fall asleep. When she was nearly sure, with a light and hesitant hand, she caressed her husband's bristly face. Bonzio had no intention of waking up and pulled away with a forceful grumble. Maddalena insisted, and she held his nose, large and ruddy from heavy drinking, between her thumb and forefinger.

It was more than he could stand. Startled, he shook and coughed. It took him a few seconds to understand.

«Woman, there are the children...»

«That's not what I meant. We have to talk.»

The conversations between husband and wife were usually about trivial matters, such as housework, cooking, firewood and winter supplies.

«We'll talk about it in the morning, I'm tired now.»

«No, we're going to talk about it right now!» persisted Maddalena.

«What's so urgent?» grumbled the resigned Bonzio.

Petite and slender, she had the gift of making even a warrior obey.

«Do you think I will be able to see my family again soon?»

The question necessarily implicated the fact that Maddalena knew of the agreements between Taddeo and Malatesta. Bonzio was not surprised. He was well aware of how clever, alert and attentive his spouse was. Peace made with the enemy, she would want to go as soon as possible to visit her loved ones in the valley of the Maricula.

«The nights are drawing in, and the journey is long and dangerous. Maybe, in the spring...»

How could he not understand?

«We have five daughters to marry off and, in Piega, there are their cousins...»

Finally, Bonzio comprehended the theory. For goodness' sake, why didn't he think of it himself?

With her belly in flames and an accelerated heartbeat, Maria couldn't fall asleep because of the wine. Huddled into a ball between her sleeping sisters, she listened to her parents' murmuring.

Cousins and marriage! The future appeared promising.

Since returning to the family, Marino had gained weight. His kingdom was the kitchen of the castle: warm, cozy, full of affectionate women and grandchildren. In one corner, near the hearth, was his armchair, old and well-worn. Before dinner, the three youngest children would get comfortable nearby to listen to him.

Regrettably, the children were sweet and sensitive little girls, and not emotionless and vivacious boys. So wars became graceful skirmishes, the horrendous wounds were little more than scratches and, above all, even having losers, winners, heroes and conquerors, no one ever died.

That valiant soldier, for which he was distinguished in many ferocious battles for courage and bravery, and who had killed uncountable enemies as if it were nothing, had turned into a loving and peaceful grandfather in his old age. Yet, at night, while he was alone in his bed, the horrors of the war returned. The faces of past enemies who died by the sword and the agonizing screams of the wounded and dying tormented him. He would often awaken suddenly, confused and worried, almost as if it were the sunrise before the umpteenth battle.

The granddaughters were new life and redemption, the only true love after the death of Tessa, his beloved bride.

Ada, Marino's favorite granddaughter, had just turned twelve. Blond, lively and very intelligent, she listened with great interest to all of her grandfather's stories. She was passing through that delicate phase of life in which she was still a child, but was rapidly learning the behavior and gestures of adults. Physically still a child, anyone would have been able to foresee the beautiful woman in her. Rosa had begun to delegate Ada some light work around the house, how to help in the kitchen, grooming and looking after the animals of the Court.

Maria, as if she feared having to compete for beauty and love with a future rival, was a bit envious of this blossoming flower. She played mean tricks and teased her with snide jokes. Even in the presence of the servants she would make fun of her, calling her names like *Ada the white-eyed fatso, lazy-bones midget* and *the fattest of the three geese.*

The other *two geese* were the younger Isotta, seven years old and Bruna, five; two beautiful girls with large dark eyes, adored and spoiled by the whole family. They had, for the time being, known only a happy life, the carefree age in which there are no problems or responsibilities.

THE SPRING OF COMBARBIO

In an excellent position to resisting enemy attacks, the castle on the mountaintop clearing of Mount San Lorenzo was no longer the powerful fortress of long ago and, even with numerous interventions of maintenance, it began to show signs of structural collapse. With the help of a scant group of stonecutters and masons brought in from the countryside, Bonzio got busy with the enormous job of restructuring. But it wasn't simple and, even with hard work and willpower, the results were inadequate. From a distance, the edifice was a castle but, the closer one came, it had the semblance of a patched together, improvised vestige. One side of the mountain was slowly caving in, and there was little to nothing to do about it. Sooner or later the foundation would collapse.

The plumbing provision was protected by an underground cistern and covered with a vault of bricks. Here, without a spring, the rainwater was collected. The tank would have allowed resistance for a lengthy autonomy, but on more than one occasion, the water had putrefied.

Even though the tank was cleaned every summer, Bonzio ordered that the purest water be consumed from the spring near the parish church. With earthenware crocks loaded onto a wagon pulled by a mule, a servant periodically made the trip to replenish the water. The most difficult part was returning up the steep and bumpy road without breaking any vases. The problem was solved by stuffing straw between the containers.

Marino was bored, and feared being a hindrance.

To make himself useful, when the weather was nice he would go down to the spring in place of the young boy. It was a good walk. He needed to cross the meadow around the castle, and pass through the woods down the steep road. Above the church in a small hollow, surrounded by thick and heavy vegetation even in the summertime, was the spring.

For the granddaughters, who yearned to go with him, the excursion was an excuse to get outside of the dark walls and the gloomy rooms of the castle, and to enjoy a healthy breath of fresh air in the freedom of the outdoors. Maddalena, out of fear that the old man could fall ill or that the happy group might end up running into a vagabond, would usually join the company.

On a hot afternoon in November, the mule rigged up to the calash, Marino set off toward the spring with Maddalena and his granddaughters. Rosa stayed back at the castle to look after the servants in the kitchen. Who knew what those scoundrels would get up to, left on their own...

Marino led the mule while Maddalena and the girls followed the wagon. Behind the group, Ada and Isotta held hands. The women wore heavy wool stockings on their feet with noisy wooden clogs. The road was difficult, even if cobbled wakes kept the iron wheels of the wagon from sinking into the mud.

About a hundred yards before the spring, not far from the path and behind some thorny bushes, was an apple tree.

«Mommy, do you think there's any fruit left?» Ada and Isotta yelled in unison.

Maddalena snorted. All we need is for them to be running around the woods!

Bruna, the youngest, copying her sisters, shouted, «C'mon mommy, please!»

The little green and red apples were sweet and juicy.

Marino stopped the wagon and waited. Maddalena gave the orders.

«Maria, go have a look. If you find any, pick some without climbing the tree and bring them to the spring. It's late, so in the meantime, we'll keep going.»

The girl left the trail and disappeared into the bushes.

The water gushed from the rock and, following a little canal chiseled in the stone, flowed into a large waterhole about two hands deep. The water from the pond spilled over into a small stream that followed a downward path.

Halting the cart, Marino got busy unloading the containers. Not far off, lying on the damp grass, was the trunk of a large chestnut tree. The women got comfortable on the improvised bench while the man finished the job.

The tree was in a clearing beyond the knoll.

Free from her pesky sisters and the supervision of her mother, Maria took her time. She climbed between the rocks and passed through the old grazing land of dried grass.

After the descent among clumps of dog rose and blackthorn, in the soft grass where the boars routed around by night, there was the apple tree!

The last time she had been there was with her grandfather and they had gathered loads.

On the ground, the animals had already eaten all of them, and the last apples hung high up in the branches. She took off her clogs and carefully climbed up the rugged trunk and sat on the branch. She saw it, big red and ripe. Reaching to pick it, she lost her balance and, for an instant, was left hanging onto a leafy branch. With a shout, she fell. «Ouch, that hurt!»

Groaning, she tried to get up. Her ankle was sore, but was able to stand on her foot. She decided it was best to hurry back to the others.

She found a stick to help her walk, took a shortcut and limped down the hill.

Mother would have been angry, her sisters would have teased her and her grandfather would have consoled her.

Fraudolente was assigned to deliver a message from Corrado to his cousin Galasso in Secchiano.

Departing on horseback with the inseparable Alvisio, he knew that he wouldn't be back to Pietrarubbia within the day. They would sleep in the barn at Secchiano. A short journey in complete freedom was preferable to staying in the house as servants and bootlickers to the master.

They left for the trip in the sunshine without haste. Soon after noon, they came to an arduous shortcut in the woods that led them in proximity to the parish church.

«Do you want to stop for a bite?» suggested Alvisio.

They had bread and cheese in their bag and the usual wine in a canteen carved from a squash. With the horses tied to an old oak, they sat side by side on a smooth white stone.

Fraudolente bit into the bread and with a full mouth, commented, «Mm good, we really needed that! Let's take our time. If we get there early, Galasso could decide to send us back to Pietrarubbia at dark.»

Alvisio nodded.

Off in the distance, they could hear the confused clamouring of women and children.

Fraudolente stopped chewing.

Yes, it was surely women and children.

«Quiet! Don't whisper a single word,» he murmured as he stood. He walked to his horse and pet his muzzle to keep him calm. Alvisio did likewise.

They squeezed through the shadows of the woods on foot in order to remain hidden. The noises came from the direction of the church. With great care, they nearly reached the building. It was deserted. They continued farther up, avoiding the road. Protected by the scrub of holly oak, they crouched down by the spring to spy.

A fat and elderly man was loading containers full of water onto a cart, while a woman with gray hair and three pretty girls were sitting on a big trunk watching him.

Even with his age, the old man, whose back was turned,

seemed powerfully built.

Fraudolente warned Alvisio, «*That* one could be dangerous.» He had whispered, but didn't count on the mule that, hearing their words or possibly the stink of the intruders, would bray, shaking the cart.

Marino brought his hand to his knife, ready to unsheathe it.

Fraudolente recognized the gesture in that old soldier. They were exposed, and might as well come out of the bushes.

«Marino, is that you?»

With his hands out in the open, he smiled and came closer.

Marino, with his hand on the hilt, interceded between the man and the women. It really was Fraudolente, the bastard who had gotten him thrown out. Looking around, he searched for the inseparable Alvisio, but didn't see him.

«What are you doing here? Are you alone?»

«I'm on my way to Secchiano, on a mission for Count Corrado. Yes, I'm alone. I heard voices and, just to be on the safe side, I hid.»

He kept smiling, and the horrendous scar on his face shined in the sunlight. Marino didn't believe him, and he twitched, moving his head right, left and center, to identify the hiding place of the accomplice.

Maddalena, seeing the terrifying sneer, set Bruna on her knee and hugged the other two girls.

Fraudolente tried to distract him with kindness. «Who are the children? Your granddaughters?»

His face, even while smiling, was contorted and repelling.

Frightened, Bruna turned and, wrapping her arms around her mother's neck, began to whine. Isotta restrained herself.

Marino attempted to disengage. «Fine! It was nice to have seen you again. Now be on your way.»

Courtesy and assertiveness was called for. Fraudolente was a coward and he probably remembered what a fearsome warrior was concealed under the deceptive clothes of a fat old man.

If Alvisio had truly remained at Pietrarubbia, nothing would have happened. But this was not to be.

The arrow pierced him between his shoulder blades.

Fraudolente chuckled in the face of his wounded enemy. Marino continued to stand, stoic, but with terror in his eyes.

«Run!» he ordered the women.

He tried to unsheathe his knife, but wasn't in time. Fraudolente jumped him. He wounded him with a stab in the abdomen, which he tore while falling to his knees.

The scar-faced man pulled out the bloody blade.

«Old pig, your time has come!»

With a kick, he struck him down in a sea of viscera and blood.

Holding tight to her mother's neck, Bruna didn't watch and didn't scream. Maddalena was horrified, but kept quiet. Ada and Isotta shrieked desperately.

Alvisio, appearing out of nowhere, attacked the mother, stabbing her in the back.

Then, after tearing little Bruna away, in a quick gesture, he slit her throat like a rabbit. Blood sprayed everywhere.

Isotta and Ada screamed and jumped up to run away.

«I'll get the bigger one.»

Fraudolente slapped her hard across the face, and Ada lost consciousness. He dragged her behind a tree and, after ripping off her clothes, he raped her. The child reacted, trying to scratch him, but the scarred man hit her again.

When he finished, while getting up, his hand touched a sharp rock. After grabbing it, in an impulsive act, he smashed her temple, killing her instantly.

Then he stood and went looking for Alvisio. He found him behind a bush. To keep her from shouting, he suffocated Isotta, saving her from the horror of the rape.

Fraudolente made fun of him.

«You didn't even get any!»

Alvisio ran to get back his arrow. He broke it, and the arrow remained stuck in Marino's back.

The old warrior lay immobile with his face in the damp grass, near the spring.

The mule, unharmed, survived.

She heard voices. There was something strange going on. It sounded like other men. Maria was afraid and, before exposing herself, she spied behind the bushes. Who was that big man with the black and hideous disfigured face?

Grandfather was struck and fell to the ground. Horrified, she wanted to scream, but kept quiet and crouched low, hidden in the grass. Frozen, she watched the tragedy, crying in silence so she wouldn't be heard. She saw obscene and inconceivable things.

When it was all over, she was afraid of being found.

"They'll come and get me!" she thought.

But the black man and his friend didn't notice her presence.

She heard them joking as if it were nothing, as they left.

Fraudolente gloated, «Did you see how I gutted that fat pig? Then I *did* his pretty little granddaughter, too!»

They slowed down, and Alvisio trotted behind while they quickly descended toward the parish church of Combarbio.

«Hey, we're close to my church, and they might recognize me. We'd better get off the road.»

The parish church where Alvisio was raised was just beyond the curve. He couldn't resist his curiosity to have a look and poked his way through the hedge. Damn, wasn't that Domino Santi on the grass in front of the door? He was fatter than the last time he had seen him, maybe even shorter and, most of all, older and white-haired.

Alvisio became suspicious. «Do you think he heard us?»

Fraudolente put his hand on Alvisio's shoulder and murmured, «Hurry up, idiot! Do you want him to see you?»

They hid behind the bushes in the shelter of the woods.

Alvisio, who knew the place like the back of his hand, turned to his friend, «Follow me, I'll take you back to the horses.»

At the castle, Rosa had to wait for instruction for dinner but, to be sure to avoid making any errors, she waited for suggestions from her mother. When darkness came, she began to worry. She asked the servants and the errand boys if they had seen her or, at least, if they knew where she had gone. Then she looked around the kitchen. One boy had stoked the fire and a big trunk burned away in the fireplace. No one was there. After looking all over the castle, she stood in the middle of the court and yelled out loud.

Bonzio rushed to aid the servants and boys and the two soldiers on sentry duty guarding the high castle walls.

The first thing to do was to find out if and when they had left the castle. «Have you seen my father?» shouted Bonzio at the two up on the bastion.

Gasparino was a good man, and could have been defined as faithful and devoted to his masters. He was small, but had a lean and muscular physique, with black hair and complexion, and a low forehead with a face often devoid of any expression. His voice was graceless, piercing and adenoidal, and he always breathed with an open mouth.

Born into a peasant family of Pietrarubbia, Gasparino found himself with the pleasant job of a soldier in times of peace, under the orders of a kind master and defending a castle which, at the moment, no one was interested in conquering.

Unlike his brothers who worked hard in the fields and endured hunger, he ate and drank in abundance, and whose only duty, with the other three soldiers, was to safeguard and defend the castle from inexistent enemies. He would have liked to have a woman, at least once in a while. But one couldn't expect everything in life.

Of his two brothers, both younger than him, only one was married, and had many children.

Similarly dark-skinned, the *Gasparini* all spoke with the

same acute and nasal voice, but each with their own variation of tonality. At the festivities, they inspired hilarity from their fellow countrymen with a great commotion of guttural howling.

From the bastions above, Gasparino answered.

«They all left with the cart to refill the clean water...»

«All who?» said an alarmed Bonzio, turning pale.

«Marino, your wife and the girls.»

«Come down right away!»

Night had fallen, and they needed to move quickly. With one soldier left to defend the castle, they ran down the road. After passing through the clearing, they infiltrated their way into the woods. The metallic noise of their weapons resounded in the silence.

As he neared the spring, Bonzio hollered, «Father, father, where are you?»

Nobody answered.

The mule and the cart were nearby, under the secular oak tree. The first thing he recognized was his wife's gray hair. Face down on the soft grass, she lay in a bloodbath. He was horrified to catch sight of the slight contour of little Bruna, curled up next to her mother. He knelt and tenderly picked her up, as if nearly afraid to awaken her. Seeing her delicate throat slit, he hugged her. He stifled his tears and, with the fragility of one placing a sleeping baby in its crib, he layed her back down on the damp grass.

Maddalena had been pierced by a blade in the back. The wound was deep, inflicted by someone who knew how and where to strike. It must have been an instant death.

He appeared to perceive an expression of terror on her face for those atrocious seconds. She probably knew what was happening, and died, knowing she would pass desperate in her inability to protect her daughters.

Gasparino shook him.

«My Lord, your father is still alive.»

Marino, face down, was wheezing. Very carefully, Bonzio

turned him over, exposing the hideous slash to his abdomen. His eyes were gaping wide open, and he was breathing with difficulty. He seemed to be searching with his gaze. He moved his lips, and Bonzio leaned down, bringing his ear closer to his face. The dying man fell silent, but was able to grasp his wrist.

Lifting his head suddenly, Bonzio whispered, «Who was it?»

The old warrior made an effort to answer, but to no avail. A spurt of blood came out of his mouth while he breathed his last breath in his son's arms.

«Who did this, father, who did this?» the painfully heart wrenching cry echoed in the shadows of the valley.

They had to look for the other girls. Maybe they were hiding and safe. Whimpering incomprehensible words, Gasparino pointed to the old elm behind the spring.

Ada lay on the ground, half-naked and with her skull crushed. Out of discretion, the other men stepped away.

«Damn them,» he murmured again, grinding his teeth.

Now they had to find Maria.

No one dared call out her name out of the unspeakable fear that she might not answer. The wind tormented the highest leafy branches of the trees. Gasparino greatly feared the dark and all of the menacing noises of the woods. Grumbling a voiceless chant under his breath, he nervously wandered about, perusing his way through the bushes. He couldn't wait for the return home, safe behind the walls and as far away as possible from the parish church and its cemetery abandoned to brambles and scrub.

And if the perpetrators, the killer rapists, were cursed spirits from God, souls damned and roaming through the shadows?

He murmured some distorted prayers in an improbable Latin.

An animal, possibly a boar, made a thunderous noise and ran away. Gasparino began to shudder while, with his heart in his mouth, he quickly distanced himself, looking back for fear of being followed by someone. The fear of the supernatural was his worst enemy.

He tripped and bumped into an obstacle. Falling forward, he reached out into the darkness and scratched his face on the thorns of a wild rose. He cursed, and with difficulty, avoided a blasphemy.

Whimpering, he sat on the grass, not far from a thick bush of holly oak whose branches appeared to blur with the tufts of weeds in the dark.

Gasparino touched his face with his hands, looking for an unlikely wound. While terrified, he was unharmed.

His eyes were slowly becoming accustomed to the darkness, which gave him some courage. He cupped his ear to figure out where the others were. Nearby, he heard panting, rhythmic and fast breathing, a continual hushed sobbing.

It was too much. He screamed out in terror with a sharp cry.

Bonzio came running.

«What happened?»

Gasparino pointed to the black silhouette of the holly oak tree.

Bonzio pushed the lower branches out of the way and saw her, curled up and motionless. Through blond hair, her hands covered her face.

«Maria!» he called, falling to his knees.

The child shook, but didn't answer. She was alive, she had survived!

«I'm here, you're safe now.»

He caressed her head and, carefully picking up her wrists, almost afraid to hurt her, he drew her to him until he held her to his heart. Maria tried to cover her face with her hands.

Bonzio stood up, and she let her head fall on her father's shoulder.

Holding the small and fragile Maria, no longer unprotected in his arms, Bonzio climbed the road back home.

Gasparino and the two soldiers prepared to salvage the massacred bodies of the victims.

Rosa was waiting outside the door of the castle.

The guardian of the walls scrutinized the darkness in vain. He heard footsteps.

«Who goes there?»

«Open up!» shouted Bonzio, and two boys ran to unlock the wide doors.

Rosa saw them. Her father held Maria in his arms, with her hands covering her face. For an instant, she feared that she was dead.

Bonzio walked into the kitchen and sat next to the fireplace with Maria in his arms. The women and the boy servants backed into the farthest dark corner.

«Father, what happened?» Rosa found the courage to ask.

He lifted his head, and stared at her. The girl understood the anguish and desperation. For the first time in her life, she saw her father with eyes red from crying.

Bonzio, pretending to clear his voice, coughed. Where could he find the right words, and the heart to say them? He bowed his head and caressed Maria's hair.

Was this the price to pay? Was this the divine punishment for all the enemies tortured and killed in battle?

The anger was followed by despair and a sense of impotence. In hope of softening the truth, he ignored the horrendous details.

Rosa sat with lowered eyes next to her father, listening to his story in silence. She didn't have it in her to shout and express despair, but cried her every last tear.

«Where are they?»

«Gasparino is bringing them home.»

Rosa jumped up and, in an instant, was in the courtyard.

The soldiers were awaiting their orders and, at the moment, the bodies of the victims were piled on the wagon.

Gasparino held a torch and, seeing the daughter of his

master, approached to guide her. In close proximity of the cart, by the flickering light of the flame, Rosa recognized Isotta and Bruna next to their mother. Bonzio's cloak pitifully covered Ada. She lifted it.

It was too much. She fainted, collapsing to a heap on the ground.

Without uttering a word, Maria curled up into a ball with her head in her hands. Her sister lay down next to her and, for the entire night, was unnerved by convulsive and muffled crying.

Even though she was suffering, Rosa gathered herself and took care of recomposing the bodies of her mother and sisters. She dressed Maddalena in her finest clothing of raw linen, like her petticoat. Ada, Isotta and Bruna were wrapped, with their faces uncovered, in course cotton cloths. Marino was taken care of by his son.

The funeral rites were celebrated a couple of days later by Reverend Santi, the elderly priest of the parish church, in the chapel of the castle with the presence and assistance of the young clerics. Gathered in sufferance, servants and masters wept together for the victims of the atrocious evildoing.

After the ceremony, Bonzio accompanied Reverend Santi.

Awaiting the moment of farewells in front of the parish church, he hoped to inquire what he had been mulling over on the day of the catastrophe.

The parish priest stood out from the clerics with his prominent *gut* of the well-to-do religious. Afflicted with a high-pitched stutter, he was completely unable to restrain himself, especially in the presence of the noblemen and of Bonzio.

Maddalena had confided in her husband that she considered him sly and sneaky, even if most likely, there was nothing to fear for their own children from him. The suspicion, due to her prominent woman's intuition, was that he was a sodomite sinner, and took advantage of his position to subject the clerics to obscene practices that went against nature.

«I wonder, if by chance, you may have heard or seen something...»

With his imposing size, Bonzio towered above the priest, who widened his eyes in an affectation of shock.

«What do you expect me to have heard? We are praying at that hour...»

«At which hour?»

Domino Santi began to falter and, stumbling over his words, lied, «At...at...at the hour of vespers!»

Even though he was a priest, he was superstitious and, like the peasants, had a mad fear of the white eyes of the demon. Unable to sustain the candid, clear and inquiring gaze of Bonzio, he lowered his head.

The vassal didn't believe him.

What did this man know? Was he aware of who was responsible and was now withholding?

The priest, shuddering, accidentally gave an instinctive and rapid glance at Bonzio's sword.

«You would tell me, in the case…?»

Rather than a request, it seemed more like a threat.

«I know nothing, nothing!» remonstrated Domino Santi before quickly returning to the courtyard of the parish church.

A young cleric hurriedly closed up, leaving Bonzio as he was, outside, suspicious and confused, with his doubts.

Maddalena was right, that one is a sodomite sinner, and one day they will hang him by his genitals and send him to the stake. As would only be fair and just.

Maria, a few days after the funeral services and burial, seemed to be recovering. She began to eat again with appetite and to look after, under the watchful eye of her sister, the kitchen chores. However, every once in awhile a pale smile escaped her lips, making her appear a bit relieved, only to close up in obstinate and absolute muteness. At first, Rosa didn't think much of it. After all, her sister understood everything perfectly and, with the exception of her absence of answering, unless with only a nod, seemed normal for the most part. With tact and caution, Bonzio had attempted to ask if she had seen and recognized the murderers. Maria, after shaking her head, ran away, and Bonzio didn't push the matter.

In early December, the weather seemed to worsen. A freezing wind blew from the north, and huge dark clouds on the horizon heralded a storm, followed by snow. Bonzio decided that the time was right, as long as weather allowed, to travel to the Count at Pietrarubbia. Meticulously armed, even if warmly, they left on horseback in the early morning. Gasparino didn't have the courage to complain; he had to obey in silence. At least he would have the chance to see his brothers.

On the slopes of the Faggiola, the two knights took the road for Macerata. Without crossing paths with so much as a dog, not to mention any of the Gaboardi, they reached Pietrarubbia unscathed.

The imposing castle dominated the valley. Outside of its walls, near the incline, there was a stone hovel village three stories high, set one on top of the other for support.

When they arrived at the castle gate, Bonzio dismissed Gasparino.

«Go on ahead to your family. I'll come back for you when I return.»

This was the moment that the faithful soldier had been waiting for. Finally, he was really and truly home, the place where he was born and raised by his own kin.

From a stall with an opening just large enough for the animals to pass through, he entered the kitchen on the first floor by the rungs of a ladder. From here, he climbed to the loft which served as the sleeping area. Wooden sawhorses held up tables for beds which were covered with rough cloth sacks stuffed with hay. The slats overhead were separated and the roof was covered with straw. During the day, even in summer, the openings filtered most of the light, where they lived in semi-darkness, and the stench that ascended from the stalls below.

In any case, it was a solid house, made of stone, built to last and very safe. At the first sign of danger, in the case of an enemy attack, it was possible to take refuge within the walls of the castle. The houses of the surrounding village, faraway and vulnerable, were made of mud, wood and straw.

Having tied up his horse, Gasparino called out loud.

«Mafalda!»

Mafalda was his brother, Bastiano's wife.

Gasparino had found her many years ago in the valley of the Maricula. Her father, the blacksmith of Piega, was a good man with a swarm of children. In those days, Mafalda was a beautiful fifteen-year old girl, who could have aspired a nice young man from a good family. Even though the bride was more attractive and wealthy than the groom, the marriage had been prolific and happy.

The children, unfortunately, took very little after their mother. With a low forehead and jug ears like all the other Gasparini, they spoke with the piercing voice of one who has difficulty breathing and with nostrils perennially closed. The marriages among the inhabitants of the village of Piega and Pietrarubbia, like that of the beautiful Mafalda and the homely Bastiano, were so numerous, that it was nearly impossible to distinguish between the various and countless generations, which were first, second or third cousins, and aunts, uncles, nieces and nephews. At the beginning of this particular custom, given that the repetitive cross breeding was well-known between intermarriage in the same town and had produced many hereditary defects, the Counts of Pietrarubbia and the Lords of Piega were in favor of facilitating marriage among the peasants of the two small towns. After some generations of arranged unions, the inhabitants of both villages had become one single family and, during wedding festivities, new and friendly relations were born, and even more happy nuptials.

With the last Lateran Council, the prohibition of marriage

within the fourth ascendent of blood relation and kin was sanctioned, and there were countless requests for exceptions to the bishop, and granted, for the arranged unions between families of Piega and Pietrarubbia.

Bastiano, a good husband and hard worker, lived in a solid house and, while he couldn't be described in any way even slightly handsome, he knew how to be a respectful, sensitive and gentle lover, priceless endowments for those times, when people were considered little more than animals.

Zanino, the younger brother with a rebellious character, was so ugly that when his female peers even glanced at him, they felt repulsion. Whenever he would happen to cross their path, especially if they were pretty, he would abandon himself to a long series of sneering faces and horrifying grimaces, and utter unrepeatable obscenities to scandalize them. He behaved like a real ruffian, uncivilized and shameless. Despite the frequent scoldings from his brothers and even a few warnings from the Count, Zanino refused to discontinue his behavior. On the contrary, he seemed to enjoy himself immensely. However, in spite of the clamor that his bad manners caused, the poor boy was completely harmless.

That old toothless gossip, Carola, wife of the neighbor, had spread a rumor that Zanino's mother died of shock when she held him in her arms at his birth when laying eyes on her hideous newborn.

Mafalda, soon after her wedding, had overcome the initial disgust for her brother-in-law, and the boy, like a charm, became as sweet and affectionate as a son.

«Gasparino, is that you?» the voice was high-pitched and cheerful.

«Of course it's me!»

It was a surprise visit.

Malfada came down to the ground floor with her oldest son, a young man of twelve-years old, identical to his father.

«Martino, run and call your father and your uncle!»

The men had taken advantage of what would probably be the last chance, before the arrival of snow, to bring the sheep to pasture on the mountain.

Martino ran like the wind. The boy stayed with the flock and the two men came down the valley.

As soon as they met in front of the entrance of the stall, the three brothers cavorted with loud thwacking on the shoulders and hearty shouting with the usual chanting.

Carola, from the window on the first floor, intrigued by the sudden chatter, was unable to peek down below.

«Gostolo, your cousins are carrying on.»

The husband went back to mixing a spluttering broth of vegetables in the earthenware pot hanging above the embers in the fireplace. With some black stale bread, this would be the meal for the entire family.

Gostolo carried on, unperturbed, as if it were nothing. Then, waving the ladle menacingly around in the air, he yelled at his wife, «You're the usual old gossip! Instead of wasting your time spying on the neighbors, it's time you got busy in the kitchen!»

He embellished the scolding with blasphemy.

«Sinner, you'll end up in hell.»

Carola made the sign of the cross, murmuring a quick prayer.

For Gostolo and Carola, work in the fields had turned to agony, and the time had come for their son and grandchildren to look after things. Imprisoned for life in the dark and damp hut, their future would be to stoke the fire and prepare the meals.

Old folks were a burden, they produced nothing and needed to eat.

In a corner, sitting on the steps of the stairway leading to the entrance of the keep, Alvisio and Fraudolente were lazing about in idle chitchat. When Bonzio entered the courtyard, they exchanged a complicit glance.

With his usual self-serving flattery, Fraudolente stood and

hurriedly grabbed the bridle of the horse of the newcomer.

«I'll take care of it!»

Bonzio thanked him, dismounted and made the proper announcement of his arrival to the Count.

After tying the horse, Fraudolente sat back down next to Alvisio. «Did you know that he has two other daughters?»

The face disfigured by the scar contorted into a smile.

The Count received him in the hall of the castle.

Sitting high up in his chair, without expressing any emotion, almost as if this regarded some unimportant episode, he turned to Bonzio, who stood respectfully staring at the floor.

«I have heard what happened to your family.»

Corrado, the elder of the Pietrarubbians, was a good looking man. Dark-haired like almost all of his brothers, and not too tall, he had an athletic physique and, at just a few years past thirty, after the death of his father, became head of the family. It was he who decided to entrust San Lorenzo to Bonzio, even though the latter was actually Taddeo's most trusted man. Despite the fact that the castle was in ruins and at risk of a devastating mudslide, it was situated in a strategic position as an outpost at the borders of the Malatesti. It would take a strong vassal, respected by subalterns and absolute loyalty to the Lords. And, for generations, Bonzio's family had always proven to have all of the requisites required to fulfill a charge of such importance and responsibility.

Even with numerous attempts to excel, the branch of the Montefeltro of Pietrarubbia had taken the dismal pat +h of decadence. Failure in the endeavors to replace the occupation of Urbino with cousins, Corrado had tried in vain to salvage the splendor and political influence of the past. Having lost the strength to influence the stability of the strongest lineages, in the arduous effort to survive, he managed with a network of alliances which were not always advantageous. He often found himself in embarrassing situations, such as, to avoid disappointing someone, he inevitably made enemies with another. This opportunistic behavior did not sit well in a period in which the difference was very clear between the Guelph and Ghibelline parties.

The ease with which those from Pietrarubbia changed their minds was notorious. In the midst of the confusion of the interests opposed by the Pope and the Emperor, it was complicated to oversee one small countship and maintain economic and political independence.

Corrado did not inherit the charisma, and political and warlord capacity of his father. Taddeo was a great man and, for his son, was difficult to emulate.

Aware of his limits, even while officially blaming the responsibility on bad luck and the change of times and conditions, Corrado suffered for the inevitable comparison between the criticism for his repetitive failures and the fame and notoriety of his illustrious parent.

He vented the frustrations of being such an unworthy descendent of his father onto the subordinates, the population and the soldiers.

He surrounded himself with a tight group of devotees, which were only present out of interest and for fear of his unpredictable angry outbursts. Vindictive and cruel, very often he would enjoy inflicting atrocious and unjust abuse. He would torture poachers with exemplary punishments, and flagellate those peasants who, to be able to survive in times of famine, hadn't payed their dues for tenant farming.

If that weren't enough to exasperate the hungry commoners, the noble family lived in luxury, within the safety of the walls of the castle, served and revered, defended by a brutal and undisciplined soldiery, and insensitive to the misery of the poor.

Corrado's wife, the noble Costanza of Azzo de' Ravegnani, an attractive woman, tall and brunette, with dark eyes and sweet delicate features, had a strong and independent personality. She was highly respected in the family; in the case her husband were absent, in war or in peace, she was capable of administering the castle. An excellent mother, she adored little Roberto, a beautiful healthy baby whose resemblance to his mother was striking.

She was loved for her generous spirit and, even more, for her unusual sensitivity and kindness in how she treated the servants and peasants. Gossip circulated around how a such a good and kind woman could tolerate being the bride of such a cruel man.

These comments, even if only whispered in front of the fire, were very dangerous. If they had reached the ears of a Master or, even worse, a spy, the consequences would have been terrible.

The Pietrarubbians were not inclined to forgiveness.

Bonzio had to tell his Lord, in its entirety and in detail, about the massacre at the spring of Combarbio.

Corrado was unmoved, as if he was being told the story of a boar hunt.

«When we have caught them, they will be handed over to you, and you may do with them as you wish,» was the Count's only comment.

The vassal proceeded with an accurate report on the progress of the restructuring of the castle at Monte San Lorenzo. He requested and obtained permission to extract the tufo from Combarbio, so as to have new stone to reinforce the old walls and the collapsing structure.

Filippuccio entered the hall at the moment in which Corrado was dismissing Bonzio. He made no greeting and no comments, only a nod of his head to his brother. The Bastard, as he was such, believed himself superior to any servant, even to those that were charged in the highest trust. In any case, he would have rather liked that his brother entrust him a countship to one of the castles, even rescinding Bonzio from San Lorenzo. To prevent Corrado from any suspicion, for starters, why not propose someone else? Fraudolente was faithful enough, and unfaithful at the same time, to be the perfect candidate. Later on, given the uninhibited ambition and the lack of inclination of the scarred man's ability to command, it would be easy to nominate himself as a substitute.

Retreating obsequiously and bowing in a sign of submission, Bonzio made his departure.

«Will he continue to be our vassal at San Lorenzo?» asked Filippuccio indifferently.

«Stop insisting! I need Fraudolente here, with me. He may be more astute and cunning than Bonzio but, precisely because of this, less trustworthy and more dangerous. Bonzio is like Marino. He has a strong sense of honor and would never betray us. Furthermore, he is a valiant, feared and respected combatant.»

Filippuccio hid his disappointment behind a false smile.

They returned to the castle just in time, right before dusk. A thin layer of snow, pure and white, had covered the road and the countryside. Dismounting their horses, they handed the poor animals over to a boy, who took them to the warmth and safety of the stall.

Gasparino, even while sad to have left the family and the beloved Pietrarubbia, was truly happy to have finally returned home, and couldn't wait to bask in the heat in front of the fire. Bonzio, impatient, hurried to the kitchen to his daughters.

1294

Even while not the coldest, the first few months of 1294 were very damp and it snowed continually. Life in the village of Pietrarubbia, despite the starving people, went smoothly. In order to maintain his modest army, essential for the security and independence of the small State, the Count had left only the basic necessities to the peasants for their survival. They got by on boiled greens, dried legumes and old black stale bread. As always happened during the harsh season, the weakest among the undernourished died, some elderly and many children.

At fifty-five years old and with many aches and pains, Gostolo survived the winter, as much as his work allowed, indoors, in the semi-darkness near the heat of the fireplace. Skilled at wood carving, he would sculpt little toys for his grandchildren. Agnolo, his first-born, was a man as good as he was unintelligent. His wife had died giving birth to a son who was named after his grandfather. The boy, a restless dark-haired child, at just three years old, insisted on fighting and winning with his older brothers, Gabriolo and Maffiolo. There was often bedlam among the children in the smokey and foul-smelling kitchen, with shouting and disturbing noise, and equally as much severe scolding from Grandma Carola. Only Gostolo, with the help of his cane, was able at times to keep a tight rein on the rambunctiously spirited children. Like all grandfathers, and not in a particularly concealed way, he had his favorite. Of course, as is often the case, it was the youngest and most vulnerable, even if the biggest troublemaker. But who could resist those resplendent eyes on the skinny little black face of that rascal?

Gostolino had no desire to stay calm and quiet in the house. He had learned to skip up and down the stairs with agility and, when he was able to slip out of the control of his grandparents, he would squeeze through the black hole of the loft so he could rummage through the straw in the stall below. There were a few sheep, some rabbits and, in a well-fenced corner, a couple of pigs.

Close to dark on a cold evening in January, after coming down the rungs of the ladder and muddling a bit in the animal dung, Gostolino seized the moment in which his father was returning to slip through the door that was ajar. Barefoot and with his legs unclothed, he mucked about in the shallow frozen snow.

Agnolo grabbed him, and immediately clutched him by his shirt. The threadbare hemp fabric suddenly ripped and the boy rolled over naked in the snow. Afraid of a scolding and a beating, Gastolino got back up and, screaming desperately, he ran hurriedly downhill. He stumbled on a rock and fell flat on his face in a ditch where he guzzled the sewage. Agnolo picked him up by his armpits. The boy yelled, kicking and screaming the air like mad, his eyes pale and wide with his little face filthy with black sludge.

Next to the buildings ran a stream that flowed into an old and deep drinking trough.

The man, without giving it much thought, plunged his son up and down in the water to rinse him off.

Gostolino shivered so hard that he wasn't even able to take a breath to shout.

When it appeared that the child had regained his normal color, Agnolo picked him up and ran into the house. Once in the kitchen, he gave him over to the grandmother to take care of.

«Idiot, what have you done?»

Carola looked for a cloth to dry the grandson who, in shock with uncontrollable tremors, complained under her breath.

The next day, the boy began to sneeze and cough with unprecedented violence. They kept him as close to the fire as possible, covered in a warm and valuable wool wrap. As time passed, he got worse. Tormented with a high fever, after a week of sufferance, he fell victim to delirium. There was nothing left to do. Despite the tender care and resorting to some magical concoction, poor Gostolino joined his mother in heaven.

Sant'Arduino was a castle built on the spur of an overhanging rock in the valley of the Apsa. Uberto, the castellan, like Bonzio had sworn his loyalty to the Counts of Pietrarubbia. Just outside of the walls of Sant'Arduino, still clinging to the mountain, there was a little village made of a miserable dwelling in stone, populated by peasants who worked for the surrounding small farms.

Ubaldo and his wife, Angelica, lived with the family in one of these hovels. Their existence would have been happy. They cultivated a plot of land alongside the river and, even in the most critical years and drought, they were able to set aside supplies for the winter.

But one can't have everything in life.

As soon as they were married, it was tradition that bride and groom make every effort to procreate. It was of vital importance that the peasants give birth to numerous offspring, with many sons destined to work the fields.

The beautiful Angelica was an excellent child bearer and birthed at least one child a year, almost always in the springtime. Healthy, strong and flourishing, she was able to sustain, in thirteen years of fertile matrimonial life, more than ten deliveries and a couple of miscarriages. Due to the scarce hygiene and disease, little more than half of the children survived the first summer, and a few who lived through the suffocating heat, died of pneumonia during the following freezing winter. It was a true hecatomb and, even worse, among the superstitious there wasn't even one single male.

Some gossip mongers commented that women, as always, were much tougher and more resistant than men, and this was why they had the courage and strength to endure the cruel labor pains of giving birth.

The six little sisters grew up healthy and, from early infancy, everyone noticed their unusual beauty. Dark curly hair and black eyes, they had high foreheads framed in little oval faces, with small upturned noses.

Ubaldo was a hard worker, and his wife, even while nearly constantly pregnant, knew how to give him a solid hand in running the land. There was so much to do. Besides working the ground, the animals needed looking after, as well as storing supplies to face the upcoming long and cold winters.

As long as the couple were able to withstand the fatigue and their funds continued to grow in abundance, Uberto wasn't worried about anything. Then, when Ubaldo's temples began to turn white and the early aches and pains set in, he realized the necessity to arrange for descendants. If six girls were nearly marrying age and, thanks to their beauty and the fertile small farm, it shouldn't be difficult to find candidates to wed them.

If in Sant'Arduino there were an abundance of females, in Pietrarubbia men were aplenty…

Baldassarre, the presbyter of Pietrarubbia, was a robust elderly man, well-fed and exacted respect. Much taller than the other parishioners, upstanding and committed, he managed the throng with the authority derived from his fame of wise and devout religion. The population of the village were made up of one unified family, and conducted a peaceful existence thanks to the reciprocal help during adverse times. The solidarity among the relatives was a determining supportive factor in overcoming hunger, misery, mourning and the numerous sufferance of life. The Domino participated as a good father to the vicissitudes of his own children, and he consoled and defended them every time they were in need. The Counts, even while holding him in high regard, did not appreciate his inclination to favor the commoners.

Gaddo, the young and inexpert Domino at Sant'Arduino, was skinny, pale and afflicted with chronic bronchitis that caused him to cough incessantly.

Shy and introverted, he was intimidated by the vassal Uberto and, even more, by the Pietrarubbians.

The responsibility of marriage was important in order to make a good impression. Ubaldo's daughters were similar to their mother and, possibly, equally as fertile.

Gaddo departed on foot on a beautiful morning in March. He was dressed in a dark wool tunic with the hood pulled down to cover his head.

The journey was short and without danger. Wading across the Apsa, he climbed the path toward Pietrarubbia. The sun illuminated the countryside, and the majestic castle reflected the warm rays of the light of day. The woods on the ridge had the thousand tones of the springtime colors.

The good Baldassarre was very happy to receive the inexperienced colleague of Sant'Arduino. It was a pleasure to converse with the young presbyter who, a true man of God, had only the parishioners close to his heart. Both cared little to nothing of honors and material goods. They only had one mission: behave *in persona Christi*.

While sitting in front of the fireplace of the rectory of Pietrarubbia, the two vicars began to talk about the delicate matter.

«I have a young unmarried man from a good family, with a house made of stone and a good piece of land to cultivate. He lives with the family of his brother. He has a bit of a restless character, but I'm certain a good wife would be able to subdue him,» exclaimed Baldassarre.

«Actually, I would need that the husband be willing to relocate to Sant'Arduino...» opposed Gaddo in a shy voice.

«With six daughters to marry off, too much can't be expected. We shall see, and in the meantime, if we are able to sort out at least one, we will see about making arrangements for the others. How old is the oldest?»

«She's seventeen, and it's time she marry...»

Typical of introverts, when they find themselves in the presence of he who instills uneasiness, Gaddo struggled to finish his conversation, and left it suspended as if, instead of affirmations, he was making suggestions while waiting for confirmation from the authoritative interlocutor.

«Oh, yes! At her age, one must know how to make do with what you've got. So, what is the child's name?»

«Gaia, and she is very God-fearing...»

Gaddo would have liked to add that she was rather pretty, and reddened at the mere thought of it passing through his mind.

Baldassarre understood instinctively. «Is she a pretty child?»

The young parish priest was taken aback and, blushing even more, turned scarlet. He covered his face with a hand and was able to nod while coughing.

Baldassarre restrained himself from smiling and, with difficulty, assumed an appropriate demeanor. He liked Gaddo, who was as transparent as water from a spring, a simple boy, incapable of hiding his feelings, pure and honest. A priest was, after all, still a man, and wasn't modesty possibly a virtue of unseemly thoughts? With time and experience, he would become an excellent pastor of souls.

«The groom that I had in mind for your Gaia, *perhaps*, couldn't be defined as a handsome young man, but you know that beauty is short-lived, I would say fleeting, while goodness is usually a quality that endures...»

The elder Domino offered suggestions to the youth in how he could argue the potential objections of the homliness of Zanino.

The two religious men then spoke of other single men and other spinsters without, however, finding anyone that, for age and benefit, would be appropriate either one for the other. At the end of their conversation, Baldassarre offered his guest a basket of little red apples, sweet and juicy, which they enjoyed with an exquisite peppered sheep cheese and crispy chickpea fritters. They drank the crystal clear water from the spring of Guiduccio.

Zanino was intimidated by the parish priest, fearing his

scoldings and, even though impossible, tried to avoid him. In Pietrarubbia the day began with the summoning of the bell. At first light, before going to the fields, the plowmen gathered in church for mass, and it was a grave sin if one wasn't present. In the hope of passing unnoticed, Zanino tried to hide amidst his relatives, but the Domino, to assure that he was there, appeared to seek him out with his eyes among the people. That severe and demanding priest had the innate ability to dig up, in an instant, the hidden secrets in the most remote corners of a man's conscience. It was useless to lower one's head or, even worse, pretend to pray. If you had sinned, it was written on your forehead, even if you were illiterate.

One cold and rainy morning, after Holy Mass, the young man was hurrying down toward his house.

«Zanino!»

He immediately recognized the deep voice of the parish priest, and jumped with surprise and fear. The day before, he had let slip a certain lascivious compliment to a cousin. Had that traitor told on him? Now he would be subjected to a long lecture, and who knows what penance he would have to endure for forgiveness. Turning around, he lowered his head and awaited his reprimand in silence.

«Son, I'll be waiting for you this evening before dark, with your brother. See to it that you are punctual.»

As soon as he arrived home, he warned Bastiano.

«What have you done this time? Who were you rude to? You'd better make up your mind to watch your tongue, before someone cuts it off!»

The brother was furious. How is it possible that this unruly boy is always looking for trouble?

They worked that day with other plowmen, cutting wood in the forest under the watchful eye of Tosco, the Count's factotum of Pietrarubbia. Time dragged on, and the hours were interminable.

Zanino kept his head down and worked hard without stopping all day.

At sunset, everyone exhausted except Tosco, they made their way back to the village.

The presbyter was waiting in front of the door of the rectory. He was smiling and didn't appear angry. Actually, he was very kind.

«Come in.»

He received them in the kitchen and, after making the accommodations, even offered them a good light wine, not the least bit acidic and not too aromatic, possibly the same drank by the Lords at the castle.

So what did he want, and why so much respect?

The Domino didn't waste time in useless digressions.

«I will ask the Count permission for Zanino to marry Gaia, the oldest daughter of Ubaldo of Sant'Arduino.»

He referred only to the older brother who, as head of the household, needed to be informed. He would have been the only one who could have any objections or oppose, even if to no avail. And who would ever have the audacity to argue with Domino Baldassarre?

Bastiano, in any case, was very pleased. «It would take a proper wife to set your head straight!»

Even Zanino seemed enthusiastic at the idea of finally putting into practice all of his amorous designs with a woman, even if he felt a bit uncertain.

«Will she really want to marry me?» he asked.

Hearing the piercing and nasal voice of the awkward and ugly little man, the Domino couldn't help but think, "Let us hope for the best..."

The arrival of Gaia inconvenienced the relative calm of the Gasparini household.

Zanino, absorbed by the frenzy of carrying out his duties as a good husband, waited with impatience every evening for the moment to climb to the low and crowded loft, where he spent blessed moments of intimate happiness with his wife.

Mafalda, a bit envious, tried to complain, claiming that all the nocturnal groaning kept her awake, and to console her, Bastiano found himself obliged to distract her by following his brother's example. Soon enough, a new generation of Gasparini would come into the world.

Filippuccio had seen her, and liked her very much. She was more or less as tall as him, young, beautiful, dark-haired and voluptuous. How could such a divine creature end up as the wife to an ugly toad like Zanino? Fraudolente realized immediately that the Bastard was attracted to the loveliness of the new bride.

«My Master, if you desire, and with certain ease, you too, could enjoy yourself with the pretty peasant. She is the wife of a servant, and you are the brother of the Lord,» proposed the scarred man.

Corrado, ruthless in implementing rules and punishment, had no tolerance for useless violence and consequential disorder.

«Lords are Lords, and should have nothing to do with the servants!» he loved reiterating to the Bastard.

Forced to obey by making the best of a bad situation, Filippuccio managed by pretending to misunderstand the reference of the doubts of his origins.

At least for now, until a favorable occasion presented itself, such as the momentary absence of Corrado, it would be advantageous to avoid mounting the new mare. But, sooner or later...

Gostolo had commissioned Mafalda, his cousin's wife and daughter of the blacksmith in Piega, some arrowheads.

Gasparino, ever the shrewd and well-connected trafficker with a multitude of relatives far and wide, was able to get them for her.

Before the arrival of the snow, Gostolo had cut a nice branch from a yew in the woods, resistant and light, perfect for making a well-proportioned bow, eighteen fists tall between the two tips of the cord and very easy to manage.

He worked with precision, as the true artist he was. He braided a cord of hemp that he rubbed over and over with beeswax. Then he went to work on the arrows. Seven fists long, from the nock to the barbs of the well-sharpened arrowheads, he was able to make about ten.

Every evening, before going to sleep, Carola prayed for her grandson. She whispered her prayers, asking for the protection of the Holy Virgin Mary. The husband didn't much appreciate these litanies and didn't ascribe to fate for that precocious loss.

«That miserable son of ours, soaking him like that in freezing water...»

Gostolo didn't know how to forgive, or was unable, and wanted to hold someone guilty at any cost. He was tormented with remorse for not keeping his eye on that little ruffian. If he hadn't run downstairs because he had eluded the supervision of his grandparents?

At this point, he felt like a useless old man who was a burden, not even able to look after a three-year old boy.

Tosco, the trusted man of the Counts, kept an accurate register where nothing escaped his control, noting with accuracy the birth and death of all the animals.

They nicknamed him Tosco because he was a native of *Tuscania* and was without relatives in Pietrarubbia. He was very robust and rather corpulent, with thick black curly hair, a hooked nose and a mouth crooked on one side. He lived in a small dwelling next to the stables and, being in charge of the supervision of the plowmen and small farms, was feared and respected. The rumormongers whispered that, in agreement with some of the farmers, he stole chickens and rabbits, but no one ever had the courage to spy on the Masters.

That winter, food was scarce, and people got by on oatmeal bread soaked in vegetable broth.

Gabriolo and Maffiolo, respectively little more than six and seven years old, and whose grandmother tried to leave the best morsels for them, were scrawny, pale and emaciated.

They had by now, reached the age in which there were hopes of them contributing to working around the house and in the fields, and to looking after the animals.

Gostolo feared that putting them to work might cause them to become ill, or even worse, to die.

It was necessary to procure some substantial delicacies in order to give them some stamina.

And so it was decided. Without telling anyone, a couple of hours before sunset on an evening in June, with the bow in his hand and the arrows in his belt, he walked quickly toward the mountain.

He was wearing pants and a heavy tunic under a course wool tippet with a hood. His clothes were of various light and dark tones of brown, which allowed him to be camouflaged.

He knew where to go, beyond the ridge, in a small clearing, the ideal grazing land of deer and chamois.

He positioned himself against the wind, behind a bush and, after arming himself with the bow and quickly waxing the cord, he waited.

With two fawns following her, a doe came out of the semi-darkness of the woods. She raised her ears and stopped to smell the air. Reassured, she began to graze with her younglings around her.

To avoid any mistake, Gostolo moved closer. On his knees behind a bramble of blackberries, he aimed the bow and, with a steady hand, hit the target.

He let fly and struck, on its left side and behind the shoulder, the bigger of the two fawns. The mother raised her head and saw him. They ran off.

Gostolo followed them. The wounded animal had lost a lot of blood, and was easy to track. He found it, alone and on the ground soon thereafter. It was gasping for air, with terror in its languid eyes, like those of a woman in love. He ended its life by slitting its throat with the knife.

Before returning home, he waited for darkness to fall.

After the death of her grandson, Carola had figured that her husband, sooner or later, would have done something foolish. Gostolo, introverted by nature with little inclination to cheer, had passed the winter in front of the fireplace, dazed like a bear in hibernation.

Not even the first warm days and the oncoming springtime could bring him out of his melancholy.

And now, why this sudden change? Why did he leave like that, without even saying goodbye, a few hours before sunset and in the dangers of the night?

Husband and wife, even through the hundreds of quarrels and misunderstandings, had lived and faced with courage and love the hardships, the hunger, the starvation, the disease and all of the misfortune common among the poor who had the unfortunate fate to be born peasants. Carola, without her old grumpy husband, would be lost.

Where had he gone? As darkness arrived, she started pacing back and forth from the fireplace to the kitchen window. She saw the neighbors returning, exhausted from a hard days' work.

When Agnolo came out of the hole of the stairs, the first thing he looked at was what was boiling in the pot, in hopes of finding something better than the usual broth.

«Where did papa go?»

He understood the worry in his mother's expression. «He left without saying a word.»

The last flickers of twilight were leaving some light flashes of dim illumination before the deep dark of the night, and the sky seemed to fill with stars.

«And from where do you come?»

The sarcastic voice, almost mean, without a doubt masculine and arrogant, shocked Carola who squinted her eyes to see in the dark.

Gostolo gave a start, recognizing Fraudolente, and tried to hide the fawn behind him. He opened his eyes wide and bowed his head. He had been exposed, and by he who would never conceal the crime. He didn't even give him time to explain himself.

Alvisio hit him hard in the back of the head with a heavy oak stick. He fell stunned, without a sound.

More than out of sight, Carola sensed, and let out a scream.

«Gostolo, Gostolo! Killers!»

Fraudolente looked up toward the window and the woman recognized the sneer of the scarface.

«You take the old man, and I'll take care of the bow and the chamois!»

Alvisio obeyed and dragged the victim.

Corrado couldn't wait to sink his teeth into the piglet. He was about to go to dinner when the clamour of soldiers echoed throughout the court of the castle.

«What's happening?»

More than alarmed, Corrado was annoyed.

Fraudolente made a triumphant entrance with the chamois in his arms.

«My Lord, we caught a contraband poacher red-handed!»

Filippuccio instantly stood up to get a better look at the animal.

«And a chamois. It will be tender and delicious,» he commented proudly for the craftiness as the favored servant.

Alvisio, holding up the culprit who was dazed by the clobbering and still at the mercy of his stunned condition, came in.

«Here's the hunter!»

Corrado moved toward the poor wretch. He grabbed him by his hair, pulling up his head and recognized him.

«He's the old man of the village. Is it possible that we can't trust anyone anymore? Call Tosco. Bring him here immediately!»

He was in the kitchen, so he didn't have long to wait.

In a hurry to obey, he presented himself with a greasy face from picking a bone clean, and wiped his chin on his sleeve, further deforming the crooked side of his mouth. He bowed.

«I am at your service, Lord.»

He had heard everything from the kitchen, and foresaw the orders of the Master.

«Close the scoundrel in the cell below. Tomorrow I'll tell you what to do with him.»

Gostolo was leaving as he was regaining consciousness and looked confusingly at his surroundings. The pain in his head was agonizing.

Tosco picked him up under one arm, and Alvisio the other. The guilty party remembered what he had done, and began to shake for fear. While they were taking him away, he tried to turn around to speak.

Tosco grumbled, «Quiet, imbecile! Do you want to make matters worse?»

He was right. Nothing the grievous man could have said or done would have helped. His fate was sealed.

They took him underground and threw him on the dirt floor, in a dark and damp cell.

Giovanna, Corrado's sister, was small, hunchback and had one shoulder much lower than the other. Of excellent and very noble ancestry, and even though her father would have provided a good dowry, she was never able to find a man worthy and courageous enough to marry her. At the ripe age of twenty-five years old, she was destined to remain a spinster.

Dark-haired, with thick eyebrows, a low forehead and jug ears, she looked suspiciously like the Gasparini of Pietrarubbia. Moreover, she spoke with an adenoidal voice like the peasant family, and the scandalmongers gossiped about the name of the Mother Contessa's lover. In truth, since blood is thicker than water, and the difference between nobility and plebeians is only a question of common money and power, the Counts were, most likely, closely related to their modest peasants.

With the arrival of the beautiful Costanza in the family, who boasted only virtues and revealed no faults, Giovanna, a child at that time, discovered a new sentiment, envy for her enchanting sister-in-law. In fact, until the arrival of Costanza, she never saw herself as awkward and ungraceful. But the comparison was harsh and obvious.

Taddeo's wife, Agnesina of Ugolino of the Fantolini was also attractive, even with black and crooked teeth.

Giovannina suffered over the competition of the sister-in-laws, friendly and very beautiful. There was nothing to do about it. Her looks were unappealing to the point that, defending herself from wicked people, as she grew up she became, as they say, mean and ugly. She hoped that Costanza would die of a miscarriage, but assisted her, and hid her cruelty behind the mask of kindness.

The dining companions, not bothered in the least over the unexpected event, hadn't lost their appetites.

Corrado looked askance at his sister, who was intent on choosing the best piece of pork. With an expression of disappointment, she grabbed a hock with her hands.

«So, my brother, what punishment will you inflict on the poacher?» asked Giovanna.

«We'll think about it tonight, and tomorrow you'll know.»

«Will you hang him, or cut off one of his ears?»

Filippuccio intervened, «To discourage other similar episodes, an exemplary punishment would be appropriate. I propose that he be hung in front of the entire village.»

Anselmo, the young servant, while filling the wine, spilled it out of the jug.

With a smile, malignant and malicious at the same time,

Giovanna reprimanded him, «What's wrong, maybe you're afraid? Have you, too, been poaching?»

Filippuccio sneered amusingly, and the servant flinched and turned red.

«My sister, the boy is too jittery for archery!»

Anselmo didn't speak and, as soon as possible, returned to his post in the shadows.

Distracted, Costanza picked at a bone and seemed to be ignoring the discussion. Then, unexpectedly intervened. «If I'm not mistaken, the person in question is Gostolo, the grandfather of the little boy who died last winter. He's an old man, and has only one male son and two grandsons who are children.»

It was the only way to save him. Who would cultivate the fields and take care of the animals? Everyone knew that Agnolo was stupid, unable to take the place of his father. At the moment, and to his good fortune, Gostolo was indispensable to his Masters.

At sunrise the next morning, before working in the fields, Tosco went down to the village and notified everyone that, at sunset, they were to gather at the castle.

It was ordered by the Count, and no one would be so foolish as to run the risk of not being present. Carola passed the day in tears, holding the ladle immobile in an insipid soup of vegetables.

The Court was illuminated by the flickering light of the smokey torches, and the intense scent of burnt resin rippled in the air. The peasants arrived stealthily, one family at a time, and stood around with their backs to the arched entrance.

Standing behind them with a concerned expression was Domino Baldassarre, formidably tall, presiding over his scared flock of sheep. When he learned about what had happened, for a moment, he hypothesized asking the Count to pardon the convict, but he knew Corrado. In similar cases, pleas had caused worse punishment.

Patience! There was nothing left to do but pray to God.

The last ones to enter were Gasparino who, out of spontaneous solidarity, stood beside Carola and the son.

Four armed soldiers kept watch that all proceeded without trouble. Tosco made sure that the children were in the front row.

From high above in the loggia, Corrado and Costanza, sitting on two wide chairs, appeared bored.

The Contessa had left little Roberto in the care of a maidservant, who had been strictly ordered to keep the child far from that violent exhibition. Giovanna and Filippuccio murmured and chuckled amongst themselves.

Tosco vigorously shook the pole that was stuck in the middle of the Court to make sure that it was stable and resistant.

Gostolo made his entrance, escorted by Fraudolente and Alvisio. Bare-chested, he walked with a stooped head. Fraudolente gave him a hard push, nearly like a blow to his back. He was disappointed that he made no resistance. Why wouldn't he react or try to escape? This was no fun.

Domino Baldassarre began to pray, and the whisper of his deep voice, even though he was speaking under his breath, was clearly understood by all present.

Tosco made the condemned man embrace the pole, and tied his hands tightly. Then he left him standing alone.

The poor man muttered a few groans, and to overcome the fear, he closed his eyes. He must prove himself courageous and not shout. He thought about how distressed his dear ones would feel seeing him agitated and suffering.

Tosco looked up, and Corrado gave his assent.

The leather whip was short and inflexible, and looked like a rod.

At the first blows, he was able to restrain himself and not cry out. The skin on his pale and bony back tore open under the whippings and began bleeding.

With a roar, Gostolo collapsed to his knees.

Carola squeezed Agnolo's arm and let out a desperate,

strained sob. Holding tightly to the pant leg of their father, Gabriolo and Maffiolo started to whine.

Zanino, shaking, had lost the proverbial arrogance and, with every whipping, whimpered like a puppy.

Some of the children joined in the weeping, while some of the other younger ones, unable to comprehend what was going on, were indifferent, only annoyed to be forced to watch that strange exhibition. A few even laughed, as if it were a game or some kind of entertainment.

Tosco continued undaunted, losing count of the lashes. When Gostolo, with his back reduced to bloody pulp, passed out, the executioner looked up to the loggia.

Even the worst tormenter, at times, could show mercy…

Corrado stood and, raising his right hand, he signaled that it was enough.

Tosco untied his hands, and the condemned man fell. Agnolo didn't know what to do. Could he come to his aid? Zanino looked up. The Count had left, and the Contessa, with teary red eyes, was about to follow him. It was time. With an arm, he dragged his cousin to tend to the wounds. Agnolo helped lift him over his shoulders.

Fraudolente reached out and slapped Gostolo on the back.

«Let this be a lesson to you! If it were up to me, you'd be dead,» he said, and the scar on his cheek contorted into a revolting sneer.

Alvisio turned and, with gaping eyes, commented, «It serves him right! That'll teach you not to poach!»

The following morning, Corrado and Filippuccio, escorted by Fraudolente and Alvisio, went out for a long ride on horseback. The young boy, Anselmo, was urgently summoned by Costanza. She gave him a basket full of leftovers, with pieces of white bread, good meat and pecorino cheese.

«Bring this to your aunt and uncle's house,» she ordered and, pointing to a small terracotta pot among the food, she added, «This is the medicament for Gostolo's back. Tell them that, after washing the wounds, they should rub in plenty of it, and then bandage them with a clean linen cloth. Hurry!»

Giovanna walked into the kitchen. When Anselmo stepped aside to let her pass, she scrutinized him lustfully. He understood, but said nothing.

The boy delivered the basket to Carola, who nursed her husband with the ointment of herb, mandragora, oil and honey.

And, though the concoction was evil-smelling, Gostolo survived and, after some time, healed. On the poor man's back, and in the soul of every inhabitant of the village, remained the everlasting and permanent memory of the scars.

When her brothers were gone, Giovannina usually stayed by herself, and the days, long and boring, felt interminable. To distract her from the melancholy, Costanza had attempted to involve her in the management of the household and the kitchen, but the sister-in-law refused the offer with disdain.

In September, in the early afternoon of a clear day of sunshine, was when the misadventure happened. The high-pitched screams resounded. Costanza and the servants rushed to her aid. Giovanna, lying on her pallet at the mercy of spasms, whispered, «Help me!»

She had lost copious amounts of blood.

Costanza sent everyone away, keeping only the eldest servant. Many hours passed, nearly till the night, before the labor pains expelled the fetus, and she calmed down a bit. But it wasn't over yet. For a few days, the hemorrhaging and cramping tormented the unfortunate woman until, gradually, the torture passed. Costanza, as attentive and diligent as a sister, tended her sister-in-law at her bedside.

She tried not to divulge the incident, but the village was near, and people gossip.

Filippo, the first of the brothers to be informed, made a diligent and punctual report to Corrado.

«I want to know who it was!»

The Count was not scandalized, and did not shout at his sister, nor did he give the impression that he knew. But he solved the problem.

Anselmo's mother was originally from Monte Boaggine, a castle under the dominion of Corrado.

The distance between the two castles was only a couple of hours on foot, but the shepherds of Monte Boaggine, tall and blonde, looked nothing like the short and dark peasants from Pietrarubbia.

Anselmo had inherited the best genes from his parents. With a high forehead and brown eyes and hair, he stood out like a giant among the other children. He would have become an excellent farmer, but his presence was noticed by Tosco, who informed the Masters. Taken from his family, he became a houseboy at the castle, with the prospect of a career as a soldier. But his strong physique didn't match an adequate personality. Passive, fearful and effeminate, in the masculine soldiery environment he was the target of ferocious ridicule, which he endured without resistance. His only help came from the protection of Costanza, who she had allocated definitively to the kitchen. Anselmo would be a humble houseboy till the end of his days.

Among his duties, he had to make periodic trips to Monte Boaggine, where his aunts and uncles lived. At the valley floor, under the wide and fertile highland of Carpegna, there was a big mill. Anselmo was in charge of delivering orders and messages to the castle and the mill. He liked those short journeys very much. Even if he feared encountering some mischievous troublemaker, it was still an opportunity to escape the sad monotony of Pietrarubbia and the cruel jokes of the soldiers.

«You have to go to Monte Boaggine. We need two masons right away.»

Tosco, before the autumn rain, would have the cistern cleaned and, if necessary, the crevices plastered.

Anselmo departed early in the morning. The sky was limpid and clear. It was easy to distinguish the coast and the sea on the faraway horizon. The boy walked the path toward the mount. When he reached the summit above Pietrarubbia, he stopped and shaded his eyes with his hand. The rooftops of Macerata, between the cultivated fields and villas glistened in the sun, and the other villages, castled on the mountains, stood out along the valley of the Apsa and of the Folia River as far as the sea.

He had heard the stories of the soldiers and the legends of the village. None of his relatives had ever seen the sea up close. To be able to travel there was a dream that Anselmo had cherished since childhood. There were fascinating tales about lands beyond the Adriatic, those that, after the rain on the clearest days, were difficult to grasp from the peak of Carpegna. They were inhabited by different people; dark and ferocious giants who, from time to time, crossed the sea to kill and pillage.

He shivered with fear. Monte Boaggine wasn't far but, to get there, he needed to walk up a trail in the bushy and dark woods of beech. Hidden dangers could be behind every corner and each tree, or concealed by a boulder. He couldn't help himself. He was unable to pass through that stretch without abandoning himself to anxiety and terror of the unknown and of the otherworldly.

It wasn't the main entrance to Monte Boaggine, and wouldn't even have been possible to pass through with a small cart. It was only a lane, perfect on foot or for leading mules. The ground was rocky and, in the case of rain or snow, it was easy to slip.

Anselmo began the climb. After the first straight distance, he moved behind a dried-up gnarled tree trunk. The wind whistling, high above, moved the trees. Could it be an animal?

He shouted when Fraudolente appeared.

«Here's our Anselmo! Where are you headed?»

Of all the people he could have encountered, he was probably the worst. He blocked the road and dominated him from above.

«I'm going to town by order of the Count!»

He hoped that naming the Master would placate Fraudolente.

«Really? I'm also here by order of Corrado.»

He was mocking and insolent, as usual.

«Me, too!» echoed Alvisio from behind.

Fraudolente sneered. «And to think, we took you for a damsel… But they say that you are very admired by the noblewomen.»

Anselmo understood, trembled and cried.

The two accomplices smirked. At this point, he was trapped, and they might as well have some fun.

«So, how was the Contessa? They say the ugly ones are hotter than the beautiful ones. And she is truly horrendous!»

«Have mercy!» begged the boy.

Alvisio, from behind, put a hand on his shoulder.

«Eh, see what happens when you go with women?»

Pulling out the sharp dagger, in a quick movement, he cut his throat.

For an instant, Anselmo remained standing. The last thing he saw before falling to the ground, was the satisfied grimace on Fraudolente's marred face.

They threw his body behind some broom trees, on the valley floor, far from the road and the trail. This is how poor Anselmo disappeared, as food for the animals and without the benevolence of a grave.

«Nobody can know,» the Count had commanded his assassins. But, accomplices in frequent and abundant drinking, Alvisio couldn't keep quiet. In no time, the tragic death of Anselmo was known by everyone, including his lover.

One evening, Costanza found her sister-in-law in tears in front of the fireplace. But was unable to console her.

1295

The freezing winter didn't spare the old and the young. In Pietrarubbia, four children under the age of five and two elderly over the age of fifty died from the cold and from fatigue. It wasn't any better at Monte Boaggine, where the village and castle were exposed to the cold north winds.

In San Lorenzo, there were no victims. Bonzio, as always, had accumulated sufficient provisions to face the harsh weather, and everyone survived. In the spring, there was still food and wood to burn in abundance.

Her face gaunt, pained, and a bit of gray hair, Rosa had lost weight. Yet, according to the men who patronized the castle, she was still a beautiful girl.

Maria, on the other hand, had grown into a very lovely young lady, taller and shapelier than her sister.

Since that cursed day at the spring of Combarbio, she hadn't uttered a word. In the early days, Rosa had tried to elicit her with questions, and often funny banter, to get her to speak. Then, given that every attempt was futile, she stopped tormenting her.

In early March, Bonzio decided to brave a long journey on horseback with the loyal Gasparino. They meticulously armed themselves, ready to battle any unexpected danger.

They departed at the crack of dawn, descending to the valley floor and took the path along the bed of the Conca River. From below Monte Cerignone, the riverbed was narrow and grueling, and the riverbanks were high and steep. The area would have been ideal to set a trap for an ambush to travelers. They went back up a gradual incline to the safety of a shady wood of centuries-old beech trees and, traveling the steep road north, reached the passage to the valley of the

Maricula.

From above, the steeples of the castles towered, and the view extended an intense blue endlessly to the sea.

So many battles and so many deaths in that gorgeous valley…

In the late afternoon, they reached the sight of Piega. Majestic and impregnable with its imposing towers, the castle was fortified on a summit of a hill on the eastern bank of the Maricula.

It belonged to the historic and noble family degli Olivieri for generations, and was the town where Maddalena was born, the "good" cousin of the Lords and Ladies. The marriage, truly unusual for those times, was not arranged. During one of the numerous missions that the young Bonzio had carried out for his Masters at the castle of Piega, the two youths had met. The degli Olivieri family had a multitude of children and nieces and nephews, and many young girls to marry off. Even if he wasn't *well-bred,* a vassal was a good catch and, with all those daughters to wed, it was better to make do. Without taking into account that the bride's dowry would have been proportionate to the meager wealth of the husband…

These were the valid grounds as to how their modest wedding was acquiesced. Maddalena, in love with that giant dark-haired man with eyes as blue as a clear sky, moved to San Lorenzo, and never burdened her adored husband with the obvious decline of social conditions. In any case, for his daughters, the ambition was to marry them off to wealthy and noble relatives from Piega. And Bonzio, to honor the memory of his wife and find an heir that could succeed him at the castle, decided to try.

At the guard post they began keeping an eye on them. There was no doubt they were two knights, but from faraway it wasn't possible to distinguish their emblems. First, it was necessary to verify where they were headed. When it was clear that Piega was the destination, one of the lookouts ran to warn Bartolino's nephew.

«Lord, Lord!»

He was gasping out of fear of being punished for waiting too long before sending the alarm.

Tignaccio didn't treat his uncle's soldiers with too much familiarity. As the son of one of the sisters of Geltrude, Bartolino's wife, in spite of his physical prowess and outstanding mind, he couldn't aspire to more than a mediocre military career within the small castle.

To maintain a proper and strong hierarchical order, he upheld the importance of formality with those twenty crude and obtuse soldiers under his command, which made up the entire military of Piega.

«What's happening?»

«Come, come and see! Two knights are already at the entrance, and we don't know...»

«Imbeciles!»

Tignaccio, in an instant, was on the bastions.

The two strangers were approaching, in step and calmly, toward the castle. The first, in his armor of dark, and what appeared, shining new leather layers, mounted a beautiful horse. The other, much more humble, small and cobbled together, came forward perched on a modest nag.

He figured they weren't dangerous, but it seemed foolish to run any risks, so he had the entrance closed.

The strangers moved to the walls.

«Who goes there?»

The voice was male, with the timber of youth.

The first knight, the real one, uncovered his head with the intention of being recognized. He had dark hair and light colored eyes.

«Don't tell me you're little Tignaccio!»

The boy had grown and, damn, to see him like this at first glance, he looked like a young bull.

It took a moment for Tignaccio to recognize him. In truth,

he had rarely seen this man, and certain uncles don't usually use so much coaxing to distant nephews.

«I am Bonzio, from San Lorenzo, open up!»

This is how the mission of matrimony of Bonzio in Piega began.

Bartolino degli Olivieri was a good man and a good soldier but, without a doubt, an awful politician. His castle was a thorn in the side to the Count Galasso of Montefeltro, Lord of Secchiano and cousin of the fearsome Counts of Pietrarubbia. It was about two neighboring lineages of the valley of the Maricula that, for generations and without any sense, both shamelessly changing political orientation according to the direction of the wind of the unpredictable powers that be was blowing, they gave each other a good whipping, and with alternating fortune.

As often happened in the fights between neighbors, those more frequent and caused more by pride than by valid reason, given time, rather than mitigate the bad blood, it only served to intensify it. With the passing of years, the thousands of quarrels implicated ever worsening effects and grave consequences. At first, it was the wounded. Then for vendetta, death and rape. With trespassing and pillaging as a regular occurrence, the limit between right and wrong of the adversaries was vague.

Piega, though, didn't have the strength of Secchiano, nor the strong alliances of the Montefeltros to sustain them. Therefore, it would have been better for Bartolino to tolerate, and temper his highly noble passion.. The wife, like most women, above all those of others, were in favor of dialogue and negotiation, and feared the uncertainty and the mourning of war. Geltrude hoped that her son would inherit only a castle, and not the family hatred.

But Olivieri, worthy son of his father, nursed resentment and vendetta. As if that weren't enough, he liked women, especially those of others and, even more so if they were unconsenting, and belonged to Secchiano. Antonio, the younger brother, closer in character to his mother, would have certainly been a good heir, preferable to that scoundrel Oliviero.

But, at times, destiny doesn't allow choice of the best, particularly to the second born.

Beyond the ridge, in the valley of the Conca, it was common that the population would have somatic and genetic characteristics similar to those of the Umbrians, short in stature and dark-skinned. In the wider extensions that expanded toward the coast and the Padana valley, on the other hand, blood was mixed for the most part. Men and women were often tall and blond with light colored eyes.

In the higher classes, where nourishment was better, the contrast to their small and black neighbors was even more evident, and degli Olivieri, regardless of age, were all beautiful and strong.

Though, one couldn't say likewise of the Pietrarubbians, nor of the Galassos and Montefeltros.

The hate between the two adjoining descendants had a multitude of valid motives, but the incidents and the numerous skirmishes were so many that it had become, by now, impossible to establish which were the original causes of the feud, and who was at fault. They detested each other, and that was that; like a cat and dog that lived in two adjacent yards and belonged to two different owners.

That evening, Lady Geltrude wanted to organize a banquet in honor of Bonzio, going all out on food and libation. The humble and distant cousin gorged himself, as was the custom to show appreciation.

Around the dark oak table in the big hall, after dinner they sat and talked near the dim flickering light from the flames of the fireplace.

«Well, Bonzio, it's time you tell us about Maddalena and your family.»

Bartolino wanted to know everything, and in detail. In Piega, the news that arrived was contrasting and unreliable. Like always, time, distance and the imagination of all the gossipmongers had created, from baseless rumors, some incredible variations of the brutal reality.

«Cousin, have you any suspects? Maybe the Malatestis?» asked a crying Geltrude after hearing Bonzio tell his story.

«Dear cousin, I have doubts about our presbyter, who, however, denies that he has seen or heard the assassins.»

Geltrude was serious and pensive for a moment. Then she didn't hesitate. «Years ago, your wife told me some strange things about Domino Santi. She didn't like him one bit, and that's all she said...»

To express specific opinions about a priest, even within the family, wasn't considered appropriate, but *domi suae quilibet rex* and, in certain situations, Geltrude didn't mince words.

That night, *in camera caritatis,* Geltrude confided her fears to Bartolino. It was time to stop retaliating Galasso and his men's provocations! To end the war, it was necessary that one of the adversaries, at least once, manage to suffer the consequences without getting revenge.

«Bonzio is a vassal of Pietrarubbia, and we have maximum trust in him. Why not marry one of our boys to one of his daughters? We could reinforce the family relations with who might have all the interest in helping us?»

Bartolino wouldn't speak of it.

«He is not a nobleman. He is a good man, but is only a simple castellan. I have other ambitions for our sons!»

«And if, instead of a son, we negotiate a nephew?»

Tignaccio was perfect. In Piega, he was a simple commander of the guards and little more than a servant, but marrying a daughter of Bonzio, could make him the heir of a vassal in the future.

And having a nephew in the ranks of Pietrarubbia, cousins of the hated Count Galasso, given time, wouldn't be bad.

A visit of Gasparino in Piega was always an event. The cousins arrived by the hordes, longing for news and current chatter about the latest happenings in Pietrarubbia. Gasparino ate mixed vegetable pork soup at the home of the blacksmith in front of the fireplace with a dozen noisy guests. He gossiped about births, deaths, disease, lovers and fights from the Montefeltro highland. He even arranged a few marriages between the single men and women. As acidic and evil-tasting it was, the wine flowed abundantly, and many that evening, ended up sleeping on the floor, warm, in front of the last embers of the fire.

TIGNACCIO

The following morning Tignaccio was summoned by his uncle to the stables.

The son of a plebeian, notwithstanding his mother's noble origins, the boy found himself in the ungrateful position of one who was, in reality, one of the family, yet carried out the humble charge of a servant. His physical looks and good nature, combined with his indisputable loyalty to the descendency, had allowed him a relatively peaceful life up till that moment, even if it was dedicated only to the service of the Lords. He was rather close to the two cousins, especially Antonio.

Geltrude and Agnese, Tignaccio's mother, belonged to a greatly noble ancestry from Rimini. These natives didn't coincide to an adequate legacy. The reason being that generations of involvement in thousands of ill-fated military skirmishes caused the ancestors of the two girls to squander nearly the entire patrimony of the family. The ancient dynasty was decidedly destined to a miserable decline and, with the two daughters as the last and only heiresses, to an inevitable extinction. In the cities a new and rich social class was gaining ground which, thanks to money and marriages to the impoverished nobility, aspired redemption from its mediocre lineage. In Rimini, the common merchants prospered and, even if viewed by the Lords and Ladies and by the working-class with some degree of mistrust, they had become an indispensable component for the well-being of the community.

Bonvicino had learned the secrets of the craft from his father Benaccolto, also known as The Pisano. The Pisano had been a traveling merchant who went from village to village and city to city, drawn by mules. Specialized in the buying and selling of spices, mostly pepper, cinnamon and cloves, he also dealt myrrh and incense. It was all popular merchandise, and not only as condiments, but as preservatives and ingredients for medicine.

Benaccolto had began with a few mules and a servant. Then, as the years passed, he earned the fame of an honest man and, besides having a noble and sophisticated clientele, he was able to become the supplier to some noteworthy convents in Rimini. He became wealthy, his mules escalated to many and the number of drivers increased. The Pisano scraped together a nice little nest egg, and stopped traveling around the countryside and woods, leaving those risks of continual roaming about to others. He was able to buy a house and shop in Rimini where, even though a foreigner, by virtue of important friends and in high ranks, he officially integrated himself as a merchant. But he made his true leap of quality when, thanks to the intuition and ability of his son Bonvicino, he invested in the trading of refined textiles, highly in demand and more profitable than spices. His house grew in excellence and, with it, increased his credit and prestige. He died young, leaving his entire patrimony to his only, and fortunate son, Bonvicino.

Merchants were not well-regarded. The nobility and the clergy considered buying and selling and the consequent profits dishonorable, and the people, who often suffered from hunger, were envious of the newly rich from humble origins. In order to acquire a minimum of social prestige and respect, they made some compromises. Some families, noble and impoverished, possibly drowned in debt for having persevered in a standard of living suited to their old lineage, found themselves forced, *obtorto collo,* to marry their descendants to those common, but well-off merchants.

For Benno, who had only two daughters and a nice noble title, marrying the very young Agnese to the plebeian merchant Bonvicino was a good deal; exchanging the prestige of his name for the security of the wealth of the son-in-law. He was even able to save a minimum of capital to give an adequate dowry for the other daughter, the beautiful Geltrude who, in fact, happily married Bartolino degli Olivieri of Piega.

Benno was able to continue to keep possession of his royal residence in the center of Rimini and guarantee a minimum of semblance of noble decorum. He had the good fortune of a peaceful old age, close to his daughter and grandson.

The reasons were never known, but believed to be motivated by envy or the desperation of some debtor in difficulty.

One summer in the evening before nightfall, the beautiful home of Bonvicino caught fire. Thanks to the timely intervention of the neighbors, the fire was brought under control almost immediately and saved the surrounding buildings. Serious, though, were the damages to the stockroom on the ground floor, where almost all of the merchandise was lost. Behind the shop, the cadaver of the young merchant was found, repeatedly stabbed in the chest. Fortunately, Agnese had taken Tignaccio for a visit to his grandfather. Upon his return, the boy, who was just four years old, saw the mangled body of his father.

It was due to this tragic event that, the following year after the death of Benno, Agnese decided to leave the city. She moved to Piega with her sister, who was more than happy to take in the poor widow and the little orphan.

«Accompany Bonzio back to San Lorenzo.»

The order of Bartolino was peremptory, and the boy bowed his head in obedience.

The Lord moved in closer to look at him straight in the eye.

«Bonzio is man to our enemies, he lives in a castle, he has no male heirs and has a beautiful daughter to marry off. It will be for you, and for us, an excellent solution to all of the problems.»

Tignaccio was shocked. A wife and a castle, all of a sudden and first thing in the morning, wasn't something insignificant. These were radical changes... But Bartolino appeared to have made up his mind and contemplated that it wouldn't be worth contradicting him. For the umpteenth time, he held back and nodded, gritting his teeth.

«Naturally, you will always be one of us, even if at the service of the Pietrarubbians. Your future father-in-law is in agreement.»

The following morning, the return journey to San Lorenzo was tormented by a long and violent rainstorm; when, toward noon, they reached the pass, the ridge was brightened by a thin and soft blanket of late snow.

Bonzio had some difficulty finding subject matter of conversation and, up to that moment, the three travelers remained in complete silence. Gasparino, who understood little to nothing of the news, plodded along behind on the nag. Next to a giant like Bonzio, Tignaccio didn't make a bad impression. Imposing in their armor and more or less of the same body size, they looked like brothers. They retraced the narrow valley in descent but, when they reached the ford for Combarbio, the rain had swollen the torrent, making it impossible to cross. They found shelter in a decrepit binnacle along the riverbank, where they lit a fire to keep warm during the wait. While still under the refuge of the falling roof, Gasparino provided care for the horses, and Bonzio settled in, a bit hesitantly as if he feared a sudden collapse, on an old wooden bench. He gestured for Tignaccio to sit beside him, on what was left of an ancient faldstool.

«Well, young man, as soon as the flood passes, we'll go up to Combarbio and then to the peak of San Lorenzo where you will see the famous castle. Don't expect much. We're still working with all our men to repair and reinforce it.»

He mustn't frighten him, but not delude him either. The castle at Piega was much newer and, above all, not in the least dilapidated and in need of restoration. Tignaccio would have made comparisons and it was well that he be prepared.

The boy uncovered his head of blond hair and, smiling, spoke to his future father-in-law. «Lord, tell me, instead, about Rosa, so I can recognize her as soon as we arrive.» The young man was not shy, and this did not displease Bonzio.

Geltrude had made arrangements to supply their pouches with white and fragrant bread. They also weren't without squash flasks, full of good black, spiced wine.

«You never know what can happen while traveling...» Geltrude had insisted when Bonzio tried to refuse.

Even Gasparino, crouched down in a corner and farther away from the warmth of the fire, took advantage of that improvised supper to calm his appetite.

Bonzio, to kill time and just to talk about something, boasted to Tignaccio, «Rosa, my oldest daughter, is tall, blond and beautiful. She looks like her poor mama, and you'll see that she will be an excellent wife and a good mother to your children.»

Gasparino, who up till that moment believed to be the only one of the group to have schemed wedding plots in Piega, finally understood. He shuddered over the surprise and choked on a mouthful of food. He began coughing and, causing hilarity from the other two, turned blue in the face. Like his voice, his cough also had a strange and acute nasal tone.

That bold young man would become his new master. Who would have ever imagined it?

The rain didn't cease all day. At dark, Bonzio felt the ford was still too dangerous, and decided to camp out for the night. Gasparino provided more wood for the fire.

Tignaccio took the first guard duty.

The waters ran thunderous and violent in the bed of rocks and boulders of the Conca. Covering his shoulders with his cloak, the boy sat near the crackling flames, to which he fed a few dry branches.

In one single day his entire life had changed.

And now what did his future hold?

The next morning, the fury of the storm left in its place a tepid springtime sun. The last to stay awake and guard was Gasparino.

«Wake me as soon as dawn breaks,» Bonzio had ordered

before curling up in his cloak.

The river, even though still turbid and dirty, had calmed, and was now possible to cross. They climbed with difficulty first to Combarbio and then, upward to the parish church. From a small knoll, close to the ancient structure, it was possible to distinguish the white summit of Carpegna.

«At least we won't have a drought this summer,» commented Bonzio.

They crossed the wood, and reached the clearing dominated by the castle. Tignaccio saw his new home for the first time. Yes, it corresponded more or less to the description given the night before: an old fortress in need of care and restoration. And of a new castellan.

At San Lorenzo, Bonzio's favorite room was the one, that for many years, he had shared with Maddalena. The moments before falling asleep were the most difficult to overcome. So many memories, so many disappointing hopes and so many sad thoughts tormented him before tiredness was able to cloud his mind! When he thought it was all over and the anguish had left sleep in its place, horrendous and recurring nightmares would destroy him. Besides the faces of the fallen and tortured comrades in arms in battle, he often dreamt of his father who, desperate and dying, tried in vain to speak the names of the assassins. Disturbed and sweaty, he would wake with a start before Marino was able to talk. In the next room, the daughters heard his distress and, at times, his shouts. The two girls passed the entire night next to each other in their bed. Maria, obstinately shut in her mutism, seeked comfort from the tender and maternal embraces of Rosa and had reverted to sucking her thumb like a baby.

During the day, as soon as she could find a few moments for herself, avoiding the housework, she would find refuge on the walls, and passed her time staring, almost stupefied, at the same panorama: the grass, the woods and down below, faraway, the old parish church. The first few times, Bonzio also climbed upon the bastions, near his daughter, to console her and persuade her to come down. He was awkward, timid and embarrassed. It would have been much easier to face an enemy in battle, rather than that delicate daughter in the shock of pain...As a true soldier, he felt obligated to fight a new war. His goal in life was to be the one to bring Maria back among the world of the living and to recover her gift of speech. This way, maybe, he could denounce the villains.

But the task was revealing itself to be arduous enough to force him to surrender.

After the blizzard during the night, the morning was so clear that Maria felt like she could touch the mountains with her fingers. Even San Paolo was pure white, like the roofs of Montegrimano. It was a fleeting sprinkle, a dusting that would survive the spring heat for just a few hours. She recognized her father right away, followed at a short distance by the unmistakeable outline of Gasparino and by another knight. The stranger rode a nice steed and, though he didn't reach the size of Bonzio, he had to be a strong and robust soldier. The girl leaned out, waving from the top of the walls to be seen. Raising a hand, her father returned her greeting.

«Bonzio has returned!» yelled the guard.

For the first time in his life, Tignaccio crossed the entrance of San Lorenzo. In the middle of the court, a blond girl with light colored eyes passed by. Might that be his future wife? As pretty and graceful as she was, it seemed that she wasn't a young girl, but rather a mature woman.

"Is she older than me?" he wondered.

He regretted not having thought, the day before, to ask how old the betrothed was. He took it for granted that she were young, little more than a child, and now he found himself in front of a real woman! He was surprised at the authority in which she ordered the groom to take care of the horses. Even while suave and pleasant, at the same time the voice was decisive and it was she who gave the orders.

«This is my daughter, Rosa,» Bonzio strutted while introducing her. «And this is your cousin, Tignaccio degli Olivieri.»

Rosa bowed her head, hinting at a curtsy. He was truly a handsome boy, maybe a bit young.

They had waited in vain the previous evening and, with the blizzard, they were all very worried. Now, finally, they had returned.

From above at the bastions, Maria took in the scene. The sun, in the meantime, rose high in the sky, and the air was warmer. The poor child returned to her place, back to staring, sad and without expression, at the cruel world and the faraway horizon.

In honor of the newcomer, in a mad rush, after having slaughtered the chickens, that evening a succulent dinner was arranged. Since good manners dictated that the young virgins not participate at the unbridled revelry, Rosa and Maria stayed in the kitchen. In the dining hall, by the warmth of the huge fireplace, Bonzio and the future son-in-law merrily feasted on skewered cockerel stuffed with fresh and finely ground pecorino, all abundantly dressed with spices and doused with the usual red from the valley of the Conca.

Bonzio was an excellent warrior, a good father, a decent husband and a good castellan, but despite all of his good efforts, an awful builder. The restoration works proceeded badly and slowly. Talking with Tignaccio, he realized that the boy seemed very competent in his knowledge of stone, of lime and of bricks. In Piega, various master masons of great experience lived, and the young commander of guards looked after their work to learn the secrets.

He promised that the next morning he would make an accurate inspection of the old construction and of the quarry at Combarbio.

When Maria gracefully turned around to refill the wine, the men stopped talking. Tignaccio, who was bringing a full cup to his mouth, in the presence of such a wonder, he halted, holding his arm still.

Who was that enchanting child?

Realizing the effect he had created, Maria blushed from shame and from satisfaction. She hurried to the shadow of the big kitchen.

Bonzio introduced her, «This is Maria, Rosa's sister.»

Forced to pause, even if for only an instant, the girl let slip a smile of greeting. Tignaccio set his tankard on the table.

«It's a pleasure to meet you,» he uttered spontaneously and breathlessly.

Maria ran off but, before leaving the hall, she turned around for one last consuming glance.

If Maddalena had been there, she would have surely noticed that instant of passionate understanding. Bonzio, instead, the simple and ingenuous man that he was, didn't notice.

Seeing the pleased expression and the discomposure of her sister, Rosa had no doubt: Maria liked him.

At sunrise the next day, the two men inspected the entire castle.

«The problem to solve is the landslide. It's useless to reinforce the walls if the foundations move,» judged Tignaccio.

The walls facing the sun were the most ruined. Every winter, due to the incessant alternation of the daytime heat of the sun to the bitterly cold night, made them subject to repetitive and considerable jumps in temperature. The water and the ice, besides creviced walls, had caused large cracks, and the poor quality of mortar that cemented the rocks together didn't hold. They went down to the tufo quarry at Combarbio where three stonecutters worked. The rock, as soon as it was extracted, was soft and easy to sculpt into nice straight, square blocks. Out in the open air and with time, they would have hardened, becoming much more strong and resistant. The hard part was transporting them, on a mule's back up the steep, fragmented path to the summit of the mountain. The work was slow and laborious.

After a few days, Tignaccio began to settle in and appreciate the new family. Bonzio soon became very fond of him, and took to treating him with the respect and regard that a father usually has for a favorite son.

During a long and tedious rainy afternoon, making haste with the kitchen duties, Rosa and Maria joined the two men in front of the fireplace in the hall. Until that moment, there had been few occasions to speak openly.

Tignaccio, more and more engaged in the restoration works, had dedicated little time to spend time with and get to know the future bride. Sitting on the bench in front of the fire, the girls leaned tenderly on each other.

«Why don't you tell us something about your life?»

Rosa wasn't the least bit shy, and believed it necessary, and not only out of curiosity, to know a bit more about the suitor.

Tignaccio was taken aback. While he was happy at San Lorenzo, he still wasn't familiar enough to be able to open his heart and mind to his new relatives. However, it would have been rather rude not to respond to such a direct question. So, with a certain sense of modesty and almost embarrassment, he began to narrate the sad hardships of his childhood in Rimini. Even though he was very young at that time, the memory of finding the body of his father was clear and alive.

«We entered the shop. I had difficulty breathing and the smoke, acrid and dense, brought on a violent coughing attack. My mother called loudly for my father, who didn't answer. Holding my hand, we crossed the room. In the storeroom, face down on the ground near the exit, he was laying in a bloodbath...» the young man stopped talking.

Distressed in recalling that moment, he held back the emotion and tears.

Bonzio, who considered it essential that a real man did not show public displays of certain weaknesses, came to his rescue.

«C'mon girls, don't you have anything better to do than sit here and listen to this sad story? Where's supper?»

Rosa got the hint and jumped up. Maria, instead, remained sitting on the bench and, turned toward the wall, was with her face hidden behind her hands.

Her sister called her, «Come along, let's go.»

It appeared that she hadn't heard, and Rosa was forced to place a hand on her shoulder. She took her by the wrist to make her turn around.

Only then did Tignaccio himself see that Maria, upset, was crying in silence. She was beautiful and desperate, and no one had the nerve to try to console her.

In the following days, finally in the warm springtime sun, the works on the castle began again.

«Lord, since the lime is of the best quality, it's indispensable that the sand is clean, without clay, and it would be better to use less water to pug it.»

Bonzio was ever more surprised at how competent Tignaccio was. In no time, the boy became the master builder in charge of the restoration.

By the end of June, reparations had been made to the sections that had moved and with every crevice and crack sealed, all the walls had been renovated.

Bonzio complimented Tignaccio.

«You've done an excellent job, and Count Corrado will be very happy.»

The two men departed early in the morning. While he watched them leave, Gasparino realized he felt an unexpected impulse of sudden jealousy. Bonzio reminded him to guard well, to protect the daughters and to defend the castle, and this was, for him, reason to be proud and satisfied. In any case, accompanying him now was Tignaccio. Poor Gasparino, all alone, stayed at San Lorenzo, making it impossible to visit his family. And to think, after the journey to Piega, he would have had oceans of news to share…

Reaching the part of the road that descended into the dense woods, the two knights stopped and, for a few seconds, remained immobile to admire the ancient castle. As it stood, seen from faraway, in the middle of the green summit clearing and in the warm light of the sun, it looked powerful and majestic, ready to successfully sustain a long and exhausting siege. From the bastions appeared Maria's blond hair, that fluttered about, waving her arms as usual in farewell. They both waved back raising a hand.

«Will she ever talk again?» dared ask Tignaccio.

«I'm afraid that such pain and the horror of having witnessed the tragedy has taken away the capacity to speak again. If only, in the future, she would regain her voice!»

«What a shame! A child, so lovely and sweet, tormented by such a disgrace...»

Bonzio, for the first time, realized that the boy seemed to be a bit too involved, but didn't want to become suspicious.

They reached Pietrarubbia in the late morning. Fraudolente and Alvisio were lazing about in the Court.

«Who's the boy?» asked Fraudolente.

Bonzio gave him a dirty look and, without deigning him a greeting and an answer, ordered, «Announce my arrival to the Count!»

«Our castellan doesn't know good manners.»

The scarface bared his teeth.

«Indeed, here we'd need a nice lesson!» immediately replied Alvisio, opening his eyes wide, taking refuge behind the robust shoulders of his accomplice.

Tignaccio instinctively brought his hand to the hilt of the sword, ready to unsheathe. With a signal, Bonzio made him cease.

«Lords, I will announce you to the Count.»

Fortunately, Tosco was nearby, and intervened to subdue the fight before it began.

In the hall sat Corrado, Taddeo and Filippo, while Giovanna, intrigued, peeked out from the kitchen.

Bonzio entered, followed by Tignaccio. The boy remained

prudently behind, in the shadows next to Tosco.

«Here is our Bonzio, welcome!»

Taddeo knew how to be courteous, and appreciated the great and faithful soldier.

Standing and with his head uncovered in front of his Lords, Bonzio began the usual accurate report on how things were progressing at San Lorenzo, on the development of the works, on the births and the deaths and, most importantly, his prediction on what he thought the next harvest might bring.

Giovanna immediately saw the handsome young blond boy hidden in the back of the hall. She stared at him with too much interest, and the Count noticed.

«Who is that man?» asked an annoyed Corrado.

«My Lord, this person is Tignaccio of Piega. We are here today, to request your permission to give him my daughter's hand in marriage.»

Filippo carefully scrutinized the stranger and intervened, «Is he from the degli Olivieri family?»

Bonzio had prepared his answer. To define him that way would be like admitting that he was an enemy.

«No. He is the son of a merchant from Rimini and of Geltrude's sister, the wife of Bartolino degli Olivieri. He is an excellent soldier, is knowledgeable about construction and is loyal to our cause.»

Tignaccio's fine physique stood out, and it was obvious that, at least from that point of view, he would be a worthy successor to his father-in-law.

«Are you willing to vouch for him?»

Taddeo seemed pleased.

«My Lord, for generations my family is at your service. I would never propose a man who was not worthy and capable to serve you equally as faithful. I vouch for him as if he were my own son.»

Filippo would have liked to show disappointment, but Corrado didn't give him time and, with hardly any hesitation, he ruled, «So be it! You have my blessing. Marry this young man to your daughter.»

After some courtesies, the two men were dismissed.

Filippo wasn't able to hide his disdain. «Whatever people will say, he is still a degli Olivieri, a Guelph allied to the Malatestis!»

«Yes, it may be as you say, but Bonzio vouches for him and is giving his daughter as wife, I think it is the case to trust. In fact, in the future, it might be convenient to have a soldier that is familiar with the castle of Piega... And, this, in peace and in war.»

For Corrado there were no problems. At the slightest suspicion that the newcomer were spying for the enemy, with little effort and without a lot of clamor, thanks to the services of the accustomed and swift Fraudolente, it would be very easy to get rid of him.

Taddeo restrained himself to a satisfied nod, and Giovannina did likewise.

Corrado pointed his finger at his sister. «And don't you even think about it! Haven't you already caused enough trouble?»

The poor hunchback blushed out of shame and ran off, limping to the kitchen.

«Fine, now we can organize the wedding!»

As soon as he returned, Bonzio contentedly announced the happy news.

Without any joy, Rosa gave a hint of a smile, while Maria appeared completely indifferent.

After the journey to Pietrarubbia, tired and hungry, Tignaccio and Bonzio couldn't wait to sit down at the table. Supper was the moment when the entire family united and, if there were no guests, the two girls sat with the men, while the servants brought the courses back and forth from the kitchen. That evening, they ate a delicious and tender roe deer, flavored with pepper and aromatic herbs, and accompanied with fragrant white bread. A pitcher of sweet wine, cooked with honey, cinnamon and cloves, cheered the mood and the spirit of the dining companions.

They talked about hunting, politics and battles. And then, as was just and fair, of wedding plans. It would be appropriate to summon the notary and, above all, negotiate the dowry and wedding gifts. The noble Bartolino would intervene at the nuptials in place of Tignaccio's father, adding noteworthy prestige to the ceremony.

THE PARISH CHURCH

As in any small respectable village, where everyone knows everybody's business and knows about the life, death and miracles of each family and every inhabitant, even in Pietrarubbia, after working in the fields and in front of the fireplace, one of the favorite pastimes was the ancient and entertaining art of gossip. The people, whose scarce consolation for the struggles of a wretched life of poverty and hunger, found some comfort in meddling in others' vicissitudes, mostly in well-known families, and even more in those who lived in misfortune. From mouth to mouth and from home to home, the massacre of the spring of Combarbio reached exaggerated proportions. Some attributed the responsibility first to a corps of bandits and then, even, to a monopoly of ferocious and bloody henchmen payed by the hated Malatesti family.

It was said that the presbyter of the parish church, in secret, had seen the tragedy, and could recognize the faces of the villains. So, while the surviving child was simple-minded and, out of fear, had lost her reasoning and ability to speak, she would have been perfectly able to identify the assassins.

Through Tosco, the only one who could speak openly with the servants and, with certain discretion, even with the Lords, the gossip reached the ears of Fraudolente and Alvisio.

One afternoon in the late afternoon, the two friends were enjoying the shade of a fig tree on the premises of the village. They had passed the entire day waiting for Count Corrado and, tired of the ripe fruit and conversation, they remained bored in silence. Alvisio, in any case, was tormented by a doubt. «And if the Domino had really recognized us? If he was spying on us?»

He felt no remorse, only fear.

Fraudolente, on the other hand, was unconcerned.

«That stupid old priest didn't see you and, anyway, even if he did, he would never have the courage to tell.»

«And if Bonzio put him through the mill? Exactly because he is coward, he might end up telling him anything, maybe even inventing just what he's not sure of, and only to please him...»

«Haha! It wouldn't bother me in the least to see you chopped to pieces by the executioner,» laughed an amused Fraudolente.

Alvisio, instead, shivered at the thought of that atrocious punishment.

«Joke as you like, but I wasn't alone at the parish church...» he reminded him.

He threw his round and light colored eyes wide open, staring at the black, marred face of his friend from bottom to top. Then, lowering his head, he murmured his brilliant idea. «And if, with the excuse of a confession, I went to visit him? Maybe I could figure out if he saw us...»

Domino Santi enjoyed his peaceful life at the parish church of Combarbio very much, and all of the consequential comforts of his fortunate condition of old age and respected presbyter. He was interested in little to nothing of faith, prayers and the well-being of his herd of sinful lambs. What he cared about was having his pockets lined and his belly full and, at times, even if now only occasionally, a young cleric with whom he could secretly amuse himself.

Carrying out his tasks and the role of parish priest was a tradition of little effort, and caused him no fatigue. Sometimes he had to go up to the castle, or down to the village, but they were short journeys and, especially during the day, were hardly dangerous. Next to the parish church, there was a building with a small cloister of simple columns made of heavy stone. At the center of the court, the water from the roof was gathered in a great cistern and, more often than not, was utilized only as a reserve for emergencies, such as summer droughts or a potential siege. For the drinking water, it was necessary to go up to the spring. While the presbyter enjoyed the intimacy of a bedroom, the clerics shared a long and gloomy room with a row of miserable pallets. All of the locals had only one access to the cloister, and the external walls of the building, with the exception of the heavy dark wooden door, were without entrances. It was said that from there, at one time, was where the pilgrims passed through, and was the custom to give them hospitality. In any case, times had changed and now, at the hour of darkness and for vespers, once they entered back into the safety of the walls of the parish church, the main door was closed to leave the hidden dangers and menaces of the hateful world to the demons of the forest.

More than out of habit, all those prayers had become a real nuisance. Giacinto was a young cleric, and had the misfortune to be in the good graces of his old parish priest. The boy, who recently had the honor of the tonsure, had gotten used to the sad and monotonous life at Combarbio, punctuated by the canonical hours and by unrewarding tasks.

When he heard the banging at the main entrance door, without hesitating to be summoned, he ran.

«Who goes there?»

A guest, after the sixth hour, might be unwelcome, and even dangerous.

«I am Alvisio, the foundling! Tell the Domino that I'm here and I've come to visit him.»

Giacinto ran to call the priest.

«Domino, Domino!»

The shouts echoed in the rectory.

The presbyter, hindered by the large, light-colored nightgown, appeared at the doorstep of his room.

«Well, what has happened?»

He seemed annoyed. Maybe, Giacinto imagined, he was

praying or, most likely, sleeping.

«Domino, a man who says to be the orphan, Alvisio, is asking for you and wants to come in!»

After some hesitation, the priest went to the entrance and parted the square peephole. In the grip of nerves, before looking through the small hole, he blinked several times.

«Wh...who goes there?» he asked obstinately.

«It's me, Domino. Do you recognize me?»

An unexpected and smiling Alvisio was at the door.

«Wha...what do you want?» His stutter wouldn't cease.

«Domino, I have sinned! I'm here to beg forgiveness and penance.»

The villain wanted to confess, and a good presbyter, in the face of his clerics, was morally obliged to accept.

«Giacinto, open up!»

Alvisio heard unfastening and the removal of the heavy wooden bar. He found himself in front of a cleric, seemingly little more than a child, even if tall and good-looking. He noticed the eyes and brown hair.

Giacinto, in the presence of the jovial round face of the orphan, relaxed.

«Welcome, make yourself at home!» he invited, stepping aside.

Alvisio darted a fleeting complicit glance, which revoked in an instant the painful and unalleviated memories of childhood. He gathered the flicker of the anxiety and fear that he, unfortunately, had experimented in the eyes and soul of that young man's religious formation. He wanted to run from that gloomy cloister, and felt chills.

«My son, wel...welcome home!»

The priest did his best to avoid stuttering.

Alvisio found him fat, aged, and without even the memory of hair, let alone dark hair. He had the impression that he had become even more slimy and false than before. He reminded him of an old, fat gossip from Pietrarubbia, a chubby and lecherous woman, who was spoken badly of in her youth, and had been with many men for pure entertainment.

Alvisio knelt down.

«Bless me, Domino.»

The presbyter's hands were small and white, with tapered fingers and manicured nails. The orphan recognized the flaccid touch on his forehead. He hated those hands.

Domino Santi noticed the empty scabbard of the dagger on the belt of Alvisio's cloak.

«Follow me, son.»

He preceded him inside.

In church, the sunlight filtered ethereal through the alabaster of a small double-arched window. The floor in blocks of rock exuded humidity, and the stale air smelled stuffy and moldy. They moved forward along the colonnade and toward the altar, upon which sat a ciborium, marble and ancient, protected by the pyx.

Alvisio had the impression that time had turned back to his youth, even though he remembered everything much bigger and imposing.

The priest preceded him by a few meters, stopped and turned around, murmuring an incomprehensible prayer.

When he was close, Alvisio entrusted his course and rough hands to those effeminate and delicate of the father, and repeated the usual formula three times: «*In manus tuas, Domine, commendo spiritum meum.*»

Fortunately, he remembered it perfectly. So, he bowed down in front of the altar.

The Domino prayed at length in Latin, while the penitent awaited in religious silence.

«Dear boy, have you sinned? Do you want to liberate your spirit and your conscience to be forgiven and expiated?»

The presbyter, while repeating the customary phrases, full of himself and triumphant for his undisputed authority of confessor, ceased to stutter.

«Domino, I have sinned gravely.»

Alvisio, in his embarrassment of having to confess without feeling any remorse, wanted to hurry the ritual along as fast as possible.

«Well, I will be the one to judge the entity of your sins. Now speak.»

«I have committed impure acts, and used violence against women.»

The priest began to torment himself with a long series of nervous quivers.

«W...w...women?» he asked horrified.

«Yes, Domino, women and little girls, taken by force and raped!» Alvisio clarified, twisting the knife in the wound.

He followed with a threat, «Do you promise that no one, apart from you and the Almighty, will ever know of my sins?»

The trembling took possession of the presbyter.

«W...w...we are sw...sworn to s...s...secrecy. In...in...war, ha...have you s...sinned, my son?»

Alvisio threw his light colored eyes wide open to stare at him without shame.

«No, not in war but in peace.»

«It...It's...truly a ser...serious s...sin!» stutteringly rasped the priest.

"He knows everything and saw us!" thought Alvisio.

«Serious, and not only that. We killed, and not in a battle. I am truly remorseful, and am here to beg forgiveness and repentance.»

Domino Santi blinked his eyes several times.

«M...my son, I c...can fr...fr...free you fr...from the pain inflicted by your s...s...sins, but o...o...only God c...can f...forgive you.»

His lower lip trembled uncontrollably.

Going into detail and extracting all of the truth from the penitent, a good confessor would have to examine and inquire, and the old presbyter, an expert in sins and sinners, was perfectly capable. But, aware of the motive of Alvisio's presence, the priest was anxious to conclude. He cared little to nothing if he had sinned or not, and whether or not the man was seriously interested in saving his soul. He needed to kindly send him on his way, but only after convincing him that his secret was safe. The scoundrel should be left in doubt that he hadn't been seen and certain that, even if the Domino had witnessed the massacre, he wouldn't be able to inform anyone.

He saw himself compelled to continue the confession and to consecrate himself to other sins. Alvisio played along and, with a certain satisfaction, enjoyed narrating the horrendous atrocities.

The discussion went on for some time and, toward the end, the Domino, recovering a semblance of serene dignity, was able to stop stuttering and contorting himself into odd nervous tics.

He absolved him, even if it went against every belief of his repentance. It was necessary to maintain a semblance of truthfulness, and he had to impose an appropriate penance to the seriousness of his foul sins.

Alvisio underwent the long spiel without batting an eye. At least for the moment he didn't fear the wrath of God.

Before leaving, he reminded the elderly presbyter what was pressuring him. Again, he threw his eyes wide open.

«Domino, you are the only one to whom I have confessed my sins!»

The old priest tried in vain to reassure him. «O...on...only to me, and to G...G...God Almighty!»

Giacinto accompanied the foundling back to the entrance.

«Brother, it has been an honor to meet you. I hope you will come back soon.» He smiled, young and handsome in his modest robe.

Alvisio, for an instant, was speechless. Then, on the threshold, he turned. «I know of your suffering. Remember to never confuse that with your sins.»

He left, happy to run away from that horrendous place.

Giacinto closed the main door. That evening, before falling asleep, he cried softly, so that the other clerics couldn't hear him.

In his childhood, the foundling had suffered, as well.

Dionigi, when he was entrusted to the Domino in order to embark in a clerical career, was a slender and kind child. His parents believed that a boy like him, so delicate and gentle, would find it truly difficult to deal with the life of a feudal serf and decided to give custody of him to the diligent care of the presbyter as an opportunity for a better existence. The Domino was pleased by the arrival of the aspiring new cleric and dedicated himself to the boy's religious education with great devotion. Maybe for doubt's sake, or out of fear that the little one might spread the word about his despicable desires, the priest, begrudgingly repressed the depraved instinct, and restrained himself, in spite of the various occasions of seclusion with the exquisite child.

That evening Dionigi heard Giacinto while he tried to suffocate his crying. In a faint voice so as not to wake the others, he whispered, «Hey, are you alright?»

But Giacinto pretended not to hear and didn't answer.

Alvisio walked swiftly toward the valley floor. Before reaching the village of Combarbio, he left the road to follow a narrow trail through the thick brambles and the flowering yellow bushes of broom. The hot afternoon sun of late June filtered through the leafy branches of the undergrowth. Fraudolente was at rest, laying belly-up on a soft spot of green turf, with his eyes half closed and a long blade of grass in his mouth. The two horses were tied to the trunk of an oak tree.

He didn't move.

«So?» asked the scarface.

«So, damn it!» answered Alvisio. He picked up the dagger from the ground, stuck it back in its scabbard and added, «I confessed and, in my opinion, that old pig had to have seen us.»

He told him everything word for word, without neglecting some fabrication to paint a more colorful and significant story.

«...and if he were ever to talk, we'll both be in trouble,» he concluded.

Fraudolente didn't like that *both*. He stood up and, after looking at him with disapproval, exclaimed, «Your damned priest knows only you!»

Alvisio felt a long chill run up his spine.

«Everyone knows that, you and I, are close friends and, so...»

One couldn't argue with this reasoning.

As the days passed, to the old presbyter it seemed that the danger had also passed. He had confessed and the miserable sinner, whatever he may have sensed, knew that his secret was safe.

In early July, just before noon, Bertino, the son of Donato della Villa of Combarbio, made his way up to the parish church. The man, happily married to a very distant cousin, lived in a hut with the old parent and numerous offspring. Bertino cultivated a tiny farm that barely fed the family and, to lighten the load of all those mouths to feed, was forced to place Lucia, the youngest of his daughters, as a servant at the castle of San Lorenzo. The child was put to service at a tender young age and, in the early days, had suffered for being taken from her mother and from Mina, her older sister. Bertino consoled his wife, overcome with the pain of losing her daughter, telling her that finding a position for Lucia was a stroke of luck. While male children were considered a blessing, girls were a misfortune.

A religious and honest man, Donato, widowed at twenty-five years, had lived a long life and had never left the farm except to go to the binnacle and the parish church. At the ripe old age of almost fifty years, he was worn out by the fatigue of the country. The ailments and pain gave him no reprieve and had become a useless burden to his family, another mouth to feed for those who were already struggling to survive, even the most fruitful years. Due to the first summer heat waves, he was close to passing away. He breathed with difficulty, talked nonsense, and alternated moments of quiet and dozing with others of which, in the grips of visions, he would flail in a frenzy on his pallet. To calm the anxiety of the father before his death, Bertino decided to seek urgent comfort from Domino Santi.

«Even if he weren't to notice, it wouldn't be good Christian decency not to call the priest!» he explained to his wife.

In the moment of a sound mind, Donato recognized the Domino and understood that he was on the verge of leaving this world. The fear of dying was stronger than the awareness of finding himself passing in God's grace. But the son perceived nothing.

As an apprentice presbyter, Giacinto was obliged to assist the Domino in the functions. After the sad task at Donato's hovel, he trotted thoughtfully behind the master.

«Domino, is it certain now that Donato's soul will be saved?»

«I would say yes, son. He is preparing to face the last journey and, given his state, he will hardly have the opportunity to sin again. But you can never tell…»

«And us, for our sins, will we ever be forgiven by God?»

His words came out spontaneously, almost as if he really wanted to free his mind and heart from anxiety and guilt.

The priest stopped and turned to look the young man in his eyes. Although they were climbing a very steep stretch of the path, and the parish priest stood in front of him, Giacinto was taller by a hand. The boy lowered his head to accept the scolding.

«What would our sins be? And what might we have done wrong? Shouldn't a good cleric, who aspires to become a parish priest, satisfy his teacher?»

On certain occasions, when he grew arrogant and became emotional, Domino Santi no longer stuttered. On the contrary, in front of the boy's compliance, he managed to dominate the tone of his voice, modifying it from effeminate to nearly virile, and transforming his cowardice toward the powerful into a brash insolence toward the weak.

Given that the hour was not late, Giacinto feared the moment in which they would reach the proximity of the usual clearing. It was a hidden and safe corner, though not too far from the road. The rocks from upstream formed a natural arch, invisible from above. The downstream undergrowth, thick with brambles and hawthorns, would have dissuaded anyone who wanted to approach. That little ravine was the favorite alcove of Domino Santi, where he consumed his horrendous and unnatural vices.

We know that the flesh is weak, and that the occasion makes the priest a sinner.

This is how it was that, resigned, the pious cleric left the straight path to follow the wicked master.

Alvisio didn't give them time to do anything. Unseen, from behind a boulder covered in green moss and hidden in the shadows, he darted out and struck him straight in the gut. With a sharp scream, the Domino brought his hands to the wound and remained motionless for a few seconds, standing and with his eyes wide open on his round face. He fell silent, bowed his head and looked in disbelief at the arrow. He took a step back and let go, falling slowly to one side. He turned onto his back and, between tears and lamentations, begged the young cleric.

«Help me!»

Astounded, Giacinto scrutinized the shrubbery looking for an escape route.

Brandishing a knife, Alvisio came out of the hiding place. The boy recognized him and understood. The archer smiled at him.

«Calm down, you have nothing to fear from me. I won't hurt you.»

Giacinto didn't believe him and collapsed to his knees next to the wounded man.

«Domino, Domino, what can we do?»

The light-colored dress of the presbyter, over the prominent belly, was vermilion. The old man held the arrow tightly in bloody hands.

«Help me,» he begged.

Alvisio knelt beside him and opened wide his light-colored eyes.

«Priest, do you know how many times, right here, I have hoped for this moment to come?»

The Domino writhed in pain, and his moan turned into a scream.

Alvisio had no compassion.

«Don't worry, soon you'll be finished suffering.»

He ran the blade of the dagger across the priest's face and rested the sharp point on his plump and rosy cheek.

The Domino stopped shaking.

«M...m...mercy!»

He stammered, and the knife cut into his skin as he spoke. His head immobile, he turned his eyes to the cleric.

«Forgive me!»

Quick and precise, Alvisio cut his throat.

The old man, choked with blood, seemed to want to speak, but was unable.

Giacinto felt pity, and found the strength and courage to whisper: «Domino, I forgive you.»

The foundling cleaned the weapon, passing it back and forth over the hem of the priest's pale robe. Giacinto, left on his knees next to the corpse, terrified and dismayed, wept in silence.

Now it would be his turn...

Alvisio stood up and sheathed the knife.

«That old pig got what he deserved. You're free now. I won't do you any harm. Go away and forget everything!»

Incredulous, Giacinto was on his feet in an instant.

The foundling, smiling, showed him the descent toward the road.

«Go!» he ordered.

Heedless of the brambles, the boy ran like a hare.

"Now he's going to hit me from behind," he thought.

He shivered, but didn't turn around. Reaching the path, he stopped for a few seconds. His heart was pounding hard. He realized his feet and ankles were torn by thorns and bleeding. But what did it matter? He had survived.

And now? His first idea was to continue his escape with a fast downhill run. But where to go? To seek asylum at the Villa of Combarbio? No, no! He would be safe only within the walls of the parish, protected by the brothers. He thought no more about it and walked briskly uphill. And if he had followed him?

Unlikely! Why let him go if he wanted to kill him? Why not do it right away?

In any case, just to be sure, he turned and stood still, listening, but didn't hear any suspicious noises.

A breath of warm southwest wind gently moved the tops of the tallest trees and, apart from the slight whistle among the fronds and some chirping, absolute stillness and silence prevailed.

Near the church, in the shade of an old elm tree by the roadside, he stopped for one last look.

«No one is following me,» he sighed with satisfaction.

Then, upstream, he heard footsteps in the distance. Someone was descending. What to do? He thought of hiding behind the thorn hedge. And if it had been a cleric from the parish who came looking for them, or a farmer or a servant from the castle? The idea of meeting a person, perhaps a brother, comforted him.

The traveler descended slowly, covered, despite the heat, in a dark cloak that reached down to his feet. His head was hidden by a hood that covered half of his face.

"Could he be a leper?" ruminated the young man.

The man crossed paths with him and, without saying anything, gave him an imperceptible nod of greeting. Giacinto caught a glimpse of the black eyes, and the stranger went on in silence.

«Hello,» the young man returned in a low voice, just to be polite, but in vain. He never received a response.

The blow from the sword came from behind, between head and neck, lightning fast and lethal. He fell sideways onto the path.

«Didn't even notice, like I promised you...»

Fraudolente uncovered his head, exposing the horrid scar to the sunlight.

Alvisio was silent, dumbfoundingly contemplating the last spasms of the cleric. The poor boy lay in his blood in a contorted and unnatural pose.

They left immediately. It was late now, and was essential, having retrieved the horses, to return to Pietrarubbia as soon as possible.

Along the way home, while they were wading the Apsa in front of the small cell-confessional, Alvisio, unseen by his friend, made the sign of the cross.

«Forgive me, brother,» he murmured in a low voice, so as not to be heard.

The next morning, an hour after dawn, when all the villagers, servants and bricklayers were already at work, Maria had climbed to the bastions as always to contemplate the world. From afar she clearly distinguished the child but, not knowing who it was, did not lean over to greet him.

Exhausted from the uphill race, Dionigi showed up at the door of San Lorenzo.

On guard duty, Gasparino modulated his voice in a persuasive tone so as not to frighten him. «Hey, boy, what happened to you?»

Dionigi recognized him and heaved a sigh of relief. He

caught his breath and wiped the sweat by passing an arm across his forehead.

«A misfortune, a misfortune has happened! Call the Master!»

Bonzio arrived immediately.

«What happened?»

He was concerned to see such a young cleric alone.

«Come, Sir! Domino Santi has disappeared, and they have murdered Giacinto.»

Escorted by Tignaccio and Gasparino, armed to the teeth, Bonzio followed Dionigi down the hill. The corpse, during the night, had suffered the indignity of animals' gnawing.

After examining him, Bonzio determined, «He was killed by a soldier's sword.»

«A man of the Malatestis?» insinuated Gasparino.

«I wouldn't know... A single blow, which nearly decapitated him.»

Dionigi began to whimper under his breath, and Bonzio tried to console him. «Don't worry, you're safe with me.»

He turned to the others. «You two, take the body up to the parish church.»

Small but sturdy, Gasparino loaded the body onto his shoulders. For hierarchical reasons, the thankless tasks fell to him.

Bonzio and Dionigi remained under the elm. The man was gigantic and menacing, while the boy, frail and frightened, continued to tremble like a leaf.

Without preamble, Bonzio asked, «Tell me something, maybe you have an idea where your Domino is now...»

The boy turned pale, and nodded his head, agitating his raven curls. Then he raised his eyes, black and deep, to stare at the tremendous giant.

«Sir, I know he often went to the cave.»

Bonzio placed a hand on Dionigi's slender and delicate shoulder. He saw that the boy was still tormented by a slight tremor, and he stroked his cheek.

«Don't worry, I'm here to protect you. Is the cave faraway?»

Dionigi shook his head.

«Do you feel like being my guide?»

Leaving the path, they climbed together through the thorn bushes to the grassy clearing. Torn apart by the animals, the Domino lay supine in front of the rocks, the arrow towering above the huge belly.

Dionigi let out a shrill scream and turned to flee. Bonzio grabbed him quickly and instinctively picked him up to hug the child to his chest. He stroked the back of his neck and, for a fleeting moment, it brought up the tender memory of his lost children. Dionigi buried his face on those powerful shoulders and wept. Bonzio couldn't find the courage to let him go and lulled him, whispering words that, once upon a time, he had whispered to his daughters in swaddling clothes. When he was quiet, he gently set him down and examined the cadaver.

That evening Bonzio didn't have the heart to leave Dionigi at the parish church, and the boy slept, in heaven, between Rosa and Maria.

The tragic end of the presbyter was greedy news for gossips throughout Montefeltro. With great rapidity, it passed from village to village and from castle to castle, arousing curiosity, scandal and horror. The blame, as always, was attributed to the usual perfidious henchmen of the hated Malatestis, even if someone insinuated that the perpetrators were bandits from nearby Carpegna. No one suspected the truth, or doubted the chastity of Domino Santi.

A few evenings later, during dinner, Bonzio broached the subject.

«My father and the presbyter were wounded by an arrow,» he began, freezing his daughters and Tignaccio. «I'm afraid it's a single-handed job. Domino was killed because he saw the killers of our family.»

In order not to further upset the girls, he spared them the

significant detail that the priest in the cave and little Bruna at the spring appeared to have been slaughtered by the same blade.

Maria's eyes widened in terror and she hugged her sister.

Bonzio turned to look at her and asked, «And did you, that evening, see the assassins?»

The girl burst into tears.

«Father, leave her alone. Don't make her suffer any more!» pleaded Rosa.

Bonzio, a brave lion in war but a tender lamb in the family, did not insist.

«Be that as it may, the rumor is that you would be able to recognize them. For your safety, we will need to find you a safe and distant refuge. I have discussed it with the Count and, thanks to his high-ranking connections, there may be an abbess willing to take you at the convent.»

Dismayed, Maria rose abruptly to her feet. She nearly dropped her sister and spilled the food and drink. Bonzio, terrified of her, saw her put her hands to her hair and flee in a hurry to the kitchen. Rosa chased after her.

«What did I say wrong?» he asked his future son-in-law.

«Nothing, sir.»

They had to tell him before it was too late. Tignaccio and Rosa had discussed it for a long time, but without finding the courage to come forward.

"Bonzio will kill me!"

The young man feared the wrath of the colossus.

So it was that Rosa, in a moment of silence after dinner, while Tignaccio had gone out into the courtyard and Maria seemed to have disappeared, decided to broach the subject.

«Father, I think my sister just doesn't want to be shut up in a convent.»

Bonzio was surprised at such audacity. It was not customary, on the contrary, it was downright improper and almost indiscreet for a woman, and even worse, a daughter, to have the courage to question the decisions taken by a man.

«How dare you! These are things that do not concern you and that you cannot understand!» he retaliated crossly.

He saw the girl's regret and repented.

«But how do you know? Your sister can't tell you.»

«Father, Maria is in love.»

His world came crashing down. It was unimaginable that a villain had found the audacity to undermine, unbeknownst to him, the little and defenseless Maria, so fragile, helpless and on the outskirts of life and the real world.

«Who was it?»

Bonzio cried out his horror in three words. Who was that worm who dared to pick the unripe fruit and take advantage of the innocence of a troubled mind?

In the face of her paternal wrath, Rosa lowered her shoulders and protected her face with her hands.

Since the presbyter had been assassinated, Dionigi had lived in the castle, pampered and spoiled by everyone. His sincere innocence and his acumen, combined with his vivacious nature, had conquered the hearts of Rosa and Maria. Even Bonzio, although he tried not to show it, had let himself be moved. The boy, initially shocked by the enormous size of the giant, in a short time was able to understand the goodness of his soul and altruism that hid under the false guise of the fierce warrior. Dionigi knew how to capture the fleeting flashes of sweetness that shined through with difficulty in Bonzio's light-colored and severe eyes, and who, in turn, imagined the yearned for son in the child.

The rascal ran into the room and, oblivious to the outburst, pulled at Rosa's dress. Bonzio, instead of ranting as he would have done to anyone else, calmed him down: «Son, we're talking about serious things.»

The boy embraced Rosa's waist and, disguising his lively gaze with an innocent expression, smiled.

Rosa took advantage of the opportunity.

«Father, it is not as you fear: nothing has happened and no one has committed a sin.»

Bonzio breathed a sigh of relief.

«Then what happened? Who is the man?»

Ascertaining that, thank God, the crime had not been committed, he tried to remain severe.

«You see, father, even if Maria does not speak, I understand her.»

He took the roundabout way and stalled by placing an arm on Dionigi's shoulder. It was settled.

«It's Tignaccio!» he exclaimed releasing the anxiety of the terrible secret.

It wasn't easy to get Bonzio to digest the senseless news. How was it possible that, in his house and right under his nose, the improbable affair had been born? And what kind of impression would he have made with the Pietrarubbians and the gli Olivieris?

And Rosa? Worried, he asked her, «What are you saying? He is your betrothed and your sister...»

«Father, I understood from the first day, and I never deluded myself. If I marry Tignaccio, you will make three people unhappy. He loves her and definitely doesn't have the same feelings for me. And I would be forever haunted by the thought that I belonged to a man who would have preferred my sister.»

Rosa managed to disguise her disappointment, and Bonzio didn't notice. The girl continued, «They have both suffered and, even if in the most absolute silence, they understand each other blissfully. Father, please give them your permission.»

Bonzio didn't comment. With the excuse of stroking Dionigi's curls, Rosa lowered her gaze and distracted it from the severe stare of her father.

Dionigi whined that he was thirsty, and she fled to accompany him to the kitchen. The boy drank deeply from the jug, heaved a long sigh and wiped his lips on the sleeve of his pale tunic.

He noticed her tears and asked, «Why are you crying, Rosa?»

That night Bonzio couldn't sleep a wink and continued tossing and turning in bed. If at least Maddalena had been there to discuss what to do...

Toward dawn he came to terms with it.

After all, hadn't he asked Corrado for permission to marry one of his daughters to Tignaccio? And he would have, even if it wasn't to Rosa. To protect Maria, he would have asked the cousins of Piega for help, so that, at least in the beginning, they would welcome the newlyweds to the valley *della Maricula,* safe and far from the murderers of his family.

As for the dowry, he could have ensured that San Lorenzo and the pertinent lands would, after his death, be granted to Tignaccio as the new castellan, and he would have thrown in his savings as well, if necessary.

Perhaps the Count would not have liked the newlyweds' transfer to Piega, but he would have justified it with the excuse of a pregnancy in a less impoverished place.

First of all, it was necessary to sort things out with the future son-in-law, and to define the details of his dowry with the noble relatives.

Being a stonecutter was hard work and a less desirable occupation. Whenever he found himself passing through the Villa of Combarbio, Tignaccio rejoiced at not having been born a servant, and at having been given the fate of a life of a soldier.

«Sir, the stones should be enough.»

«Yes, in any case it's a good idea to prepare some material, as backup in case of need.»

After the latest renovations, the new yellowish stones stood out conspicuously against the old gray walls.

«In a few years,» said Tignaccio, «the difference won't be noticeable.»

Bonzio got right to the point.

«Rosa told me about you and Maria.»

Prompted by Rosa, the boy had prepared a little speech. However, he blushed and didn't meet Bonzio's gaze.

«Lord, I should have… asked your permission.»

Uneasy, he couldn't find the words.

Bonzio cleared his throat.

«You know that Maria doesn't speak and that she may have lost her mind.»

«Lord, from the first moment I saw her, I was enchanted, and I feel a strong sentiment for her.»

Bonzio kept it short.

«Does Maria want you as her husband?»

Tignaccio raised his eyes and wasn't afraid to answer, «Maria doesn't speak, but she understands and loves like any enamored woman. Lord, believe me, Maria wishes to marry me.»

Rosa was nervous. Arranging her sister's wedding banquet was complicated. How many would participate?

She had made an approximate calculation of the guests from Tignaccio's family, including the gli Olivieris, and the number of the bride's guests. Then there were the commoners, who would take part in the ceremony and party without invitation. While the Lords would be received in the castle, the poor would feast outside the walls.

Gasparino would have taken the opportunity to reunite the relatives and, once word had spread to Pietrarubbia, even more inhabitants of the village would have flocked to San Lorenzo.

Piega was not that far away, and many of the gli Olivieri's servants and peasants would have come following their Lords.

Rosa estimated that she would receive about thirty people

at the castle and that she would have to feed a hundred outdoors.

For the nobles and relatives, there would have been game, chickens, pigs, side dishes of vegetables and legumes, white bread, fruit and an abundance of excellent spiced wine. The people would have had to content themselves with cheese, black bread to be dipped in vegetable broth and, in order to avoid excessive disorder, a little watered down and poor quality wine.

And what feudal serf would have turned down a day of revelry?

The public celebrations for the wedding were an opportunity to broaden acquaintanceship, and to arrange marriages with remote people, not of close ancestry or tight blood relation.

«The third Saturday in September will be perfect!»

So they established the notary Simone, the noble Bartolino as representative of the groom, and Bonzio the castellan.

The Domino Maliocco of Piega was present at the stipulation for the agreement for the nuptials and the dowry.

The parish priest, chaste and pious, lived the priesthood as a mission. Well into his sixties, he was as small and twisted as a vine branch.

The small church of Piega and the rectory were in front of the keep, but the gli Olivieris had a private chapel, and the Domino, to better serve the Lords, lived in the castle.

As always, the news spread throughout Montefeltro, from godmother to godmother, even reaching Fraudolente. The scarred man thus saw the prospect of stealing Bonzio's job vanish. With the placet of the Counts, the vassal would have had heirs and descendants.

The attempt to recommend himself to Filippuccio was useless. In fact, the bastard was even indignant, «Who do you think you are? That which my brother, Corrado, decides is the law, and it is useless to argue!»

The stab wound that Fraudolente had taken in Cesena to save his life was only a distant memory and, as was fitting for any self-respecting bastard, the handsome Filippuccio hardly cared anymore about the fate of that sort of vile and impertinent Squire. To hell with him, damn it!

Fraudolente swallowed the bitter pill and did not insist. He umburdened himself to Alvisio, «It's not worth being faithful and courageous! That pig Bonzio is too well liked, and we'll have to make him pay for it.'

But even his friend, rather worried about Bonzio's size and sword, seemed to hesitate and didn't encourage him.

So it was that Fraudolente realized how much, at times, wounded pride hurts more than a stab to the side.

Maria, under an elegant blue dress, cinched at the waist by a thin belt, wore soft shoes with leather soles. From a white cap, tied under the chin by two blue strings, protruded a rebellious lock of blond hair that gleamed in the sun. She was beautiful.

Proud and upright in his formal dress, Bonzio advanced alongside Maria as far as the portico of the old chapel of San Lorenzo. Slovenly and humble in a brown dress, Rosa followed them holding little Dionigi by the hand. The boy, in a new white tunic, looked like a cherub.

Next to the noble Bartolino, Tignaccio waited for his betrothed. Behind them, as befitting, were the groom's mother and aunt moved to tears, while Agnese and Geltrude secretly whispered trivial comments.

When Bonzio and Maria were in front of him, the notary Simone began with the deed of endowment and betrothal in a solemn and regulated voice.

«I give reading of the *consensus de futuro* stipulated between these two families.»

Thus Bonzio bade a final farewell, even if without any regrets, to a large part of his wealth.

After the succinct and official *escursus,* the notary turned to Bonzio, «Let he who delivers the girl come forward!»

Awkward and clumsy, the giant advanced holding the bride's delicate hand. He joined it to that of Tignaccio, who proclaimed his intentions for him, «I receive you now as my wife.»

Maria was silent, as always, but she nodded with a radiant smile. The notary hesitated; would such a silent consent have been considered valid?

In confirmation of her will, as was customary, the new wife bowed down to submit herself to her husband.

They entered the church, where Domino Maliocco blessed the bride and groom before celebrating the Holy Mass for the wedding.

After the ceremony, the merry, festive crowd, made up of about thirty people, just as Rosa had foreseen, moved to the castle hall for the banquet.

The people, about eighty hungry men and just over twenty women from the neighboring surroundings, took advantage of the beautiful sunny day and rushed to celebrate the wedding. Those who could had dressed up in party dress, outfits that were worn for religious functions, weddings and funerals.

To keep the peasants from the summer heat, Rosa had a wooden arbor erected, leaning against the walls and supported by sturdy poles which sustained some mats and course cloths for shade.

The Gasparinis flocked en masse and distinguished themselves, in the midst of the general confusion, by their inexhaustible appetite of having known hunger very well, and by the unmistakable chanting of their incessant chatter.

The real surprise was the arrival from Piega of a crowd of distant cousins, all more or less related not only to the Gasparinis, but to most of the peasants of Pietrarubbia. Mafalda, as she embraced her father, the old blacksmith from Piega, was moved to tears.

The people of Pietrarubbia and those of Piega, as usual,

took advantage of the opportunity for a reunion. It was a large family, the fruit of innumerable marriages between blood relatives. Although the similarity was evident, the inhabitants of Piega were much more beautiful than those of Pietrarubbia. Fairer in complexion, some of them even had dark brown hair and not jet black like their cousins.

Despite the bad and watered-down wine, there were those who went overboard, some throwing themselves into a rage, others toppling to the ground, or even vomiting.

For two agitated men who came to blows for futile reasons, the intervention of Gasparino and two soldiers was necessary. It was enough to call Bonzio to subdue the brawl before it started.

As the sun went down, the time came for the couple to retire to the alcove. Rosa helped her sister undress and perfume her with a sweet essence of violet. After comforting her with some improbable recommendations, she left her, wrapped in soft quilts, waiting for her husband.

Tignaccio entered the nuptial chamber with Domino Maliocco.

«God of Abraham, Isaac and Jacob, bless these spouses, and may the seed of eternal life be in their hearts.»

The presbyter's voice, unlike his old and tired physique, was firm and virile like that of a strong young man.

Finally alone, the two were able to consume that simple rite which, since the dawn of time, had always been celebrated in the same way.

Outside the castle, the people celebrated until late at night, when even the most resistant survivors gave in to tiredness and the heavy drinking . Someone ended up falling asleep by the fire of an improvised encampment, while most, wrapped in cloaks, sought shelter from the humidity under the arbor or in the village barn.

It was an anomalous marriage, where the husband, contrary to the customs of the time, would have moved to his wife's house.

The possible transfer of the spouses to Piega, even if justified and momentary, would have given rise to the criticisms of Filippo and Fraudolente.

«Sir, if I left San Lorenzo now to return to Piega, we would incur the wrath of the Counts of Pietrarubbia. They would annul us and we would lose our castle forever.»

Tignaccio's mother reluctantly resigned herself to the umpteenth abandonment. Two days After the wedding, Agnese took her leave, crying over her son and returned, followed by her sister's family, to the distant valley *della Maricula*.

After the wedding, the castle of San Lorenzo and its people enjoyed a period of serenity, dedicated more to agriculture than war.

While servants and peasants worked with their heads down, gentlemen like Tignaccio spent entire days having fun with their wives.

Despite repeated and very pleasant attempts, it seemed that the beautiful Maria couldn't get pregnant.

Bonzio began to worry. Was the infamous fate that persisted with his family the same as his destiny to remain without offspring?

Rosa began to get worn out, to wrinkle and to look more and more like her poor mother. While Maria, even if in her perpetual silence, was ever more beautiful and radiant, her sister was aging precociously, as if she had lost the zest for life.

After the massacre of the spring at Combarbio, Bonzio had gone through a period of mourning and pain. However, despite the tragedy, life had to go on.

At the castle of San Lorenzo there was a young girl, still

inexperienced but very promising to be put to practical use. Entrusted by her father to Maddalena and her daughters to take into service, the girl, a perky and very pretty brunette, soon became a member of the family.

Bonzio had always considered her only and simply a child, without ever imagining her as anything more than a humble servant. Then, on a hot August afternoon, after going to the Combarbio quarry, he went down to the river to cool off. The pretty girl had had the same idea. Bonzio saw her while, in the company of a sister, splahing half naked in a pool of fresh water. Enraptured, he slipped beteen the bushes and lingered for a few moments. It seemed to him that the girls were looking in his direction. He gave up the bath and retraced his steps without making a sound. As he walked away he heard a few, but significant words, «He's old, but he's still a handisome man...»

The pretty servant and the gruff vassal confessed to Domino Ubertino, the new presbyter of Combarbio, more or less the same unforgivable sin.

Rosa had grown very fond of little Dionigi. Ever since the death of the lustful old priest, they had shared the same life and, during the long, gloomy nights at the castle, the same bed. The boy had found in the young woman the distant memories of his mother's warmth, while Rosa's anguishing loneliness, caused by the immense suffering for the tragic death of her loved ones at the Combarbio spring, had been soothed by the naive familial affection of Dionigi.

«Father, let us keep him with us, I beg you.»

The poor thing implored him in vain when the time for parting came.

Bonzio reassured her, «Do not be afraid, my daughter. I have been informed. The new Domino, compared to the *other one,* is a good man, and you will see that the child will be well cared for.»

On a humid and misty afternoon at the end of September '96, they accompanied him together to the parish church. For the occasion, the boy wore his most beautiful and immaculate tunic, with a light-colored cape and hood over it.

Fresh from a bath, he smelled like a cherub.

In front of the door, before knocking, there was a moment's hesitation.

«Father, do we really have to?»

«Yes, Rose. It is his destiny, and this is what his parents had decided for him.»

The Domino opened, a good man, much younger, kinder and more humble than his predecessor. He smiled as he welcomed them.

«Welcome. Here's my new son!»

Rosa fell silent.

Dionigi grabbed Bonzio's hand. His lower lip began to tremble, but he held back the tears. The Domino bent down to better look into his eyes. The child perceived the softness of one who is good and has the gift of faith. No, he wasn't a bad priest. Dionigi abandoned the trusted hand of Bonzio and clung to a hem of the dress of Domino Ubertino.

«Welcome home!»

The presbyter stood up in farewell.

«Thanks for bringing him back. May God grant you merit.»

Bonzio pulled the child's hood away with a quick gesture and stroked the curly-haired little head.

Dionigi darted with raised arms towards the giant, who pressed him to his heart. The Domino left them like that for a few seconds, until Bonzio resigned himself to handing him over again.

When the heavy door closed, Rosa wept.

«She didn't even say goodbye to me.»

Upon returning to the castle, she sought refuge and comfort in the silent embrace of her sister, while Bonzio, a course man accustomed to hardships, appeared to everyone to have no need of any sentimental and inconvenient consolation.

PIEGA

It seemed that fate wanted to have its way. Was it possible that Tignaccio and Maria were unable to procreate? Domino Ubertino, in the hope that the Lord would help them, continued to pray for them and, whenever he had the opportunity, to bless them. At the Villa of Combarbio lived an old hag, widowed and childless, who survived by begging and, above all, from the meager compensation received thanks to her reputation of knowing how to cure the sick, predict the future and remove the evil eye. She wasn't a real and true witch that worshiped the devil or, even worse, that didn't love God. Destiny had simply given her a *gift*. When the poor were in need and desperate, and when not even prayers worked, they resorted to her help.

The Domino, while inviting them to persevere and to have faith, hadn't succeeded for the moment, and Tignaccio decided it was time to try Piccarda. One afternoon in May '97, having wrung the neck of the oldest hen in the henhouse, went down to the village with Maria.

When she saw the them arrive at her miserable hut with the gift dangling from Tignaccio's hand, the horrid crone languished into an obsequent and toothless grin of welcome. «What an honor for my house!»

She bowed awkwardly on her wiry, twisted legs. The poor thing was so ugly and battered that Maria reacted by clinging to her husband's arm with unusual vigor. To hide her shock, she made a dull attempt at a smile. The old woman was white-haired and balding like a dog with mange. Her nose, crooked and hooked, almost reached her chin, and a repulsive white tuft sprouted from a mole on her cheekbone. She gave off the stench of someone who hadn't gone down to the river to wash for at least five years.

They sat down on the uncomfortable bench in front of the house.

«My wife can't have children,» Tignaccio began, handing over the chicken.

Piccarda grabbed him. Then, with her lively black eyes, she scrutinized the young couple intensely.

«My Lord, there is a blessed spring that offers miraculous results. Before going to bed you will have to drink its water at length and you will see that a child will arrive.»

«And where would this spring be?»

Tignaccio snorted all of his doubts.

«And don't think of going to Piccarda!» the Domino had warned him.

But, at this point, there was nothing left for him but to listen to the sibilant old woman. Also because the chicken had already been sacrificed.

«Sir, I'm talking about the miraculous spring of Val de Teva,» Piccarda managed to say before being shaken by a violent phlegmy cough. Maria was horrified and withdrew. Tignaccio, whispering a painful «Thank you», got up, promptly followed by his wife, who tried to say goodbye with a more credible smile than the one with which she had introduced herself.

«Have a safe journey back, my young Lady and Lord!» croaked the poor crone in farewell.

When the newlyweds disappeared around the bend in the path, the old woman ran to her neighbor with the chicken. «Bertino! Bertino!» she called.

Due to her toothless mouth, Piccarda exchanged the sinewy payment for some excellent goat's milk and, that evening, she finally had enough to eat.

It is not known whether it was due to the miraculous water, or to the prayers and blessings of the Domino, or even to Tignaccio's greater efforts, but, to everyone's happiness, after a few weeks Maria exulted, «I'm pregnant!»

The Domino rejoiced sufficiently, and invited the young

couple to give thanks to God. However, when Tignaccio confessed to him the visit to the hag and the little trip to Val de Teva, he really didn't like it. He didn't get angry, but came very close.

«Son, it's a grave sin to have put your trust in that woman! You were right to give her a chicken, but know that the water from Val de Teva has nothing to do with Maria's pregnancy!»

And, so that he would never forget to commit such foolishness again, he inflicted a heavy penance on him.

«You will fast on dry bread, legumes and water for a week.» Then a doubt came to him. «Only you alone, and not your wife! She is not to blame.»

Ah, yes! Domino Ubertino was truly a good priest.

Drought was a serious problem. More and more frequently, the springs and autumns were as dry as much as, and more than the summers and, during the winters, despite the biting frost, it snowed little and very seldom. Luckily, the spring at the parish church of Combarbio continued to give a weak but constant gush, just enough to satisfy the needs of the people of the castle and nearby villages. However, Bonzio feared that, sooner or later, if the seasons did not return to what they once were, the ancient spring would dry up.

Then the miracle happened: in the first cold days of October the sky darkened menacingly, and big clouds, carried by a furious southwest wind, stopped on the ridges of the mountains. The wind stopped, and it rained. It looked like the Great Flood.

«Too much water, and all at once!» Bonzio worried.

People sheltered in houses and in the castle. Fireplaces were lit and people waited patiently for the fury of the storm to run its course. There was no thunder and lightening, just a long, incessant rain. After two days, the first thin but well-defined cracks began to appear in the walls of some of the buildings.

On the northeast wing of the castle, near a small window, from the roof to the foundation, a long crevice opened. On the third day the light could be seen from one side to the other and the fracture widened to the point that one of Bonzio's arms would have easily passed through it. Tignaccio wanted everyone to move to the *solina* room of the building.

«It's safer to stay here. I wouldn't want there to be a collapse.»

And that is exactly what happened. After a week of nonstop and heavy rain, the landslide moved the part facing *della Conca*.

It happened at night, and it woke everyone because of the enormous crash. Not only did it ruin part of the castle, but the curtain walls, as well. Those that had been restructured with so much patience and effort, came down in a sea of mud and clay.

«Thank God, no one was hurt,» was Bonzio's laconic comment. Months and months of hard work and sacrifice nullified by the fury of the elements!

«We'll rebuild everything, Sir, don't worry!» attempting to console his father-in-law Tignaccio.

Ironically, in the late morning of the day after the collapse, almost suddenly the rain stopped and, as the clouds dissolved, a warm sun appeared.

Gasparino, ever the superstitious one, let slip: «It's a curse! The downpour ends when the castle collapses.»

Bonzio heard it. «You are stupid! The landslide happened because of the rain, and we all knew that, sooner or later, it could happen. Curses have nothing to do with it. In fact, it's a stroke of luck that it's sunny now.»

As always, even in the face of misfortune, Bonzio saw the tankard half full.

Rosa was desperate. Her house was half-destroyed and, moreover, right at the worst time of the year, that of the bad weather. The old oak beams, which once held up the loft, now hung sadly in the void or, worse still, had rolled to the ground on the rubble. As soon as it was possible and with the help of all the capable men, they began to clean up, recovering, among the debris and rubble, beams, epistyles, stones and bricks.

«Let's hope that the winter is mild and that it doesn't snow too much,» said a worried Tignaccio.

It would not have been a simple restoration, but a reconstruction. Although the wing on the roof of the castle had remained standing, everywhere there were infiltrations and frozen drafts.

Rosa talked about it with Bonzio, «Perhaps it would be good for Maria, at least until the birth of the child and, in any case, until the end of the works, to move elsewhere, to a drier, warmer and safer place.»

Also for safety, with that huge hole in the walls, was a serious problem and not easy to solve.

Bonzio arranged night watch shifts beyond the perimeter of the castle, where, in defense, an embankment had been hastily erected. But, no matter what was done, the old manor would have remained exposed, until the completion of the entire wall, to possible assaults by the enemy and to the usual threat of incursions by the Malatestas.

As if all this were not enough, at night packs of famished and brutal outlaws roamed the countryside, to whom it would have seemed too good to be true to sack the castle.

«By their nature, the outlaws are cowards, and they wouldn't dare attack us openly. The Malatestas, on the other hand, if they knew about this situation, could exploit it.»

And the Malatestas, ruthless allies of Piega, Tignaccio knew them well...

Submissive to her husband, Maria accepted resignedly.

«My child will be born in Piega!» Tignaccio decided.

Before leaving, they waited for the dawn of a beautiful autumn day, one of those which, if it hadn't been for the warm, rosy colors of the woods, could have been defined as spring.

Rosa wept desperately on Maria's neck.

«Come back soon, please! Remember that this is your

home and that I will be here waiting for you.»

Bonzio remained in San Lorenzo, but decided to accompany them as far as Combarbio. Four men held up the comfortable litter, with the escort of Tignaccio at the head and Gasparino at the rear on his humble nag.

They took a short break at the parish church. Domino Ubertino wanted to bless Mary.

«Daughter, Saint Anne will protect you. I will pray for you and your son.»

He was moved to tears at their farewell.

Bonzio dismounted and caressed Maria.

«I'll come and see you,» he promised her unconvincingly.

When her father bent down to kiss her on the forehead, Maria abandoned herself to tears. Hiding his embarrassment in a cough, Bonzio looked away and moved on.

The small procession left for Piega.

Bonzio waited motionless, standing beside the Domino, until they had disappeared around the bend in the path.

Little Dionigi came running out of the convent door in his fluttering tunic.

«Bonzio, Bonzio!»

He climbed up on the giant to throw his arms around his neck.

Ah, yes! Domino Ubertino was truly a good priest.

Geltrude and Agnese looked so alike that it would have been easy to confuse them. Only a good observer would have noticed how Geltrude, the eldest, was slightly thinner, with a more pronounced nose and thinner lips.

Agnese, on the other hand, had the right curves in the right places, less pronounced features but full and sensual lips. Geltrude's voice was of a higher-pitch and less soft and persuasive than her sister.

Although in their thirties, they were still two beautiful ladies, and Bonzio would have gladly enjoyed being entertained by them.

The arrival of Tignaccio and his wife in Piega made the two sisters happy. Agnese and her daughter-in-law shared a bedroom, and Geltrude ordered that Maria be treated as a guest of high status.

Tignaccio spent a beautiful evening in the company of his uncle and cousins. In front of the fireplace in the castle hall, enjoying the dinner prepared to celebrate his return, he recounted the latest events in San Lorenzo.

Bartolino, prodigal of almost paternal suggestions, to avoid any doubt confirmed the relationship: «This, my boy, is still your home.»

Oliviero hid his jealousy and confirmed in turn, «You and your family will always be welcome.»

The young future Lord and heir of Piega had never liked his cousin, cumbersome and much too liked by his father and brother. Now, damn it, he was back with his pregnant wife, mute and stupid!

Antonio, on the contrary, was happy to see his cousin again, and he hoped that he could stay in Piega for a few days. But Tignaccio disappointed him.

«Tomorrow we will leave at dawn to return to San Lorenzo.»

«What, so soon? Tomorrow morning?»

«Yes, we must all return as soon as possible. Days of hard work await us.»

Oliviero could not hide a smirk.

«Will you be able to rebuild your castle?» he asked between irony and envy.

«It's not my castle.»

Bartolino didn't notice, or pretended not to. Antonio, on the other hand, cast a reproachful look at his brother. Was it possible that he was so stupid and jealous?

The next morning, after a long and passionate goodbye to his wife, Tignaccio set off again with his men for San Lorenzo.

Gasparino, as always, had overindulged and slept at his cousin's blacksmith's house. With red eyes and a dry mouth, after his hangover he was suffering a ferocious headache.

Maria, pampered and spoiled by her mother-in-law and her aunt, spent a peaceful time, despite the lack of her husband's love and Rosa's affection. The days passed happily, and it was very pleasant to while away the time in the company of Geltrude and Agnese. Even though she didn't participate in the conversations, Maria listened to their intense chatter, and she expressed her approval with silent complicit laughs.

A warm February anticipated spring.

With a big belly, Maria had run out of time and Geltrude gave the midwife an early warning, «You never know. We must be ready!»

Tessa's mastery was frowned upon and tolerated only when needed. Domino Maliocco doubted her because he only saw her at church on Sundays and on the obligatory holy days, and because she preferred the company of prayer of other godmothers.

The superstitious folk handed down ancient legends about midwives. They were witches, in agreement with the devil to kill children. And sometimes even mothers.

Labor was a female affair, from which males were excluded because witches only enjoyed the company of other witches. Even childbirth was exclusive to women and, in a male-dominated society, highly suspect.

Tessa worked as a midwife to make ends meet, but also out of passion and to feel less of a spinster.

It was late at night when she heard a loud banging on the door.

«Who is it?»

Tessa thought of an urgency, but given the times, it was better to be cautious.

«It's Gaia, hurry up!»

She found herself facing an out of breath maid of the castle.

«Come up now! The Mute is already having labor pains.'

Clinging to the hands of her mother-in-law, Maria suffered in silence. When Tessa and Gaia entered the room, Agnes breathed a sigh of relief.

The water was tepid and the hot cloths ready. Geltrude went back and forth restlessly from the fireplace to the chair of the woman in labor.

Maria breathed her silent desperation. Aside from the crackling of the fire and the girl's moans, the room was unnaturally quiet.

Everything went well, and the matter was resolved in a short time.

The baby was healthy, big and beautiful. He cried and yelled everything his mother hadn't been able to yell.

Once the umbilical cord was cut, Tessa carefully washed the newborn in the tub and wrapped him in a warm, oiled cloth.

«It's a boy!» Agnes rejoiced.

Geltrude tried to refresh the new mother: «Drink a little hot broth. Or would you like some potato bouillon?»

It was important that Maria ate and was strong enough to breastfeed.

The mother embraced her son to bring him to her breast.

That evening, at dinner, she celebrated. The Domino Maliocco, who seemed to appreciate the excellent cuisine, expressed an atrocious doubt, «I have not heard the mother cry enough, and I fear that she has not expiated her guilt.»

Geltrude retorted, «Domino, she is mute, and she has suffered as much as any other good woman, but in silence.»

The presbyter was enjoying spelt soup, overflowing with pork rinds. Old and frail, at the table he ate as much as a teenager and, what's more, he didn't disdain wine, especially if it was very spiced. A grave cardinal sin! But it is known that priests don't practice what they preach. And even that evening the Domino ate with his usual voracity.

Geltrude's answer did not seem to have satisfied the priest, «But did she really cry over the labor pains?»

It was not simple morbid curiosity, but an actual desire to know if there had been a suffering such as to allow her to make just amends for all her guilt. In fact, childbirth had to be experienced as a punishment for the pleasure of conception.

Agnese was silent, trying to understand. Would the Domino have liked the sufferings of his daughter-in-law? What could a male know of the spasms and torments of a woman in labor?

Geltrude cut it short, «The poor thing suffered the pains of hell, much more than I suffered to bring my two children into the world.»

After these words, the insinuation that Maria had not suffered was an offense to the mistress of the house and to her husband.

Bartolino, until then devoted to the appetizing soup, raised his eyes from the bowl to stare grimly at the Domino.

The priest fell silent and immediately resumed eating.

Antonio was very excited about the prestigious assignment. For the first time in his life, he would be in command of an important mission. In the early morning, escorted by four soldiers and dressed with the insignia of his noble family like a true knight, he set off on his steed for the valley *della Conca*. The journey was exciting. At the sight of that handful of armed men, villagers and settlers fled in terror. It was true power; the people feared the sword.

His father had flanked him with one of his most trusted men, the brave and expert Lapo, who had distinguished himself in countless wartime skirmishes in the soldier's pay of the Malatesti allies.

«You will be in charge, but Lapo will be your guide.»

Shortly after noon, they reached San Lorenzo.

Gasparino sounded the alarm.

«Five knights in arms are coming from the parish church!» he shrieked as he spotted them.

Tignaccio rushed to the battlements and ordered: «Close the door and lower the gate!»

When the strangers were close, he yelled, «Who are you? Who goes there?»

Antony turned his horse to show the insignia on his shield and showed off his manliest voice.

«Antonio degli Olivieri with his men!»

The timbre of his cries betrayed his youth.

«Open up!»

Tignaccio ran down to the courtyard to receive his cousin.

Lapo held the young man's bridle while he dismounted.

Antonio uncovered his head and his blond hair to the sun.

«Cousin, I'm here to bring you good news. You are a father! Your wife gave birth to a beautiful, healthy boy.»

Bonzio arrived at that moment.

«A male!» he yelled as he slapped his son-in-law on the back vigorously. Tignaccio staggered and almost lost his balance.

«And how is my wife?» he asked worried.

«Maria is fine. My mother and aunt are taking care of her,» Antonio reassured him.

That evening, the men of the castle feasted on delicious game and deep red wine from the Valley *della Conca*.

Rosa, after the kitchen chores, fled to her cheerless pallet, where she cried all night long.

The next morning Tignaccio took his cousin on a tour of the castle and carefully explained the restoration work to him. Rebuilding the fallen walls was a difficult and thankless undertaking; no one could be certain that the landslide had stopped.

«For the moment it's not a good idea that I come to Piega. I have to wait for the work to be finished, and it will take a few more months, provided that the warm season holds and that the spring rains don't arrive early. In the meantime it is best for my wife and child to stay with my mother and aunt.»

«You don't have to worry about anything. Your wife is like a sister to me, and I will take care of your son as if he were my own.»

Antonio wanted his cousin to be assured in this way.

The knights of Piega left shortly before noon, and Tignaccio accompanied them to the parish church. After the goodbyes, he stayed for awhile with the Domino.

«We'll have to arrange for the baby to be baptized and find a godfather,» said the presbyter, taking Rosa for granted as godmother.

Tignaccio had already decided on the name. «As soon as my wife and little Bonvicino have returned home, they will immediately come down to the parish church.»

It would not have been appropriate to wait too long. Infant mortality was very high, and the limbo was full of newborns.

The land of Galasso reached the river and, on the other bank, the property of the Olivieri began. The border was subject to change according to the whims of the course *della Maricula* which, in dry periods, was reduced to a stony trickle.

It was customary to entrust grazing animals to children who were not yet strong and grown up enough to work in the fields. Carlino was a real pest. To educate him properly, his parents would usually give him a few slaps, but the boy was an incorrigible brigand and showed no signs of repentance. At the age of six he should have been much more obedient and cooperative.

Instead he took advantage of every opportunity to hide out and loaf about. He helped his mother poorly and reluctantly around the house, and he hated the hard work in the countryside. Uguccione, his father, had given him the task of looking after the flock, about twenty sheep in all, and to lead them on nice days, to the stony pasture near the river.

Uguccione's family, always at the service to that of the noble Galasso, cultivated a farm in the valley floor, with room and board guaranteed even in times of famine and drought.

Handsome Oliviero loved long gallops on his majestic roan. Out of fear of running into Galasso's thugs who occasionally trespassed across the river, he never went out alone, and was always accompanied by Lapo or at least a couple of other soldiers. Sometimes, to amuse themselves, they dared to skirmish in the villages subjected to the hated Montefeltro. Fortunately, thanks to the peacemaking intervention of the priests of both families, and above all of the wise Domino Maliocco, a conciliatory settlement had always been reached in order to live quietly and not to upset the delicate political balance between Malatesti and Montefeltro. Upon which, however, the oppressive shadow of impermanence still weighed. In fact, it is well known that, if you frequently light a fire near a haystack, sooner or later you risk setting something ablaze.

At sunset on a splendid day at the end of April in 1298, the temperature was particularly mild, and the sky clear and serene. Escorted by Lapo and a soldier, Oliviero was preparing to return to Piega. That afternoon he was bored: they hadn't met anyone, with the exception of a few farmers.

The riders rode up the river. There was little water and, in some stretches, *la Maricula* gave the impression of having become a modest torrent.

On the property of Galasso on the other bank, in a stone quarry with a few tufts of grass and some sparse bushes, a shepherd boy, immersed in who knows what thoughts and sitting on a white boulder staring at nothing, looked after a small flock. Soon it would be time to go back to the fold and go home to mom. The boy did not so much as look at the three men on the other side and did not even notice that they were passing by.

It is known that beasts are not intelligent, at least not as much as man. The sheep, then, would be especially stupid. All it takes is it is just one of them to take the initiative for the whole flock, without thinking, to follow it everywhere, even into a wolf's mouth.

Carlino noticed when it was too late. A little sheep, perhaps attracted by the greener grass of its neighbor, crossed the stream, immediately followed by all the others.

«Hey, stop, stop!»

The boy shook himself from his stupor, and quickly stood up to chase after the fugitives. He waded, pattering barefoot in the shallow water.

«Snotty nose, this isn't your land!» shouted Oliviero, stepping between the shepherd boy and his flock. Carlino's face went white with fear. The three men on horseback were gigantic and menacing.

«Sir, the sheep have escaped...»

With a small hand in his dark curls, the child sobbed in fear. He backed away until his feet were wet again.

«The sheep? Which sheep? I don't see any!» sneered Oliviero ironically.

«My sheep, sir,» Carlino whimpered through his tears.

The knight with the light-colored and mean eyes dismounted.

«Servant, how dare you speak to a gentleman like that?»

With her gloved hand he gave him a tremendous slap, which sent him sprawling onto the cobblestones. The blow was such that the boy lost consciousness. When he came to it was dark, and the riders and sheep were gone. His head ached, and he felt the bitter, unpleasant taste of blood in his mouth. The tunic was soaked, and he shivered. The farmhouse was not far away and, after a few minutes, shaking and wet as a kitten, he arrived safely.

«Father, they stole my flock!» Carlino despaired.

Uguccione ran to the sheepfold and was astonished to see

it empty.

«Who did it?»

Carlino managed to stammer out, «A knight hit me.»

The boy was lucky. Alina, his mother, was in the kitchen, intent on preparing vegetable broth. She had a baby in swaddling clothes, a restless little urchin who resented being immobilized and often left abandoned hanging from a ceiling beam. When this happened, the poor child expressed his disappointment by screaming at the top of his lungs.

Hearing her husband's cries, the woman went downstairs to the farmyard, just in time to see him as he kicked Carlino's backside.

Dark and petite, but young and strong, Alina strove to defend the victim. «Don't hit him! Don't hurt him!»

The son had a black eye and a broken and bleeding lower lip. He thought it was all the work of Uguccione.

«Scoundrel, what are you trying to do? You'll kill him.»

«This good-for-nothing had our sheep stolen!» Uguccione raged.

Everyone was screaming like mad, including the baby hanging from the kitchen beam. Even the dog, a mangy mutt the color of mud, began to bark wildly.

Uguccione, a big, thick and simple-minded boy, in fear of his wife's fury, limited himself to mimicking the threat of further blows to the child.

Carlino took cover behind his mother's worn and greasy dress.

The three older brothers also left the house, simpletons like their father, couldn't believe they were witnessing such an unexpected spectacle. Alina didn't even give them time to breathe.

«You three, get to the kitchen now!»

The boys, with their tails between their legs, went right back in the door of the house, and the dog, too, crouched down behind a bush.

«So, Carlino, what happened?»

It was amazing how the woman went from anger to sweetness in an instant.

«Mother, a rider down in the pasture struck me. And then the sheep disappeared.»

«So it wasn't your father who hit you?» inquired Alina, staring at Uguccione with a stern expression.

«Dad just kicked me in the ass,» the boy complained, massaging the injured part.

Uguccione breathed a sigh of relief.

Having clarified the reproach from the wife, what was he going to do with the Master? Anguished, he couldn't sleep that night.

Called to podestà at Cesena, Galasso left old Paolino with the task of looking after the small farms of Secchiano.

The farmer lived at the castle, ate abundantly every day, and worked much with his brain and little with his hands. Fat as a piglet ready for the butcher's blade, he had a luxuriant nape, with several rolls of lard, covered with sparse black down. The double chin, flaccid and unsteady, made the face look small and the eyes thin as two slits. His nose was pudgy, with upturned nostrils, and his mouth had almost nonexistent lips.

The pig-like appearance matched a fine brain, and he knew the tricks of the trade. He noticed the peasants who reaped prematurely to steal a bundle of ears, who thinned out the vineyard to steal a bunch here and there, and who secretly gathered the unripe fruit. He counted well, and it was difficult to steal even one chicken, let alone a whole flock of sheep.

«What's up? Where are the Count's sheep?» he yelled in a shrill, effeminate voice.

Uguccione attempted an impossible defense.

«I had nothing to do with it, it was Carlino.»

«You were the shepherd, and you will have to answer to the Master!» threatened Paolino.

He sent a messenger to Cesena to notify Galasso.

«Hey, no! Now enough with the provocations! Let the sheep be returned to me, and the thief handed over to punish him!»

Galasso didn't take long to understand the crime. The Olivieris, in addition to plotting intrigues with the Malatestas, dared to raid their livestock! It was immediately necessary to publicly reaffirm the dominance of his family and to force Bartolino to submit definitively. He sent the messenger back to Secchiano with two written orders for Paolino.

He banished Uguccione and his family, with the death penalty if they returned to Secchiano.

He had the soldiers stationed in the valley ready, about thirty in all, for an imminent war campaign.

Uguccione begged for mercy.

«It's not my fault, it was the Olivieris, and God damn them!»

In an instant, the poor man found himself out of the house and without any sustenance.

They loaded the household goods onto a handcart. The swaddled baby in her arms, Alina cried aloud. Her other children were frightened, but not aware of the situation.

Paolino moved with pity and let them take away two loaves of black bread, a jug of milk, dried fruit and eggs.

«Leave us at least one goat...» pleaded Uguccione.

«I can't, the animals are counted,» replied Paolino.

With anguish in their hearts, they set out on the path downhill alongside the river.

Two soldiers escorted them to the border.

Paolino, tormented by remorse, wanted to dine with the priest.

«I obeyed the Master's orders, and I could not do otherwise.»

Domino Giovanni, intent on nibbling on a succulent leg of roast chicken, wiped his mouth on the greasy sleeve of his robe.

«Galasso's will is law, and you cannot disobey. Otherwise...»

The priest of Secchiano appreciated good food and wine. He loved the quiet life and, albeit a young age, peace of mind, while he hated the insecurity of war.

«Do you really believe that Galasso wants war with Piega for just twenty sheep?» he asked.

Arrogant and shrill, Paolino explained, «Domino, it's not a question of sheep, but of an ancient grudge. Galasso wants Piega, and we're at the final confrontation.»

The pastor was afraid, «But will we win?»

«War is not an exact science, and anything can happen. If the Malatestas help Bartolino, who knows how it will end up...»

Leaving the discussion unfinished, Paolino nibbled at the bread and sipped the wine.

«Domino, you teach me that the future is in the hands of the Lord. Our Uguccione, who was until yesterday a sharecropping farm, today is a beggar.»

Was he enjoying frightening the priest?

The following morning, accompanied by Gano, a young cleric of the parish church of Secchiano, Domino Giovanni set out for Piega. The journey was short, but not without risk. Having crossed *la Maricula*, they entered the territory of the degli Olivieri, a parish priest and an unarmed cleric at the mercy of the enemy.

Giovanni heartened himself, "Whoever beats or kills a priest commits a mortal sin, and will end up in hell. No one will dare to touch me."

Strengthened by this conviction, Domino Giovanni presented himself safe and sound at the gate of Piega.

The soldier on watch did not recognize the strangers. To

avoid any doubt, while noting that they were undoubtedly two harmless religious men, he called out in a loud voice, «Lapo, Lapo!»

Lapo ran and cordially greeted the parish priest of the nearby church.

«Welcome, Domino! Who are you looking for?»

«Would you please announce me to your priest?»

The voice was firm, but betrayed emotion. Much taller and, apparently more vigorous than the presbyter, Gano hunched over to hide behind him. They were in the enemy's lair.

Maliocco made them sit on the bench in front of the oak table. A boy served a jug of red wine.

«Well? To what do I owe the good pleasure of seeing you?» Maliocco began unceremoniously.

«It's certainly not a pleasure, rather quite the opposite!» replied Domino Giovanni before consoling himself by guzzling. Then he continued, «Count Galasso is preparing war because of the sheep ...»

He was about to add "stolen", but he managed to stop himself just in time: his words could have been interpreted as a provocation and, as an unarmed guest in someone else's house, it was better to avoid being rude.

The wise Domino Maliocco recognized the crime and the fault.

«If I could convince Bartolino to return the flock, you would help me…»

Both parish priests had difficulty finishing the speeches, as if suggesting that the other continue with the right approach.

Gano, quietly, convinced that no one noticed him, tried to take possession of the jug.

«Idiot, what are you doing? A young cleric does not drink wine! Were you hoping I wouldn't notice?» his Domino scolded. The boy withdrew his hand too late, and Giovanni hit it with his fist.

«These young people still don't know what respect and good manners are.»

Domino Maliocco nodded to confirm.

The two priests, under the longing eyes of Gano, who remained sober and with a dry mouth, drained the jug. Between one sip and another, they agreed that Maliocco would try to convince his Lords to compensate the damage with the return of the sheep, and that Giovanni would intervene, in favor of peace, with Count Galasso.

After the merry drink, which lasted a couple of hours, Maliocco accompanied his colleague and the cleric back to the door.

The old parish priest admonished Lapo and the guard: «Ensure that they return safe and sound!»

He watched them walk home, the lanky, uncertain Gano supporting the reeling, drunken little priest. With an unpredictable twist of irony, he commented, «*Ganus clericus beverendissimum dominum presbiterum Johannem, Seclani plebis rectorem, difficillime ducit atque sustinet.*»

Lapo and the guard concluded the prayer with an "Amen".

THE SEIGE

After months of hard and incessant work, the walls of San Lorenzo returned to their former glory.

«Now we will be able to defend ourselves as in the past,» Bonzio congratulated his son-in-law.

«Sir, we still have to rebuild part of the house and the keep.»

The old warrior looked the young man up and down: «It's time for you to go to Piega, and bring your wife and my grandson home.»

«But... And the work?»

«Most of it is done. If you're missing for a few days, I'll take care of it. I'm old, but I still manage.»

On a splendid spring morning, one of those that don't make you regret the mist and heat of summer, Tignaccio and Gasparino left for Piega. The golden tufts of blooming laburnums defined the limit of the cultivated fields.

They went up the ridge, where the road went into a forest thick with hornbeams, and turkey and durmast oaks.

«Sir, this path is ideal for an ambush,» Gasparino complained.

Tignaccio consoled him, «And who do you expect to attack us...»

More than worried, the young man was in the throes of the euphoria of seeing his wife again and taking his heir in his arms for the first time.

Once at the pass, they dominated the valley *della Maricula* with its castles from above. The clear sky seemed to merge on the horizon with the darker blue of the sea.

«Here's Piega!» exclaimed Tignaccio pointing to a hill near the river.

«But it's still a long way off,» Gasparino complained.

The first to spot them, when they were still very far away, was Lapo, who was on watch. He distinguished Tignaccio's armor and horse, and imagined that the more battered soldier was Gasparino.

He yelled to give the alarm. Antonio climbed onto the battlements and, recognizing his cousin, dismounted and jumped on his horse to run towards him.

«Tignaccio! A little longer and your child would have started walking,» he joked. If Gasparino hadn't been there, he would have made some wisecracks about the bride.

Maria, curled up on the soft cushions in Geltrude's room, heard the clanging of a soldier's iron on the stairs.

«Maria! Maria, it's me!»

She recognized her husband's voice and got up to run towards him. Agnese had arranged her hair in a braid which, from a white silk cap, descended to below her shoulders. After a polite bow, she tried to resist the urge to throw her arms around her neck and blushed. She then relented and, much to the scandal and amusement of her mother-in-law and aunt, she stood on tiptoe and kissed her husband on her lips. Tignaccio pretended to withdraw, but ended up reciprocating. He stroked her face, caught his breath and ordered, «I want to see my son!»

Agnese approached with the baby in her arms.

She entrusted it to his father.

«See how it looks like you? He looks just like you when you were a kid.»

As soon as he was in the stranger's smelly hands, the child began to scream in despair.

«He's hungry, as always. He eats like a wolf!» exclaimed Agnes.

Tignaccio handed her screaming bundle back to Maria who untied her dress to attach it to her breast.

«We'll call him Bonvicino, like my father,» said Tignaccio,

ecstatically contemplating his wife and son in that tender moment of intimacy.

That evening, the newlyweds were left a room all to themselves, with a soft and comfortable bed.

It was an unforgettable and very short night.

Shortly after dawn they were awakened by shouts and noises.

Tignaccio recognized his uncle's authoritative voice: «Close the front door! Lower the gate!»

Everyone shouted, and the castle resounded with a thousand noises of men and weapons.

Antonio looked out at his cousin's room, «Hurry up, quick! Galasso and his men are attacking us!»

Tignaccio put on his leather undercoat in a flash, belted on his sword, and set off running towards the walls. He didn't even give the young bride the opportunity to say goodbye.

He crossed the court, where there was a great confusion of people, soldiers and animals: most of the peasants had managed to get back into the castle before the door closed.

Reaching the bastions, he found his uncle in control of the countryside. To understand what was going on, Tignaccio looked out. The peasants lay on the lawn in front of the castle, those further away killed by sword, those below the walls pierced by archers. Men, women and children had suffered the same merciless fate.

«Cowards! They took us by surprise. They waited for the servants to leave for work in the fields.» Bartolino was horrified. «We were forced to close the door. They looked like so many,» he explained to his nephew.

Gasparino appeared behind the men. Pale as death, he approached Tignaccio. Despite the fear, the curiosity was too much. He leaned out from the stands, and recognized blacksmith, his cousin in front of the portcullis.

The poor fellow had been hit by an arrow a few meters

from the entrance. After Bartolino's order to let go of the hoist, the heavy grate, which suddenly fell to the ground, had separated the living from the dying. With all his breath, before being hit over and over again, the blacksmith had screamed in despair. Mortally wounded, he had dragged himself to the gate, in the vain hope that one of his own might help him. He had left a long trail of blood on the dusty ground.

Gasparino let out a guttural yelp.

«Hey, that man is screaming like an animal,» said a surprised Bartolino.

Other soldiers were dumbfounded at hearing the shrill and, at the same time, deep cry. There were some exchanges of looks, some ironic and some fearful.

An archer, a slimy and superstitious guy, one of those who fight from cover, let slip a rash comment: «For me, that little black man who screams like a wild boar is cursed and bad luck!»

Some men put their hand on the hilt of the sword. Others, a custom inherited from the Jews, touched their genitals, and still others, hurriedly and secretly, made the sign of the cross.

«What is this nonsense!» Tignaccio rose up indignant. «Act as if you were all as brave and fearless as Gasparino!»

Bonzio had told him that, when in the past, things had gotten serious, Gasparino had always proved to be a good soldier, even if a bit whiny. Now, though, he was whimpering softly like a little woman, and he looked overtaken by fear.

Then, however, he astonished everyone, «We will make those worms pay. They are relentless against the defenseless people and we will do justice, and without mercy!»

His angered words at once calmed all the gossip and the superstition.

Only the reckless do not feel fear, while the brave know how to dominate it.

It was difficult to estimate how many enemies there were.

«In my opinion, there will be about forty soldiers from Secchiano, and at least as many from Cesena,» Bartolino muttered aloud.

«Uncle, and how many of us are there?» Still a little confused, Tignaccio tried to understand.

«Thirty-six soldiers and about twenty other men capable of fighting. And we have plenty of supplies.»

An unusual calm reigned on the walls, a patient waiting for events.

«I don't think they'll attack us, at least not right away. They will first want to understand if we have the possibility of resisting, and for how long,» said Bartolino.

Tignaccio leaned out to scan the horizon.

«For now, we can't see any catapults or ladders,» the boy limited himself to ascertaining, lowering his head again.

Oliviero went up to the bastions. He was fully armed, as if to fight on horseback and in open fields.

«Those bastards killed women and children!» he exclaimed furiously. «And they raided the livestock.»

«They took back their herds, and all the animals they found!» Antonio intervened.

«The sheep have nothing to do with it! They want our lands and the castle.»

As usual, Oliviero wanted to start a fight.

Bartolino defended his eldest son, «Yes, the sheep have nothing to do with it. Galasso wants Piega and our land.»

The men remained alert all day, but the enemy gave no battle.

In the first shadows of the evening, in the countryside and in the valley, all around the walls, a long line of fires appeared, more than thirty. From Piega the crackling of the flames could be clearly heard and, carried by the wind, the acrid smell of the smoke reached the castle.

Bartolino and his family were at dinner when Lapo burst in to sound the alarm, «Lord, there are so many of them, and they've surrounded us!»

They all ran to the bastions.

Bartolino reassured the men, «They are fewer than they might seem, and they have lit many fires to scare us. You will see that tomorrow they will come to negotiate.»

He gave orders that they double their guard, and recommended that they not hesitate to call him in case of need.

«You never know with the Montefeltros...» he snorted before returning to the keep.

For supper the cook wrung the necks of two fat geese. While the men were served their delicious meat, the poor people had to settle for a soup of legumes, where rancid pork rinds floated here and there which, rather than adding flavor, made the miserable meal smell foul.

In the large room, Domino Maliocco did honor to the food as always, and applied himself with passion not only to the big pot, where the geese wallowed in a sea of vegetables, but also to the white bread and the jug of wine.

«Domino, how did you like dinner?»

Heedless of the uncertainties and restlessness of the diners, Antonio felt like joking.

As he kept chewing, the priest looked up from his meal with a wry smile at the boy.

Geltrude, supported by her sister, reprimanded her son.

«Blessed youth! We are at war, and you enjoy making fun of it.»

Having swallowed his morsel, the Domino pronounced, «The supper is good, my boy, and it would have been excellent if your brother hadn't plundered the Secchiano flock.»

Oliviero stood up and shouted: «How dare you talk like that in my house! Thank God for the respect I owe your Holy Office, otherwise...»

Geltrude jumped, and Agnese squeezed her arm to silence her.

All the diners looked at Bartolino. The Master took a few moments to find the right words. Then, calmly, he said, «Sit down, son. The Domino is not wrong. Taking possession of the sheep was not prudent on your part. Galasso was looking for a reason to attack us and you, without first thinking, gave it to him.»

Humiliated, Oliviero was on the point of continuing the scene and leaving with a curse against his father. But he sat down shaking his head and, overcoming his anger, hated Bartolino in silence.

Alluding to the Domino, Antonio whispered in his cousin's ear: «*In vino veritas…*»

After dinner, the parish priest retired to the upstairs chapel, officially for night prayers and, in reality, to digest better away from the hustle and bustle of the hall. After the psalm and the readings, as he went out he ran into Antonio and Tignaccio.

«*Mala tempora currunt*!» the parish priest addressed them.

«*Sed peiora parantur*!» Antonio, promptly and with a pinch of sarcasm, answered back.

The religious nurtured a profound esteem for the two cousins.

«Young men, I had made an agreement with the presbyter of Secchiano to try to nip the war in the bud, but we didn't have time. Let's hope that common sense prevails, and that the Lord helps us. You two, if you have the opportunity, advise Bartolino to do the best.»

«Domino, Tignaccio is no longer of this house. You'd have to talk to my father for him to authorize him to go out. I believe the Montefeltros would also be pleased.»

As always, Antonio tried to protect those he loved.

Tignaccio almost got angry, «Nobody knows that I'm here and, if they did, since I'm a man of Corrado, I would pass as a traitor. And even if that were not the case, I would never, in the future, want to have to fight my uncle and my cousins.»

«Son, here are your wife and your firstborn, who have nothing to do with these people and with this battle. And you, as if that weren't enough, have obligations, and no longer with the degli Olivieri of Piega, but with the Counts of Pietrarubbia.»

The parish priest wisely wanted to distinguish the Pietrarubbia family from that of the Montefeltro cousins.

«Domino, it's just a skirmish, and no one will notice me,» Tignaccio said.

The thought of having put his adored Maria and little Bonvicino in danger made his insides twist with nervousness and a sense of helplessness. However, he managed to find a positive note. Instead of being with Bonzio in San Lorenzo, and completely unaware of the siege of Piega, he was here, ready to defend his family.

In dismissing the two young men, the Domino exchanged a knowing look with Antonio, as if to say: «I'll try to convince him.»

Lapo did not sleep, and he spent the night on the walls watching the enemy's fires from above. In the first light of dawn, Galasso's troops lined up on the plain in front of the walls.

«Here we are! Run and call Bartolino!» Lapo ordered an archer who was gazing at the multitude of Montefeltros in astonishment.

Antonio arrived first.

«There must be at least a hundred,» the boy estimated, «but I don't see any catapults, battering rams, or ladders.»

The two knights advanced towards the castle.

Galasso would have liked to stay out of range, but it was essential to get close. Nervous, the horses struggled to keep pace.

When he was within earshot, the count uncovered his head: he had dark and very short hair, and he surprisingly resembled his cousin Corrado, although the latter was twenty years younger.

«Bartolino!» he shouted authoritatively. «Give me your son, so that he can be punished for his wrongdoings.»

Standing in the stands, Bartolino answered without hesitation: «If you want my son, you'll have to come and get him!»

Oliviero, next to his father, grinned satisfied.

Galasso insisted, «I claim Piega and its villages! If you resist, we will show no mercy and kill all of you!»

On the walls of Piega the men let themselves go to a worried bustle. Bartolino glared at them and, suddenly, silence returned.

Then, showing no fear, he contemptuously dictated his terms, «Withdraw in an orderly manner, otherwise we will destroy you! Piega will never give up!»

Galasso murmured between his teeth, «This is the showdown. We will exterminate all the degli Olivieri and their people.»

And he turned the horse.

Cavalca, the favorite son who had escorted him under the walls, agreed, «Yes, my father.»

«There are about fifty horsemen, thirty infantrymen and twenty archers» Tignaccio, as a good strategist, while everyone was agitated in anticipation of the next battle, had assessed the forces of the enemy army.

«Perhaps, if we attempted a sortie, we could could chase them off,» suggested Oliviero.

«No, we have solid walls to protect us and enough supplies to hold out for a long time. When they attack, most of them will die before they get under the fence. We just have to push them back.»

Bartolino was confident that, after the losses of a bloody and useless assault on the castle, the morale of the enemy would not have been through the roof. It was enough to defend oneself, and save as many men as possible for a possible final battle.

Towed by mules, two truncheons on wheels were positioned by the besiegers on the grassy plain at Solina of Piega, just over three hundred yards from the castle and right on the edge of the bush. Tignaccio, who knew the structure of the manor, heaved a sigh of relief.

«They think the walls are fragile near the gate.»

The side from the *solina* was the most solid and robust and, right near the entrance, the wall was two times thicker and much wider.

If, on the other hand, they had bombed from the northeast or from sunset, from the side of the river, the matter would have been different.

They began hammering at the walls, aiming close to the gate. The stones struck with a thud, dull and impressive, which resounded darkly throughout the castle. The bullets scratched the scarp of the walls and bent the grate in front of the door.

«Incompetent!» exulted Oliviero.

«They will continue like this for a little while longer. Then the archers will start. Inform the soldiers that they be ready to take cover with their shields, and make sure that the people and the animals are under cover» ordered Bartolino to his eldest son.

Oliviero hastened to give his father's instructions. Two peasants reinforced the closure of the stable and that of the enclosure for the animals under the canopy, while, in the meantime, the church in the courtyard was filled with faithful kneeling in prayer before God and Domino Maliocco.

The first arrows, not to kill, but to burn, came whistling from above. Everything that could burn, the wagons in the yard, the hay and the thatched roofs, burned, and the men with buckets came out into the rain of fire.

Galasso's soldiers took advantage of the confusion and, protected by shields and capes, ran with the ladders under the walls. Many fell as they crossed the open ground, slain calmly and precisely by Piega's archers. They succeeded in supporting the ladders, but, pushed back with the poles, they fell backwards. Very few, under the pitch and boiling sewage, reached the battlements, but ended up torn to pieces from the swords of the degli Olivieri.

Tignaccio, one of the best in combat, killed two enemies by throwing them back down, and Gasparino, who was screaming like a madman, cut off the hand of a giant who was taller than him by a palm. The poor man, distraught with pain and desperate, begged for mercy, falling to his knees.

Gasparino finished him off with a tremendous blow.

«This is for my cousin!»

The high-pitched, croaking cry amazed the fellow soldiers.

The Montefeltros beat a retreat and, under an incessant rain of arrows, they abandoned the field leaving behind many corpses.

«Galasso, step forward and fight!»

Oliviero, standing on the walls with a drawn sword, challenged the enemy. Targeted by a cloud of arrows, he was forced to return to cover.

Tignaccio summed up the battle to Bartolino: «We have a farmer whose foot was pierced by an arrow, and a hay cart was burned. The fire is out and everyone is safe.» Then, pointing towards Secchiano, he concluded, «I counted fourteen fallen in the ranks of Montefeltro and five or six wounded.»

Oliviero looked forward to the final victory.

«Father, this time we will be able to defeat them and, perhaps, then take Secchiano!»

«This was more of a skirmish than a battle. Galasso underestimated us and he won't repeat the mistake. He has lost many men and won't want to lose any more. He will try to starve us out, and we'd better prepare for a long siege.»

Bartolino's prediction came true. Galasso's men made no further attempts and remained at a prudent distance for the rest of the day. At sunset, like the previous evening, the fires surrounded Piega.

After dinner, Antonio and Tignaccio went up to the bastions. They found the guards peering into the shadows of a night of keeping vigil and waiting.

«Cousin, taking advantage of the darkness and the escape route, someone could be sent to look for reinforcements. What if we try to talk to my father?»

The escape route, a twisted and narrow tunnel, allowed only one man to pass at a time with difficulty. From the cellars of the keep, the tunnel descended, with a steep brick staircase, to a natural cave, which opened onto the overhanging cliff towards the river with a tiny opening hidden by vegetation. From this hole, to reach the grassy plain at the level *della Maricula,* it was enough to descend to the ground with a rope or a rope ladder. Only the degli Olivieri and the most trusted of the household knew of the existence of the passage, which was said to be older than the walls of Piega. The inner part of the keep wound under a brick vault, and the steps below all had the same regular rise, except for a couple, one higher and one lower than the others. In the dark and in the agitated phases of a battle or an escape, they would have made anyone who did not know of their existence tumble down, thus exposing the unfortunate person to the blows of the enemy.

«For the moment, the situation is not hopeless. Galasso has lost many men and the Malatestas could help us, even if their intervention would entail obligations for which it would cost dearly to repay.»

«You will see that your father will want to try and resist on his own. At night it shouldn't be difficult to cross their lines and, with the Malatesta troops, we could do away with Galasso and his dregs.»

Tignaccio felt like an Olivieri of Piega, even if his cousin kept reminding him of his new condition, «You're here almost by chance to fight a war that isn't yours. We would all understand if you and your family left, perhaps taking advantage of the escape route.»

«And do you see me, with a woman and a child, fleeing by night among the enemies? Better to stay here. Tell Bartolino to send someone else for reinforcements, a man alone and unhindered.»

At dawn the castle seemed revived from the torpor of the night.

After the rotation, the soldiers who had stayed up all night could enjoy a few hours of rest. The peasants tended the animals, and the courtyard resounded with the traffic of men and animals: shouts, clanging of weapons, shrieks of women and children, grunts, bleating, bellowing, the clucking of hens and the crowing of roosters. There were those who cooked, those who waited their turn at the well to drink, and those who, in the midst of the chaos, argued and came to blows. The constraint in a confined space exacerbated spirits, and fear agitated the peasants.

Tired and sleepy, Antonio went in search of his father. He found him in his room getting dressed to go out.

«Father, the night was quiet, and the enemy only kept the fires going. I've already arranged for the changing of the guard and, for the moment, all is well.»

After a long sleep, Bartolino was optimistic.

«We could hold out for months, even years. They don't have enough strength to conquer the castle and, sooner or later, they will have to give up.»

«And if we took advantage of this moment to ask for reinforcements from the Malatestas? A couple of men are enough for the escape route at night, now that there is no moon. Rimini's army could take Galasso's thugs by surprise...»

Antonio did not speak of help, but only of reinforcements, and took advantage of the absence of Oliviero, who did not like his brother's initiatives. Bartolino could have argued that it was his idea, and no one would have had anything to say about it.

Oliviero, without meaning to, looked out the door.

«Father, what are we doing today? We could attempt a sortie.»

In trying to make a good impression, the boy did quite the opposite.

«We just have to wait, without facing them in an open battlefield. They have us outnumbered, but not enough to conquer the castle,» retorted Bartolino. He didn't raise his voice, but Oliviero felt mortified all the same.

Antonio slipped through the door and left secretly.

Lapo's physique betrayed his Tuscan origins. Well into his thirties, short, thin, dark-haired and fair-eyed, he was a brave and experienced soldier. Unmarried and without children, as a trusted family member, he was treated by the Olivieris like a relative. Bartolino consoled his wife, in distress over the restless nature of her eldest son, saying to her: «He is always in the company of our Lapo, who knows how to defend him in case of need.»

Geltrude, aware of what the boy was up to with the women of Piega, and sometimes even with those of Secchiano, lived in the constant fear that, sooner or later, a husband, a father or a brother would avenge with blood the maidens' honor taken by force. Submissive to the men of the house, and forced to pretend nothing happened, she had tried to confide in Domino Maliocco. The priest had confined himself to reminding her that often the girls were only apparently unruly. Or, at least, not apparently enough.

«Sooner or later they'll hurt him or worse, they'll kill him!» Geltrude had wept in despair.

«My lady, Oliviero is strong, much feared, and is always with Lapo. And later, he repents and confesses his sins.»

To discuss the war and the siege, Bartolino dismissed the women after dinner.

«Today was a calm day. Galasso's men just watched us, as we did with them. They are realizing what the costs and losses would be if they tried to attack us again.»

Oliviero, who continued to underestimate the enemy, hoped that his father was planning to come out to do battle.

«What if they're waiting for reinforcements? Cesena isn't that far after all,» suggested Antonio, who, on the contrary, feared the arrival of new soldiers and, above all, more efficient catapults.

«We'll be the ones looking for reinforcements. Go get Lapo right away!» ordered Bartolino.

Out of breath from the run, Lapo arrived shortly after.

«Tonight you will go down the escape route, cross enemy lines and go to the Penna in search of reinforcements. This letter is for my cousin. If they catch you, you must destroy it. Choose a soldier to accompany you.»

Oliviero was unable to hide a gesture of surprise. However, he noticed an exchange of complicit glances between Antonio and Tignaccio. How dare they interfere in his father's decisions?

In a surge, without even reflecting, he suggested, «Father, if the men of the Penna come to help us, they will want to be rewarded. Why don't we wait to see how the siege proceeds?»

«If the Malatestas and the soldiers of the Penna intervene, this will be the last battle of Galasso and the victors will divide the lands of Secchiano between themselves», replied an annoyed Bartolino.

Oliviero swallowed the pill and cursed his brother in a low voice.

Tignaccio waited until Bartolino was alone.

«Uncle, what would you say if my Gasparino went with Lapo? Once we get to the Penna, he could go to my parents in San Lorenzo. Bonzio will be wondering why I haven't returned yet, and he will be very worried.»

Tignaccio did not say that this was not the war of Gasparino and Bonzio and, perhaps, not even his.

Bartolino remained thoughtful for a few seconds. He considered the possibility that Bonzio, as a half-relative, could intervene in favor of the besieged, but he was forced to rule it out. San Lorenzo was a castle of the Pietrarubbia family, Ghibellines, enemies of Piega and allies of Secchiano. He thought that if Galasso asked Corrado for help, Bonzio might make an attempt to convince him to remain neutral.

«So be it! Prepare a letter for your father-in-law, so that he knows about the siege. Ask him to ensure that Pietrarubbia remain impartial, and not mention our request for reinforcements from the Malatestas. If they succeed, as I hope, in escaping the encirclement, Lapo will go to Penna and Gasparino to San Lorenzo. In case of capture, they will have to pretend to ignore each other's mission.»

The two men wore light traveling clothes, comfortable breeches, and leather-soled boots. As their only weapon, they put a knife on their belt. The bags with bread, cheese and the rolled up letter were slung over their shoulders. Wrapped in black cloaks with a large hood, they descended the twisted ladder and walked along the tunnel until they looked out over the overhang. Tignaccio, who had followed them, checked the knots in the rope.

«Once on land, you will have to cross the river and continue toward Secchiano. The soldiers guarding that side will be fewer than those on the *solina*, where there is the castle door to keep an eye on. Try not to go near the fires, and take advantage of the trees and bushes to avoid being discovered,» Tignaccio advised with an air of worry as he lowered the rope into the void.

First, agile and silent, Lapo slipped down into the darkness and, after less than a minute, touched the damp grass. Having reached the shelter of a bush leaning against the bank, he curled up in his cloak.

Tignaccio laid a hand on Gasparino's shoulder, «Now you go too, and tell Bonzio that the situation is serious, but not desperate.»

Gasparino went down. Before reaching Lapo, he looked up and regretted the safety of the solid walls of Piega.

As expected, Galasso's men on the river side were few and far between. Wrapped in cloaks with hoods to hide the dim luminosity of their faces, they chose a passage between the two fires distant from each other, and managed to reach the shore. Avoiding the habitual and well-known ford, they crossed at a point where the water, even if scarce due to the drought, reached waist level. Silently and sheltered in the thorny undergrowth, they walked up the course along the opposite bank. Once at a safe distance from the enemy, they turned to look back. In the distance the fires around Piega shone, macabre gleams on that night with clear air and a starry sky.

«Well, the time has come for us to part ways. You will go up to the pass and cross towards San Lorenzo. I, on the other hand, will continue along the river to the Penna.»

It was obvious that Lapo was giving the orders. Garparino, before preparing to wade across *della Maricula,* whispered a brief whiny goodbye.

The strong and intrepid Lapo, on seeing the frail little man who, having climbed the opposite bank, ventured alone into the darkness, murmured to himself, «Good luck!»

The life of Uguccione and his family hung in the balance. After the two soldiers had accompanied them to the border of Secchiano, they had gone down to the valley as far as the first village, but hadn't found the courage to enter and ask for help and seek refuge.

«They'll take away even what little they have left us!»

Alina, as always and even in that desperate situation, distrusted strangers. It was she who decided, «Let's go back through the woods. Those from Secchiano know us and, above all, they know what happened. If we are seen, they won't report us.»

Anxiety had dulled Uguccione's brain, of which was already rather lacking. Without thinking, he obeyed his wife. Helped by his sons, he towed and pushed the cart with the household goods up and down the path that climbed up the valley into the bushes. Even with only the strength of a six-year-old boy, Carlino gave it his all and suffered the fatigue in silence. How to make dad ever forgive me?

«Oh, slow down! And don't come out in the open,» exhorted Alina, at the head of the group with the swaddled baby in her arms.

«Mama, where are we going?» asked Magnino, the eldest and most mature of the boys.

«Children, we must find shelter for the night. I think we could hide in the caves under the riverbank of Talamello.»

«Why are we hiding? What have we done? Who is looking for us?» asked an alarmed Magnino.

Grim, her mother gave him a sign on her lips with her finger to keep quiet.

In a small clearing among the broom trees, a narrow fissure hid a humid and cramped cave. Alina believed that a fire would signal their presence and, at least for the first night, they would only suffer the cold, but not hunger. Over the next few days, once the supplies ran out, it became essential to find food.

«Go south into the woods. Don't let yourself be seen and look for something to eat,» Alina recommended.

She stayed in the cave with Carlino and her youngest son, who was exhausted. The cold, the nocturnal humidity and the scarcity of mother's milk had reduced him to a pile of fetid clothes, in which one could glimpse his little black face, haggard and suffering. Without strength, the child no longer screamed, he kept his eyes closed and only emitted a few faint moans. When evening came, Uguccione and the boys returned almost empty-handed. They had picked some berries, some small unripe cherries, a small bunch of asparagus and some various edible sprouts. No one was able to get their fill, and wives are known to become mean on empty stomachs.

«You are miserable, incompetent, a worthless man! I curse the day I married you!» yelled Alina before breaking into hysterical sobs.

That little woman, physically weak, knew how to be ferocious and brutal with poor Uguccione, big, heavy and trembling. Her sons made a desperate effort to maintain a manly attitude, but when Carlino began to whimper, Cecco and Renzo couldn't help themselves, and wept without restraint.

Lapo expected to arrive at the Penna before dawn. Hidden in the darkness of the bush, at first he avoided clearings and cultivated fields. Tired of scratching himself in the brambles, he decided to try to walk a few stretches out in the open, on the gravelly bed of the river. Here he walked faster, even if much less confident. The black cloak stood out on the clear pebbles, and the footsteps were far from silent. He judged that it would be safer to go back into the woods. After crossing, he found a path, hidden by thick and impenetrable shrubs, which continued for a good distance along the bank. At the edge he found a boulder that appeared to have been placed there for a traveler to sit down to rest.

"Just a few moments, just to catch my breath," he thought panting.

There was so little water in the river that he could barely feel its flow among the stones. The almost absolute silence of that dark night was interrupted by sporadic rustlings and the cries of animals in the woods. Although accustomed to the cruelties of war, Lapo was endowed with remarkable sensitivity. How much violence and how many atrocities he had committed! While his body rested, his mind wandered in a multitude of feelings and sad thoughts. What would have been his fate? Within a few years he would be an old soldier, one of those who survive in battle only by experience. As time went passed, the situation would get worse. Remorse gave him no respite. How many people had he killed, and how many women beaten and raped? On the other hand, as Oliviero's companion, he could only share his vices. At times he envied a very hard life, serene and full of affection, of poor people, of servants, of sharecroppers, of those who, every evening, overwhelmed by fatigue and brutalized by the immense effort, returned to a hearth and to the love of a wife. Domino Maliocco, to whom he had confessed his sins, despite the absolution, had not managed to free his heart and soul from the weight of remorse.

«Domino, but did God really forgive me?»

The atrocious doubt never left him and he lived in terror of hell. But what can be done to redeem oneself and deserve a place in purgatory?

Absorbed in his melancholy thoughts, Lapo rested for a few moments in the quiet of the darkness.

The cudgeling was very violent, between head and neck, and not at all muffled by the hood of the cloak. Dazed, he rolled to the ground, but retained a flicker of consciousness.

«I'm dead!» he thought, terrified, before receiving a second blow.

«Father, is he dead?» his voice was that of a child.

Lapo stirred slightly, without reflecting that that slightest movement would have been the end of him. He glimpsed the silhouette of the man kneeling next to him and hoped, for a brief moment, to find the strength to react. When he saw the stone that was about to give him the finishing blow, he tried to at least save his soul.

«Pardon!» he wanted to cry out to God and to men, but only the murderers heard him.

«Father, why did he ask us for forgiveness?»

«Help me undress him and shut up!»

Under the cloak, they found the purse. Uguccione opened it in search of food. He bit into the cheese and bread, and chewed frantically. He offered the leftovers to Carlino.

They took possession of the knife, the tunic and the precious boots with leather soles. At the bottom of the bag, Carlino found a roll of yellowed parchment tied by a leather strap. He untied it and, curious, unwrapped it.

«Father, what is this?»

Uguccione snatched it from his hands.

«It will be a message or a letter. Maybe he was a man of the church.»

At night, in the woods, not even a priest would have been able to read and, for an illiterate farmer, that writing had no value. He returned the parchment to his son.

«If you want it, you can keep it. You can brag about it to your brothers. Now help me move him.»

They dragged the body away from the path, so as not to leave it where anyone might find it. Maybe they would look for him, and then go after the killers. Uguccione went up the slope dragging the corpse by the legs. As they crossed a stony ground, Carlino, who was trotting behind trying to help, recognized him.

«Stop!» he shouted.

«What do you want?»

Tired, Uguccione stopped.

The boy bent down to look at the dead man's face.

«He's one of the sheep thieves!» he exclaimed. «That's why he begged for forgiveness!»

They climbed the steep slope in the dark and threw the body into a crevice between the rocks. After covering it with stones, dry branches and leaves, they set off with the meager booty to return to the cave.

Alina was waiting for them on the grass in front of the cave. In her arms she held her baby, wrapped in filthy, stinking rags.

«Look at what you've done! And may you go to hell!» she shrieked as she held out the smelly bundle. Her anger and pain twisted her face into a hideous grimace. Her eyes, even in the dark, seemed to shine with their own light. The baby was dead. Killed by hunger, hardships and inexorable and cruel destiny.

Uguccione swore, cursed, shouted his anguish to the clear and starry sky. Placing the little body on the damp grass, he ran into the cave. In the background, lying on a bed of leaves, Magnino, Cecco and Renzo held each other tightly. They were shaking and shivering with very high fever. Only Magnino was alert, and recognized him.

«Father, when are we going home?» he whispered, and coughed as he tried to get up on his elbows.

«Soon, son, very soon.»

Uguccione delicately covered the boys with Lapo's cloak. Then he turned, and fled into the open air to breathe deeply.

Alina, sitting on the lawn, was lulling the child in vain.

«He hasn't been baptized,» she complained under her breath.

Carlino coughed violently.

«Father, is my brother in limbo now?»

Gasparino knew that his journey would be long and dangerous. For the first time in his life he found himself at night and alone in a wood, far from home and with no one to cover his back. Stories and legends about bandits who took advantage of the dark to attack travelers and pilgrims came to mind, but what really terrified him was the fear of spirits and the devil. As he struggled up the slopes of Mount San Paolo, every bush, every boulder and every tree took on the appearance of a lurking demon. Slow and attentive to the slightest noise he proceeded rattling off Our Fathers and Hail Marys. Having reached the pass, he thought he saw the profile of Mount San Lorenzo against the starry sky on the other side of the valley.

To avoid bad encounters, he took a path beaten by animals. He had passed there the year before with Bonzio to chase a roe deer. Brambles and bushes blocked the undergrowth, and he walked stooped under the branches. Rounding a bend, he heard a mighty shuffle in the rustle of leaves. He stopped.

The foul beast grunted like a beast. Gasparino shouted, turned and ran up the slope to the pass.

Silence! The devil hadn't come after him.

The boar, solitary and majestic, for his part ignored the

strange animal that howled like a sow pursued by wolves. He turned his rear end and trotted downhill.

Wrapped in a cloak, Gasparino crouched in a crevice among the bushes. He decided to wait for dawn, in the hope that the evil spirits would vanish at first light and return to hell.

When the guards realized that the strange traveler was Gasparino, they giggled between insolence and amusement.

«Like that, wrapped up in your cloak, we thought you were a friar, or a knight on foot!»

Bonzio, on the other hand, had no desire to joke.

Where was Tignaccio? He feared a disaster.

«So what happened to you?» he asked gruffly.

«Galasso besieges Piega, and Tignaccio, with your daughter and your nephew, are inside the castle!»

In the adenoid vernacular of his family, Gasparino told his Lord the story of Piega.

Curious like most women, Rosa left the kitchen. She kept calm.

«Father, what can we do?»

Bonzio did not find an answer, and alarmed his daughter even more. The situation was complicated. Piega was strong and, since time immemorial, had resisted and endured the assaults of the enemy. And, in all likelihood, it would have been like the past this time too. Unless...

As a vassal of Corrado, he could not decide anything without first consulting him.

And of Tignaccio, what would he tell the Count?

Nothing! Nothing should and could not be done.

«My daughter, let us pray that God will protect our loved ones.»

Rose obeyed. At the parish church of Combarbio, she found the affection of Dionigi, the comfort of DominoUbertino and the support of faith.

After two weeks in a state of siege, with no other battles and only a few mutual exchanges of shouted insults from a distance, it seemed that the stalemate would continue indefinitely. Galasso, in order not to pay dearly for an uncertain result, did not sacrifice other men. Hatred and desire for revenge were curbed by the fear of exposing themselves politically to criticism for having abused the position of podestà to pursue a personal end. The siege could still last for months and months and, if so, he would have to bear the cost. Meanwhile, who would look after Cesena in his absence?

Bartolino, on the other hand, in the hope that reinforcements would arrive, remained with his men at the castle, without attempting sorties to go into battle.

Cavalca was a good young man, a good soldier and Galasso's favorite son.

His older brothers, Guidobono and Bonconte, resembled his father, an ambitious and fearless warrior.

Cavalca, on the other hand, would have liked a life without politics, intrigues and wars. He loved hunting, good food and beautiful women. To the vulgarity and violence of the troops, he preferred culture and art.

Galasso had many other projects planned for him and, for a good son, it would have been inconvenient and dangerous to escape his father's wishes. Sometimes opposites attract. Galasso adored Cavalca, and the boy, honored to serve under his command, reciprocated his sentiment.

«Choose two men and go with them to Corrado in Pietrarubbia. You will tell him that Piega has rebelled against our house, and that he will have to help me defeat the rebels. As a reward we will divide up his lands. Tell him to round up his men and be here as soon as possible.»

Happy to indulge his parent, Cavalca left for Pietrarubbia.

«Father, you must go to the Count. Tignaccio could be useful to the Montefeltro cause...»

Rosa's suggestion reminded Bonzio of his wife's wisdom.

Although it was inopportune and annoying for a father, and for a man, the advice of a daughter and a woman, Bonzio had the humility and intelligence to accept it, and decided to go to Pietrarubbia.

He arrived late in the morning, pretending not to notice Alvisio and Fraudolente idly gossiping in the courtyard.

Tosco went down the keep's stairs with a young man who sported weapons and clothes that betrayed his belonging to a noble family. He nodded to the vassal and accompanied the stranger to the castle door. After the farewell bowing to the young gentleman, he turned to Bonzio with his usual cordiality, «What good pleasure brings you to Pietrarubbia?»

«I need to speak to Count Corrado...»

He was received shortly after.

Corrado didn't get angry. Indeed, he seemed happy to know that Tignaccio was in Piega.

He stared at Bonzio and asked abruptly, «Can I count on your son-in-law?»

The question was precise, embarrassing, and Bonzio avoided uncertainty or hesitation.

«My Lord, Tignaccio is a man of San Lorenzo, a faithful soldier and submissive to the Counts of Pietrarubbia. Order and he will obey.»

Corrado seemed very satisfied. He had answered properly.

What a problem war was! Forced *obtorto collo* to participate in the siege, Corrado thought, to get rid of the embarrassment, to propose an advantageous agreement without bloodshed. As a relative of the besieged and son-in-law of Bonzio, Tignaccio would have negotiated an honorable peace treaty, but similar to the surrender of Piega.

To achieve this goal, it was essential to rally all the soldiers, even those of Taddeo, in order to demonstrate to Bartolino and his sons that the enemies were many, fierce and determined to conquer Piega.

Furthermore, and here came the most difficult part, Corrado wanted to persuade the cousin to settle for a meager victory on paper, and not to persevere in a siege with an uncertain outcome.

Corrado, having gathered his soldiers, left his castles practically undefended. While Gasparino was forced to leave against his will, the Count decided to leave Bonzio at San Lorenzo. He was a valid warrior, irreplaceable in terms of ability and experience, but if he had found himself fighting against his relatives and, perhaps, against his daughter's husband, how would he behave?

After a few days, Corrado and Filippuccio arrived in Piega in command of about a hundred men.

As soon as the dust raised by such a movement of men and animals appeared on the horizon, the lookout posts of Piega, the first, from the top of the walls to realize it, sounded the alarm. Antonio ran to the bastions and, at the sight of the army descending along the valley, shouted his enthusiasm.

«Lapo is coming with reinforcements!»

Tignaccio joined him with Oliviero who commented, «This is the end of Galasso!»

«They are too many to be those of the Penna,» grumbled Bartolino.

When he recognized the blue-and-gold banded shields of the Pietrarubbians, Oliviero cursed.

Depressed, Antonio cast an evil look at his brother and shouted: «Those are enemies!»

Oliviero grit his teeth and looked for a scapegoat.

«Tignaccio, here is your new master! Father, we have a traitor among us, a servant of Galasso!»

Tignaccio raised his hand to the hilt of his sword.

«Stop!»« Bartolino's imperious scream froze the blood of the two boys. «Oliviero, enough! He's your cousin, he fought for our cause and he's not to blame.»

Oliviero kept silent, and his father ended up humiliating him.

«It's your fault! It was you who raided the sheep of Secchiano!»

There was no time to reply.

Thus Tignaccio knew that he had a new and formidable enemy. Antonio took refuge silently and quietly in a corner. When Bartolino got angry it was better not to keep a low profile.

«At last, cousin!» Galasso exclaimed.

Corrado turned to his cousin with the respect due from a poor relative to a rich one, «I have more than a hundred soldiers with me!» he exclaimed.

Filippo ordered the camp to be prepared and the men to be refreshed.

As Corrado's servants, Fraudolente and Alvisio had no other duty than to escort their Master. A tent was set up for them close to Corrado's and, that evening, they shared the dining table of the Counts. They stuffed themselves with game and drank without restraint some excellent spiced red.

Gasparino ate rancid boar stew with the troops, and drank a cloudy wine that flowed like oil.

A soldier commented: «Those bootlickers Alvisio and Fraudolente eat with the gentlemen, while we get the watered down wine and pork scraps!»

That evening, the morale of the besieged was low.

The people had taken refuge in the church. Domino Maliocco confessed sinners, women prayed and wept, and children, with their mothers in that state, were terrified.

Oliviero alternated moments of euphoric madness, in which he threatened to go out into the open to face his enemies, with others of deep depression, «We will die with honor, taking the filthy bastards of Secchiano with us to hell!»

Bartolino kept calm: «No one will die. Piega is strong and

if they attack us, we will resist. We mustn't lose our heads.»

Oliviero comprehended who he was alluding to.

After dinner, Galasso and Corrado, escorted by Cavalca, Fraudolente and Alvisio, passing from fire to fire, went on a horse ride around Piega. The two cousins argued animatedly in whispers. Back at Corrado's tent, Galasso and Cavalca said goodbye on their way back to Secchiano. Fraudulent noticed a glimmer of satisfaction in the gentleman's eyes.

Later, sitting in the warmth of the bivouac fire, the scarface commented with gratification, «We'll take Piega without a battle.»

Alvisio shivered at the mere thought of an armed combat. That night Fraudulent reposed, while his friend could not sleep a wink.

THE TRUCE

Early in the morning Antonio broke into Bartolino's room.

«Father, hurry, run!»

They joined Tignaccio and Oliviero on the bastions, who were having a lively discussion.

In the distance, on the southern clearing, behind the two truncheons and a large new catapult, Galasso's army seemed lined up for the imminent battle. Covered by a solid canopy, a mighty ram was ready to attack. It was an impressive and fearsome sight at the same time.

Four horsemen left the enemy lines to advance at the pass towards Piega.

Tignaccio recognized the arms and insignia.

«Uncle, that is Corrado of Pietrarubbia, my Lord, and he comes to negotiate.»

Bartolino shouted, «Prepare the horses! Tignaccio, you will come with me.»

Oliviero grumbled, «And me, father?»

«You and your brother will remain here and, if we do not return, you will command the defense of the castle.»

Corrado and his men, meanwhile, had stopped halfway between the army of Secchiano and the walls of Piega.

The winch creaked up the heavy, twisted iron portcullis, and the door swung open. Armed, but bareheaded as if for a walk, Bartolino and Tignaccio advanced calmly, on their war horses, towards the enemy.

Corrado took off his helmet, and Cavalca did the same.

«Get back in!» he ordered Fraudolente and Alvisio, who turned their horses and hurried to obey.

«We will take Piega, and my cousin will have no mercy for

the defeated,» threatened Corrado.

«We will hold out, and this meadow will fill with corpses!» Bartolino answered resolutely.

For a few seconds they studied each other in silence.

Corrado and Cavalca had dark eyes and hair, while Bartolino and his nephew were lighter and more robust.

«Well? What do you propose?» asked Bartolino.

Corrado, without dwelling on useless digressions, replied, «Galasso demands double the value of the sheep, and he wants the four lands of Piega along the river, with houses, animals and farmers.»

They were the most fertile lands of the Olivieri family, a few thousand acres of territory cultivated with grain. But was this enough?

«My cousin expects guarantees that Oliviero, in addition to making a public apology, is banished from Piega.»

The loss of the farms along *la Maricula* would have led to considerable impoverishment, and the river was the border and the first bulwark to defend the castle.

Bartolino stared into Corrado's deep, dark eyes and spoke, «My Lord, you tell me what your cousin is asking for, but asking and obtaining are two very different things. Without getting lost in delays, why don't you tell us what would be enough for Galasso to stipulate definitive peace between Piega and Secchiano?»

The direct and precise question surprised Corrado. He studied the interlocutor, older and shrewd, to sense if it was the case to reveal the margins of negotiation imposed by Galasso, and answered.

«This is not my fight and, perhaps, not even my war. I'm here to find a peaceful way out that allows Galasso, and myself, an honorable agreement. I wouldn't want to go back to my cousin without having reached an understanding. I will tell you the conditions and limits beyond which I could never go. Know, beyond a shadow of a doubt, that any further request for modification by you would, for me, be equivalent to a refusal. In which case we would just have to fight this war.»

«You have my word, Lord,» agreed Bartolino.

«Well, the acres Galasso wants are only two, the ones closest to the northeast. He knows that you would never give up the others, too close to Piega. He also demands your public apology, sanctioned in an act, with your formal commitment not to harm Secchiano's rights any more. And, of course, you'll have to return the sheep.»

Bartolino, who had feared unacceptable agreements, disguised his relief with the skill of an old fox.

«These are extremely burdensome conditions but, in order to spare the people the suffering of a long conflict, I think I would do well to accept them.»

Bartolino liked the enemy's loyal smile.

Corrado did not hide his satisfaction.

«Well! How do you suggest we proceed?»

«I propose giving the priests the task of preparing the treaty of peace. Tignaccio, who benefits the trust of both parties, will be the guarantor of the safety of your messengers in Piega. I think we'll be ready before noon tomorrow.»

Corrado accepted, «So be it! We will send our presbyter to you as soon as possible, and tomorrow it will all be over. The agreement will be signed in Piega.»

It was an honor for the Olivieris that the pact be stipulated at their castle, and bestowing honors cost nothing.

«There's Domino Giovanni over there!» Antonio exclaimed as soon as he made out the round shape of the young priest.

«Who's accompanying him?» Tignaccio asked.

Three unarmed men were advancing on the back of a mule. Two, very plump, were heavy even for mules. The third, in a gray tunic and tonsure gleaming in the sun, was a young cleric.

Galasso had demanded that the farmer Paolino participate in the mission. He had dismissed him with a few direct words. «You know what acres I am entitled to, and how many servants there are and the animals belonging to them. Make sure you don't get deceived.»

Domino Giovanni had brought the cleric Gano, harmless but imposing, as an escort.

When Galasso's delegation crossed the Piega gate, Oliviero commented aloud, «Two fat pigs and an effeminate clerics. These are the representatives of Secchiano!»

With a grin, Giovanni ignored the offense.

Domino Maliocco invited the guests to the rectory, «Welcome, we've been waiting for you.»

There were three representatives of Secchiano, and as many would have been for Piega. Oliviero came forward, but his father grabbed him by the arm, forcing him to stop.

«Antonio, you have studied, and you will participate with your cousin in the meeting,» he ordered.

«But, father...» Oliviero objected.

Bartolino interrupted him, «You will stay with me. We are soldiers and we cannot read, write or do arithmetic.»

The boy didn't understand if it was an insult or a compliment.

They sat down around the table set with a pitcher of spiced red wine.

Domino Giovanni, sensitive to the charm of the divine nectar, turned his languid eyes to Paolino, who, shaking his head and his throat, made him clearly understand not to indulge in premature revelry.

Catching on to the wit of Domino Maliocco, Tignaccio gave the hint of a smile.

Gano, diligent and almost jovial, expertly carried out the arduous function of scribbler, and wrote down the dictates of the parish priests.

At the time of defining what and how the two acres were, a small problem arose regarding the quantity of pigs entitled to the smaller, but very fertile and subsidized farm.

Paolino disputed the number, claiming to be aware that there were three and that a fat and pregnant sow was missing from the inventory.

Domino Maliocco, with an intimidating and deep voice, intervened to mediate.

«You say a sow is missing, but we have to stick to our inventory, and Antonio can guarantee it's true.»

Indifferently, Tignaccio reached out and shook the pitcher in the center of the table. He was clumsy, accidentally spilling the elixir. Seeing that wasted bounty, Domino Giovanni hissed an appropriate and almost blasphemous curse, «Be careful, for Bacchus!»

The young sprightly priest cared little to nothing about the fate of a pregnant sow, presuming that she even existed. He cut it short, «I don't see why we should doubt the word of a nobleman.»

Paolino, with stubby fingers and almost no nails, scratched his nose, from bottom to top, exposing his horrid nostrils even more. For a second, Antonio feared that he was about to grunt a protest. The poor fellow, on the other hand, unable to contradict his parish priest or, worse yet, question the counterpart's word, kept silent.

Seated around the table, three religious men, a shrewd accountant and two soldiers, found no other disputes. They transcribed the agreement, and Gano's clear handwriting sanctioned the agreed clauses and commitments on the parchment.

Once the drafting was completed, Domino Maliocco smiled with pleasure at Secchiano's colleague, «Now we can drink!»

Gano's face lit up in an ecstatically happy expression.

When Domino Giovanni shook his head meaning no, Paolino gave in to a long, shrill laugh. His double chin quivered like the swollen tits of a running cow.

The young cleric was excluded from enjoying the spoils.

Bartolino continued to fidget, prey to a thousand thoughts, without enjoying the excellent dinner.

«Domino, do you think Galasso's word can be trusted?»

The question betrayed concern and his wife, who believed all the danger was in the past, became horrified.

Domino Maliocco replied, «My Lord, what interest does Galasso have in staging a useless performance? Two farms, with modest costs and losses, are a bargain. Why give up on a good deal and prefer a war with an uncertain outcome?»

«Galasso is very sly, and I don't trust him at all,» said Bartolino.

He dismissed Antonio as if he were leaving on a hunting trip, «My son, have a good trip!»

Bartolino cursed Galasso, Corrado and the war. He had only one single hope, «At worst, my lineage will not die out in Piega!»

It was the middle of the night when Tignaccio followed his cousin into the tunnel.

«Once on the ground, stay in the shadows, and don't run or make any noise...»

Obvious recommendations, but it was hard to suppress the anxiety.

«You'll see that nothing will happen to me, and that, before dawn, I will have reached Penna safe and sound,» said Antonio.

As his only weapon, the boy wore a short, sharp knife at his waist. His blond hair hidden in the hood of the black cloak, he lowered himself into the escape route. Like his predecessors, as soon as he reached the meadow he took refuge and disappeared into the darkness of the brush.

«May God protect you!» Tignaccio wished upon him, narrowing his gaze to see where he had ended up.

After many nights of idleness and boredom, the enemy soldiers guarding the river were tired and distracted, and Antonio crossed *la Maricula* without anyone noticing. Having reached the other bank, he threw his cloak into the bushes and remained with the dark hood over his tunic and breeches. He made sure he had the dagger sheath firmly on his waist and, agile and oblivious to the thorny shrubs, he ran into the undergrowth. He had to hurry. Perhaps the mission would have been useless, but his father had been adamant.

«You will go to the Penna to ask for refuge and help. Our cousin will be happy to help us…»

Fast and almost without taking a breath, Antonio went up the river. It wasn't easy running in the dark, and though his eyes had become accustomed, he came close to falling over again and again. When he felt far enough away from Galasso's army, exhausted by his effort, he stopped to rest in the bushes.

«I made it!» he gasped.

Before dawn he would arrive at the Penna.

Wild boars are afraid of man and, if they meet him, they flee in fear. They are not silent animals and, in the undergrowth or in the meadows, thrashing and rooting, they make a lot of noise. This boar was strange. Instead of running away, he was coming closer.

«What if he's not a boar?»

In doubt, he reached for his belt and gripped the handle of the knife. He distinctly heard a dry branch break. No, it wasn't a boar.

He turned and unsheathed. In the shadows, a couple of meters away, he sensed the silhouette of a man and the vague glow of his face. The stranger pounced without giving him time to think. So, instinctively, he reached out with the dagger and struck him in the belly. With a strange, yelping sound, the attacker froze. Antonio caught his anguished expression before he fell.

He peered into the darkness of the brush. Nothing moved and, apart from the gasp of the wounded man, he heard no other sounds.

«You're alone?» he asked leaning down.

The poor man, with a breath of breath, pleaded, «Don't

kill me. Have mercy!»

«Why, would you have any for me?»

The wretch grabbed his arm with a bloodied hand, «My son... my son...» he whispered before losing consciousness.

«May God have mercy on your soul.»

Antonio was in a hurry and didn't have time to waste. However, he wanted to check who his enemy was. He wore a dark cloak over his robe and, at his belt, carried a sharp dagger. He was wearing luxurious leather-soled boots. His bony legs in his baggy breeches betrayed a long period of fasting, and he smelled like goats.

Having cleaned the blade of the knife on a corner of the unknown man's cloak, Antonio stood up.

The sky was clear and full of stars. A cool, light breeze stirred and quivered the scrub.

"It's not a bad night to die," he thought before continuing on his way.

The brothers had been gone for a few days, killed by fever, hunger and cold. The mother, destroyed by grief, had followed them shortly after. Only the father was left, and he had promised not to abandon him.

Holed up behind a prickly bush of holly, Carlino watched the whole scene. When he was certain that the man had gone, he came out.

«Father, father!»

Uguccione lay motionless and silent. Before approaching, the child looked around him, restless and hesitant. At first he had hoped that, in the confusion of the dim light, everything had gone well. Now, seeing his father on the ground, he was almost sure that he was dead.

He leaned over him and felt his breathing.

«Father, are you alive?»

He stroked his face gently, as he never would have dared before. He crouched down and, both of them wrapped up in the warm mantle with no more tears or even the strength to cry, hugged him. Still and silent, he waited for the night to end.

Galasso was happy. His war with the Olivieris was about to end and everyone knew who the winner was. His arrogant neighbors would have given him the two most luxuriant farms in the valley, and the new peace treaty would have sanctioned the submission of the Olivieris to the Montefeltros. After centuries of continual exhausting disputes, it was a first and important step towards the definitive annexation of the small neighboring feud to Secchiano.

At the head of about thirty knights, and with Cavalca and his cousin Corrado at his side, Galasso crossed the meadow in front of the walls.

«They are arriving!» shouted Oliviero impatiently and, at the same time, annoyed. «Father, we could still reconsider! Antonio will soon return with the men from Penna. Why don't we wait?»

Bartolino, on the other hand, was resigned. The Montefeltros were too many and very determined. While waiting for better times, the important thing was to survive and, in the future, with the help of the Malatestas, everything could change.

«Boy, calm down! By now the terms of peace have been agreed upon, and we have given our word. Let's get ready to receive Galasso honorably.»

From above, Tignaccio recognized the unmistakable shape of Domino Giovanni, who jolted and started without respite. He rode a stocky bay with a blond mane and small ears. Apart from the unusual size for a soldier, more than a priest he looked like a real escort knight to his Lord. For the important occasion, he had dressed up with his best cloak.

The appointment for the stipulation of the treaty had been agreed upon by the two parish priests after the third canonical hour, and the Montefeltros were punctual. The shutter was raised and the door opened.

Tignaccio had placed men on the walls, ready to intervene in case of need.

Secchiano's army, under the command of Guidobono, as the eldest son of Count Galasso, had remained deployed at the extreme limit of the meadow south of Piega. In front of the church, Bartolino was waiting for his bitter enemy. Beside him, Oliviero displayed an irrepressible trembling the nervousness and anxiety that were distressing him.

Galasso entered Piega first, followed by his son, his cousin and the notary Raniero da Vico. The latter, a good man with a cheerful and peaceful character, had found himself forced to participate reluctantly in the dangerous stipulation of that improvised peace. Tall and well-fed, he hated any danger that disturbed the tranquility of his life. With the inseparable seal tied around his neck with a thin cord, among the soldiers he looked like a fish out of water and he couldn't hide his fear. His Lord, Count Galasso, had demanded that he act as notary, and he had to obey and thank him for the important task.

Fraudolente, the first of the men of the escort, raised his eyes to the enemies in the stands as soon as he crossed the entrance.

«We're trapped!»

Alvisio, behind him, nodded. If they closed the door, they would have been exposed to a violent attack from above and with no means of escape.

Bartolino and his son hadn't worn armor. They were wearing swords, but it was clear that, in the unfortunate event of a skirmish, they would have been the first to die.

From the stairway of the keep, Tignaccio controlled the soldiers of both factions. Corrado looked at him while raising a hand. It wasn't a greeting, as one might have misunderstood, but a way to remind the boy who he really was, and which side he should have been on in case of battle. With a nod of the head, the young man let the Lord comprehend that he understood the message. He was a man and a soldier of the Pietrarubbians, and would remain so.

Fraudolente noticed the exchange of glances and understood the meaning. He hated Tignaccio, guilty of having taken away his place at San Lorenzo. Sooner or later, he was going to make him pay, even if it was preferable that for now he was an ally.

The nobles, the notary and Domino Giovanni dismounted. The men took off their helmets and uncovered their heads. The young presbyter looked around. Where was Domino Maliocco?

Bartolino turned to Galasso, inviting him to take a seat in the church, «Welcome to Piega.»

They crossed the threshold together. Inside, in the humid half-light, the stale stench of death reigned, barely diminished by the scent of incense.

Domino Maliocco waited in front of the altar. For the solemn meeting he had worn the chasuble, while Secchiano's colleague wore a dark woolen tunic, tied at the waist by a cord, under his traveling cloak.

Domino Giovanni approached Maliocco. Both short, the first was fat and jovial, while the second hunchbacked and bony. Bartolino, standing in front of Galasso, taller and more robust than the enemy, feigned a proud and determined attitude. Between the two contenders he was the loser.

The witnesses joined the Lords, while the notary and the religious stood between the parties to represent the impartiality of the Church and the Emperor.

On guard in the parvis and in the courtyard, Galasso's men, with nerves on edge, kept an eye on Piega's soldiers. Removed out of caution, the people had found refuge in cellars and stables together with the animals.

Not a breath of wind was blowing in the courtyard, and the air was saturated with a thousand different and disgusting odors.

Strangled by the leather gorget and oppressed by the chain mail, Fraudolente thought of taking off the helmet and the *infula*.

«Let's hope they hurry!»

Alvisio, at his side, was in the grips of itching. The heat and lice gave no respite and, under the red-hot scrap metal, it was impossible to scratch.

The noblewomen of the Olivieri house were safe in their rooms on the first floor of the keep. Maria, thanks to the gossip of Geltrude and Agnese, was aware of the situation. How to resist the temptation to take a peek? She waited for her son to fall asleep and went down the stairs to the hall. The gate was open and, at her door, her husband, armed but without a helmet, stood on the lookout. Despite the fear of being rudely kicked out, she took a peek. In doing so, she touched the arm of Tignaccio, who scolded her.

«What are you doing here? Go back upstairs to my mother.»

The imploring gaze of his wife forced him to give in. After all, what could happen? It would have been enough to give her a push, before closing it again, to keep her safe, and only in the unfortunate event that the situation degenerated.

In the church, after a few coughs, the notary began to recite the treatise. His voice echoed in the dim light.

The presbyters followed the river of archaic and unfeeling words attentively, while the nobles and the texts were too ignorant and too intent on controlling each other to understand their meaning. The pact was clear and known to the parties, and the ceremony a formality.

«*...et magnificas viros dominos comites Galassium et Corradum...*»

In the churchyard, astride under the heavy harness and half suffocated by the helmet, Fraudolente grumbled, «Enough!»

He dismounted and, leaving the bridle to Alvisio to stretch his legs, he approached the keep's stairway.

Tignaccio snorted. What was the intention of the scarface?

Fraudolente climbed the first steps and saw someone retreating in the dark behind Tignaccio. He thought it was a soldier ready to close the door in case of need. He stopped on the balcony in front of the entrance.

Tignaccio raised one hand to his sword and with the other pushed the soldier inward towards the door.

«Hey, Tignaccio, don't you recognize me?»

Taking off his gloves, Fraudolente took off his helmet, uncovered his head and breathed deeply. He smiled and continued.

«It really seems that, at least this time, we won't be fighting...» he didn't say anymore, but only fell short of him to ask, «And you, which side are you on?»

Tignaccio would not have known how to answer. Raised in Piega, but a vassal of Corrado and son-in-law of Bonzio, his heart was in the valley of *la Maricula,* but his honor elsewhere. And honor, for Tignaccio, was sacred.

Maria was too curious to be able to remain long in the shadows, and her husband too busy following the moves of all those armed men to be able to stay with her. The young bride reappeared at the door. She wore a white linen dress, trimmed with precious scarlet fabric, and two long blonde braids hung on either side of a blue hood.

The divine vision surprised Fraudolente.

Maria recognized the slimy and repulsive grin of the scarred man. She pointed at him, her eyes widening in horror. She forced herself to scream her hatred of him, but didn't breathe a word.

Fraudolente felt lost. It was her! The beautiful, stupid and mute daughter of Bonzio, the survivor of that day at the parish church... Damn!

There was no time left for anyone to notice and understand. She pushed Tignaccio who lost his balance and tumbled down the stairs.

«Betrayal!» yelled the scarfaced man at the top of his lungs before pouncing on sweet Maria. He stabbed her in the chest with brutal ferocity. The young woman collapsed lifeless to the ground and died without a cry.

«Maria, Maria!» Tignaccio called in vain.

He tried to get up. Alvisio drew his sword and struck him in the chest and on the head. The blow knocked Tignaccio unconscious, and fell heavily to the ground.

«It's him, he's the coward who betrayed us!» yelled Alvisio.

He looked up and saw the enemy archers in the bastions. He spurred his horse and galloped away from the castle gate.

The court was filled with excited shouts and commands.

In church the notary was finishing reading: «*Et ego Raniero da Vico de Seclano, de auctoritate Imperiali Notarius, ut legitur rogatus scribere scripsi et...*»

Distracted by the noise, he left the sentence hanging.

Cavalca ran to the churchyard.

The battle had begun, and the spears and arrows of Piega's soldiers were raining from the sky on those of Secchiano.

In the church, Galasso and Corrado pounced on Bartolino who, taken by surprise, fell and was immobilized.

Oliviero tried to react but his father, under the threat of arms from the Montefeltros, shouted, «Stop!»

The boy cursed and obeyed.

The notary and Domino Giovanni took cover behind the altar.

In a severe manner, Domino Maliocco began to pray, «*In nomine Patris, et Filii, et Spiritus Sancti...*»

Corrado disarmed Bartolino and made him stand up.

«Order your men to surrender!» he commanded, pushing him towards the door of the church. He jabbed his back with his sword to force him to face the court.

«Stop! Drop your weapons!» ordered Bartolino going out into the sun in the churchyard. Oliviero, in a fit of anger, threw himself against Galasso. More accustomed to battle than the young man, the Count shielded the cutting blow, and wounded the boy's side. With a wild cry, Oliviero let go of his sword and collapsed to the ground.

Piega's soldiers obeyed their Lord and surrendered.

Alvisio, meanwhile, screaming like an eagle, had reached

Secchiano's troops, «Run, they have betrayed us!»

Guidobono saw door to Piega open. What if it had been a trap? If, once near the walls, exposed and without protection, the gate had closed again, how many men would he have lost in a senseless attack? He decided to wait and did not advance.

Fraudolente had remained covered inside the keep. He reappeared as soon as he was sure the fight was over. Everything had gone well. Piega had surrendered and, what's more, the last witness to the massacre at the Combarbio spring had been eliminated. He was truly satisfied.

As if that weren't enough, Tignaccio was on the ground, perhaps dead. And, as far as everyone was concerned, he would have been the traitor.

Several of Secchiano's knights were on the ground, wounded or dead.

Galasso, making sure that there was no more danger, went out into the churchyard. In a corner under the walls, pierced by a spear, Cavalca was dying. The boy recognized his father. He tried to talk to him, but could only wheeze phrases.

Galasso knelt beside him.

«Don't move, my son. It's nothing, you'll get better...» he lied to console him. Cavalca's fear-filled eyes widened before breathing his last breath.

Livid and distraught with anger, Galasso turned to the sky, «You will all pay for this!»

Tignaccio, still stunned, was put in chains and dragged into the church, next to his uncle and cousin.

Corrado didn't even deign to look at him.

Secchiano's army took possession of the castle. The women, the servants, the people and the soldiers were herded into the court.

The first was Tignaccio. Corrado wanted him to be conscious, and ordered a bucket of icy water from the well to be thrown on his head.

When he saw the axe, the young man pleaded with Corrado, «My lord, have mercy on my wife and son!»

The Count pretended not to have heard.

Tignaccio screamed in despair under the pitiless blows of the captors.

Oliviero, in front of the sharp stake and the executioner's club, despaired and wept. Galasso, before ordering the execution, turned to Bartolino.

«Today, Lord, your descendency will be extinguished!»

The father witnessed the execution of his son, to then shared his fate. The noble Bartolino and his eldest son died impaled in front of the people of Piega.

Galasso, not satisfied with the blood shed, conceded the sack of Piega to the men.

«The village is yours, and let none survive!»

The soldiery went wild. There was no mercy, not even for women and children.

Fraudolente and Alvisio gave yet more proof of their ferocity. They were the first to enter the keep and Bartolino's nuptial chamber. Breaking down the door, they found, terrified and helpless, Geltrude and Agnese. Awakened by the deafening noise, the child screamed at the top of his lungs. The women tried to protect the cradle, but there were no scratches, screams or blows that could stop them.

Alvisio killed the newborn with a clean and precise dagger stroke.

Fraudolente, after having stunned them with slaps, raped the two sisters on Bartolino's bed.

«Now they're yours...»

Alvisio, like always, was able to accomplish nothing, but unburdened himself otherwise. He stabbed Geltrude and suffocated Agnese.

All the people of Piega were exterminated. They spared only Domino Maliocco, left alive so that he would pass on to posterity the horrendous end of his flock.

Piega burned for a long time before being definitively razed to the ground.

It was 29 May, 1298.

Millesimo CCXCVIII die XXIX mensis Madii Comes Galassus de Seclano cum Caesenatibus, et suis Amicis de Monte Feltro, obsedit Castrum Plegae, et vi accepit illud. Bartholinum et Aulivarium filium eius turpissima morte, scilicet affixos in palo, fecit perire; et Tinacium, qui erat de ipsa Domo, et multos alios, gladio fecit interimi, qui ipsius Galassii Comitis erant capitals inimici.

On the return to Pietrarubbia, Filippuccio, Fraudolente and Alvisio rode behind the Count.

The Bastard, whose hands dripped with innocent blood as much, and perhaps more than those of the scarfaced man and his companion, took advantage of the opportunity to plead his candidacy for vassal of San Lorenzo.

«That Tignaccio was a traitor, and Bonzio pledged for him.»

Corrado ignored him.

At Piega, Corrado had lost about ten knights and, given the small size of his army, it was no small matter. The lands of the Pietrarubbia family were not fertile and, apart from the farms at the bottom of the valley, they consisted of woods, arid gullies and high hill pastures.

The real wealth of the ancient lineage was the strength of the sword at the service of the powerful. Bonzio had pledged for Tignaccio, calling him a faithful subject of the Pietrarubbians, but Corrado was anything but naïve. Filippuccio, with the excuse of favoring Fraudolente's candidacy for castellan, in reality was plotting to take Bonzio's place and to deserve a more independent and prestigious assignment, especially for a bastard.

Bonzio would never have aspired rebelling to undermine the Master. Even though, for generations, his family had served the Counts faithfully and with honor, he was only a humble castellan, and without even a drop of the blood of the Counts in his veins. Filippuccio, on the other hand, even if only half, was a Pietrarubbian, and wasn't history full of illegitimate children who had killed their half brothers?

However, Bonzio had pledged for Tignaccio.

Who had caused the fight in Piega's court? Could it have been Tignaccio? Why would he have renounced the title of vassal of the Pietrarubbians?

If things had gone differently, if Cavalca hadn't died, Corrado would have tried to pardon Tignaccio. But, in the face of Galasso's wrath in front of his son's corpse, he had been unable to do anything.

Corrado only knew that Fraudolente claimed to have been suddenly attacked by Tignaccio. The scarred man was a sneaky, cunning and very ambitious man. But was he also loyal? And if he had provoked Tignaccio to eliminate a rival? Or if, instead, it was Fraudolente who had started the battle?

Filippuccio insisted, «San Lorenzo needs a vassal of indisputable trust, someone who...»

Corrado lost his patience and cut it short, «It is I who must evaluate who is worthy of my trust, and what will become of Bonzio is my business!»

The bastard admitted defeat and fell silent.

Fraudolente, who followed the men closely, heard the entire conversation.

Gasparino was distant, but he saw the knowing look, full of disappointment, between the bastard and the scarfaced man.

«What are those two up to?»

As soon as he got home, he would report to Bonzio.

When Corrado and his men arrived in front of the church of Combarbio, Gasparino made the sign of the cross and thanked the Lord who had brought him home safe and sound. For the most violent, faith was a weakness, and some of the knights grinned. Most of the soldiers, however, followed Gasparino's example.

Despite the afternoon drizzle, Bonzio went down to the courtyard to welcome the guests. He didn't see Tignaccio and imagined that, waiting for a sunny day to start the journey, he had stayed in Piega with Maria and the baby.

Corrado dismounted and, without much preamble, serious and drawn in the face, ordered, «Let's go in!»

He took a seat on the bench in the living room. Bonzio stood respectfully, and the Bastard leaned against the fireplace.

«Piega is destroyed. Tignaccio betrayed us and was executed,» Corrado said.

The Count's black eyes, in an attempt to read his soul and feelings, scrutinized those of the vassal.

Bonzio felt the blow. Still, he found the strength to ask, «My daughter and grandson?»

The Count shook his head.

Like an ancient oak under an axe, Bonzio collapsed to his knees. Pain and anger prevailed for a few moments, but he dominated his anger to protect Rosa. In his heart, he cursed Tignaccio. And to think he'd seemed like a good boy... he regained his senses and kept calm.

«My Lord, I am your servant, and my life is in your hands.»

Corrado hesitated. Bonzio was a good soldier and a faithful vassal. Who would have benefited from his death?

«Tignaccio didn't keep his promises and paid for the mistake with his life. But he also betrayed you and your family.»

Bonzio cursed under his breath, «Damn him!»

Corrado, satisfied, decided, «When you marry off your last daughter, we will choose a better husband for her.»

Bonzio had been pardoned.

Filippuccio remained silent in the shadows.

As soon as the count and the bastard had gone, Rosa came

out of the kitchen. She threw her arms around her father and wept. She would never see her sister again! She was all alone.

Gasparino knew that, in a short time, he would be called to report.

He had taken advantage of the journey to try and rearrange his ideas, preparing to answer the most embarrassing questions. What would he tell Bonzio? And how to describe the end of Piega to the relatives of Pietrarubbia?

The mighty call of Bonzio echoed in the Court, «Gasparino, come here immediately!»

The poor fellow ran to Bonzio in the keep.

«What was my son-in-law been up to in Piega?»

In a high-pitched voice, broken at times by emotion, Gasparino also recounted even the most raw and violent episodes. Seated in front of the fireplace with his daughter beside him, Bonzio listened without interrupting him.

Having finished the report, Gasparino was silent, embarrassed.

Rosa ran the sleeves of her shirt over her eyes to wipe away the tears.

«So you weren't present at the start of the fight, and you didn't see who started it?» Bonzio inquired.

«My Lord, it is said that it was Tignaccio who attacked our soldiers first. It seems that he attacked Fraudolente by brandishing his sword, but was unable to strike him. But the scarfaced man's word, as you teach me, has very little value.»

Bonzio burst out and unburdened his long-repressed anger, «That worm wants my place in San Lorenzo and, to get it, he killed my heir and my descendants!»

Frightened by the grim expression on Bonzio's face, Gasparino began to shake like a leaf.

The Master, instead of punishing him, dismissed him with praise, «You are a good soldier, a faithful servant and I am very lucky to have you with me.»

Gratified by the unexpected praise, Gasparino politely

backed away and, after making repeated bows, reached the door and went out.

PIETRARUBBIA

Corrado's men, after the siege of Piega, returned to their homes.

With only the escort of his half-brother, Fraudolente and Alvisio, the Count returned to Pietrarubbia. He preferred that the rest of the soldiers remain stationed for a few days in Sant'Arduino, on the other side of the valley, and made an agreement with the castellan Uberto to provide food and assistance.

«It's best the servants don't know yet what has happened to their kin in Piega. You never know how they might react, and we have no interest in fueling discontent,» he recommended to Filippuccio.

Before leaving for the valley *della Maricula,* Corrado had left four soldiers to guard the castle, more than enough to guarantee order and safety in his absence.

At just over a couple of months, Gaia was pregnant again. Her pregnancy had made her even more florid and beautiful in the hungry eyes of the soldiers and Filippuccio, in order not to incur the wrath of the Count, had not yet passed from words to deeds about her.

Constanza asked Corrado to keep Filippo in check, and Domino Baldassarre, with discretion and a lot of tact, invited Zanino not to expose his wife in public.

«Make Gaia leave the house with only you and your brother!»

Even without any reference to the Bastard, Zanino understood perfectly.

«It doesn't matter if he is the Count's brother. If he tries to touch her, his neck will meet the blade of my scythe!»

«And then your neck, instead, will end up on the block and under Tosco's axe.»

Zanino, jealous but not stupid, treasured the advice of the Domino.

A few days after returning to San Lorenzo, Gasparino asked Bonzio for permission to go to Pietrarubbia. In the hope of returning during the day, he left at the first light of dawn on Sunday 8 June 1298. The journey was neither long nor dangerous. He decided to travel off the beaten track that he knew like the back of his hand. He wanted to be alone, and to avoid houses and villages of people curious to know other people's affairs. Riding his nag on paths bordered by yellow-green broom hedges, he crossed the cultivated fields that waved in the warm climate. Thus he had time to reflect on what he would tell Pietrarubbia. How to tell Mafalda that her family had been exterminated? Better to keep silent about the crudest episodes, even if everyone knew how atrocious the war was.

The Domino ensured that Sunday was a day dedicated only to the Lord. Manual labor and unworthy acts were prohibited.

«Woe to anyone who touches the almighty coin or indulges the vices of the flesh!»

Convinced in his heart that rest and prayer were the best cure for the soul and body of the poor, the parish priest had absolved the peasants to be forced in bad weather to reap on the Lord's day, but with a long fasting as penance.

On a splendid sunny Sunday, a strong southwest wind heralded the probable arrival of rain for the beginning of the following week. It was too early to harvest, and if it rained, the farmers would enjoy a few days of quiet.

After so much fatigue, idleness and rest!

Gasparino arrived in Pietrarubbia late in the morning, as the villagers left the church. The women and men wore their best clothes, less worn out and consumed than those they usually wore during the rest of the week.

The children wore the rough tunic that had been passed down for generations from older to younger siblings, and from parents to children.

Gasparino immediately recognized the merry caterwauling of his loved ones. Yes, he was home!

Zanino warned Gaia, «My brother is back! We have to celebrate...» and she ran to hold his bridle.

He touched the ground and was surrounded. In the uproar, the grandchildren clung to the robe to attract attention.

Gasparino returned kisses and effusions, but Bastiano noticed that he did it with little enthusiasm. He looked strange, sad and restless.

«I wonder what happened?» he thought.

He wanted to know right away, but he didn't spoil the celebrations. He was even more worried when, in a moment of calm in the midst of the chaos, Gasparino asked, «Do you know where the Domino is?»

«Maybe he's still at the church.»

With a bit effort, Gasparino managed to free himself.

«I have to speak to the parish priest,» he excused himself. «Wait for me at home. I'll tell you about everything later.»

The little church was damp and dark, despite the fact that, from above, a weak ray of sunshine filtered through a small window and the semi-darkness, near the altar, was enlivened by the flickering flames of some candles. Gasparino, who came from the blinding light of the sun in the churchyard, had to wait a few moments for his eyes to adjust. The sudden change in temperature sent a shiver down his spine.

The building, severe, bare and with a single nave, had a semicircular apse and a small stone altar.

Gasparino heard a low muttering coming from the darkest corner. Standing, dressed in dark, Baldassarre was absorbed in prayer. To get noticed, Gasparino coughed slightly. The parish priest raised his head, recognized him, but continued to whisper in Latin. After a few minutes, he came over and, as he used to do with his parishioners, blessed him with a sign of the cross on his forehead.

Gasparino's eyes filled with tears. He fell to his knees.

«My son, what has happened to you?»

Baldassarre feared a confession, one of the terrible ones that only soldiers could make.

In a high-pitched, plaintive voice, broken by emotion and, at times, by tears, Gasparino described the end of Piega and its people to the Domino. He found the comfort he badly needed.

«It's not your fault, my son, and you don't have to torment yourself like this for the sins of others. One man alone cannot prevent a war!»

The presbyter hid his dismay. How to help his flock to forgive in a Christian way? Would he succeed?

«For the good of your kinsmen and of us all, do not feed hatred, and know how to silence the horrors that might do so. I'm not advising you to lie, but not to tell everything.»

They left the church and it seemed that the torment and anguish had remained inside, in the dark and faraway from the sun.

Moretto, a distant cousin of Bastiano, as all of the Gasparinis, was an ugly little man, black, with protruding ears, a low forehead and a shrill, nasal voice. As the stockiest brother of the brood, he had been chosen as a child to become a soldier.

On watch for several hours at the gate of the castle, Moretto saw Gasparino arrive, witnessed the welcoming celebrations and, since they would soon be taking over from him, got ready to take part in the Sunday meal to celebrate his cousin's return.

Mafalda and Gaia put to boil in an abundant vegetable soup, a stew of fatty pork which, though over-aged, would have made the diners happy.

Bastiano sacrificed the cask of wine, sour but very alcoholic, which he kept in reserve for important occasions.

In front of the little house, a crowd of hungry and joyful cousins gathered. The threshing floor was packed, and everyone was waiting impatiently for Gasparino.

Moretto sat down on a stump next to the cistern in the shade of the fig tree. He couldn't wait to hear the war stories.

«There he is!» shouted Zanino's oldest son, jumping up and down like crazy.

His mother caused laughter from the other children by giving him a slap. The boy grimaced, but without complaining. Gaia settled down on the wooden bench in front of the house and, to console him, she took him on her lap and stroked his curly black head. Gasparino pushed his way through the relatives in the farmyard. Everyone was hanging on his every word.

Moretto broke the ice, «We won, didn't we?»

The survivor began the story. Faithful to the suggestions of the Domino, he left out the horrors, violence and rapes, but he could not keep silent about the destruction of the village and the castle. He concluded with the truth.

«No one survived!»

Incredulous and shocked, the women remained silent for a few moments. Then Mafalda screamed and, after her, all the others.

The men cursed and blasphemed God and the saints. The children yelled and ran to cling to their mothers.

It seemed that a revolution was about to break out.

«Calm down, calm down.»

Gasparino tried in vain to appease their spirits.

Filippuccio hated idleness. After the violence and the raid at Piega, a long period of inactivity awaited him, without even the amusement of a graceful girl to delude his boredom.

«Leave the women of the village alone!» Corrado had ordered.

Rightly convinced that he was a handsome man, Filippo could not tolerate Gaia continuing to ignore him undeterred. Was it possible that that ugly toad of a husband was enough for her?

Collected in the village cistern, the rainwater was used to quench the animals' thirst, but even the people were forced to drink it, despite the stench and intestinal problems, when the spring of *the good water* dried up due to the summer drought.

Even in bad weather, Gaia used to go down to Guiduccio's spring every morning to fill a pitcher for the children. The journey was short, but out of fear of a dangerous encounter, she had her nephew and Mafalda accompany her along the impervious path in the thick bush. Filippuccio, convinced that he had more chance in the absence of her husband, sometimes lurked in vain near the spring.

Gasparino was forced to answer. Everyone was asking and everyone wanted to know what had happened to their loved ones. As much as he tried to sweeten the story, the sad and raw truth about the horrendous end of the people of Piega ended up being clear and obvious: a true massacre.

Perhaps because her parents weren't from Piega, Gaia kept her cool in the general bustle. It was very hot and her children were thirsty. She left them unattended just long enough to run into the kitchen. The spring water had run out in the usual jug. In another moment she would have taken advantage of Mafalda's escort, but it seemed, at the very least, indelicate to ask her sister-in-law's favor in such a predicament. In fact, the poor thing had other worries on her mind.

She stepped out into the commotion in front of the house, undecided what to do. Who to ask for help? If she had turned to her husband he would have sent her up the famous creek. He glimpsed Carola intent on checking Gostolo through the half-open window. The old man had been among the first to go down to the farmyard, looking for trouble as he usually did.

«Carola, would you mind the children while I go to the spring?»

«I'll send my nephews down to pick them up!»

Before leaving, Gaia glanced at Zanino. Among the men, caught up in the discussion with Gasparino, he didn't notice her.

Careful not to trip over the cobbles and stones of the path, with the large earthenware jug by the handle, she hurried down the slope.

She did not reach the spring.

He appeared from behind a tuft of broom bush. She recognized Filippo's chestnut hair and cursed the moment she had decided to venture out on her own.

Incredulous at the unexpected stroke of luck, the Bastard unleashed the charm of his best smile, «Finally we meet!»

He advanced upon her, and forced her to stop. Gaia could no longer ignore him.

«Lord, please, I'm going to the spring to fill the jug for my children.»

«What if I fill your jug instead?»

Filippo positioned himself in the center of the path to block the passage. He kept smiling, but she realized that he was checking that no one had followed her.

Gaia was wearing a pair of wooden clogs, which would have been a hindrance in her escape. She decided to look nice.

«My Lord, my husband, who is very jealous will be arriving very soon...» her voice was now persuasive and her gaze mischievous.

Filippuccio, amazed, deluded himself for a few moments. The young woman was wearing a tight Sunday dress, which highlighted her full breasts. The Bastard couldn't take his eyes off her. Was it the right time?

Distracted by the vision of all that abundance of her, Filippo didn't see her take off her clogs.

Gaia opened her arms, as if it were an invitation. When he got close, she hit him on the head with all her strength. The jug shattered.

Filippo cursed, bringing his hands to his forehead, and Gaia took the opportunity to turn around and run uphill. She got ahead by a few meters, but the Bastard, over the shock, gave chase. He joined her at the entrance to the lane in front of the town. In the heat of passion, wild with rage and oblivious to the world around her, he pounced. They tumbled to the ground. Gaia, as the Bastard's hands touched her everywhere, screamed.

Despite the confusion in the yard, Gasparino saw them. Zanino realized that his brother was distracted, and turned his head in the same direction. He let out a high-pitched scream, and everyone fell silent. Filippo heard it too, and froze.

Mafalda, with all the breath she had in her body, shouted, «It's him, it's the murderous bastard!»

Gaia took advantage of that moment of uncertainty, and she wriggled free and escaped. Filippo tried to get up, but the villagers surrounded him while he was still on his knees. He reached for his dagger, but didn't have time to draw it from its scabbard. They started kicking and punching him, and then went on to beat him. He tried to shield his head with his arms, but it was useless. A well-aimed blow to the back of his neck made him lose consciousness.

«Stop!» shouted Zanino, and everyone obeyed. He ran into the house and came right back out brandishing the sickle.

Filippo lay motionless upside down in the grass. Zanino bent down, grabbed him by the hair, and lifted his head. Quick and precise, he slashed it with the sharp blade.

«I promised you!» he murmured satisfied.

THE REVOLT OF THE GASPARINI

Moretto had not taken part in the lynching and remained seated under the fig tree, uncertain what to do. His duty as a soldier would have required him to intervene in Filippuccio's defense, even if, had he tried to oppose the enraged people, in all probability would have shared the same fate. But it wasn't out of cowardice that he didn't even try to save him from the wrath of the people. It was simply because his instinct would have been to get up and run, together with his family, to execute the infamous murderer.

Gasparino was the first to realize the situation. In Filippuccio's veins, even if only in part, flowed Pietrarubbia blood, and Corrado's revenge would have been inexorable and cruel. Moretto, in the shade of the fig tree, looked blank and lost.

Gasparino decided, «Moretto, warn the other soldiers, without letting the scarred man and his friend hear you.»

Moretto didn't seem to understand, and didn't answer.

«Hurry up, damn it! We must hurry and take them by surprise!» he persisted in trying to shake him out of his torpor.

«What if they don't want to?» Moretto tried to retort.

«Either with us or against us! Tell them what happened in Piega, and they'll take our side. Are we, or are we not all of the same family?»

Moretto, even if a little hesitant, finally understood and went towards the gate of the castle.

Bastian took the bastard's body by the legs and dragged him behind the bushes.

«And now?» he asked Gasparino.

«Now everyone run into the house, arm yourselves, and get ready to fight.»

The men and women of Pietrarubbia recognized their

leader in Gasparino and, aware that the only hope of survival would have been to take the castle, they obeyed him without any question. Before long, they were back on the street brandishing scythes, pitchforks, axes, and sticks.

Carola accompanied her son and husband downstairs.

«Gostolo, I will pray for you!»

When she saw her grandchildren, Gabriolo and Maffiolo, armed with scythes and pitchforks, she was in despair.

«No, for God's sake, leave them here! They're too young to fight.»

The boys pretended not to hear. Gaia reached Carola and led her back home.

«Come, my children and I will stay and keep you company, and we will pray to the Lord to help our loved ones.»

Gostolo tried to console her, «Don't worry, we'll make it and, in a little while, we'll be back safe and sound!»

The Domino intended to go as soon as possible to the Gasparinis.

As he left the rectory, he saw his flock go by in arms. Only a few women and younger children were missing.

«My children, what do you intend to do?»

He held back the powerful voice for fear that the soldiers on guard might hear it and become suspicious.

The people stopped. Gasparino went within an inch of his face.

«Insolent!» said an astonished Baldassarre.

«Domino, it's too late. We've already killed Filippo... and there's no going back.»

The presbyter read in the servant's eyes the awareness of ineluctable destiny. «*Alea iacta est,*» he murmured before joining his warlike parishioners.

Fraudolente and Alvisio were taken by surprise as they sat, chatting about this and that, on the bottom steps of the access stairway to the keep. And just imagine that fellow soldiers would have attacked them treacherously? Almost without realizing it, they found knives at their throats.

They surrendered without reacting.

Moretto and the other three soldiers did not have the strength to kill them in cold blood and, when the others arrived, the Domino opposed, «You are not assassins!»

Gagged and bound tightly, with their necks tied in a noose hanging from a beam in the stable, they were left at the mercy of a small boy armed with a pitchfork.

«At the slightest movement or attempt to untie themselves, kill them!» ordered Gasparino.

To make the young man understand how to do it, he snatched the fork from his hand and pricked Alvisio's belly with a certain vigor. The sharp points pierced the chain mail and slightly wounded the victim, who, in the throes of terror, yelped for mercy.

«Don't let his lamentations make you feel sorry for him. If he had been in your place, this worm would have killed you! You two, thank the Domino. Without him, you would be dead already!»

Alvisio peed in his breeches for fear.

They entered the keep. About thirty villagers, many barefoot, but some with noisy wooden clogs, although they tried to make little noise, were heard in every corner of the large building. The men were on the first floor, while the servants and Tosco were in the kitchen. An apprentice, looking out on the threshold that gave access to the room, let out a frightened cry. Tosco stepped forward.

«Well, what's going on?»

In the midst of so many thin people his enormous belly stood out like a fat sow in a brood of piglets. The Tuscan was not a warrior and the only reason the villagers were afraid of him was his undisputed authority as factor and the Count's executioner. Gostolo, who was brandishing an axe, made his way up to within an inch of his nose.

He grinned satisfied, «What do you want, old man? You scared, huh?»

A slight tremor in the voice betrayed the emotion of Tosco, who brought a hand to cover the crooked side of the deformed mouth.

«Afraid of whom, and of what? Are you crazy? You all know what the consequences will be...» in terror, he tried to stop them with a threat.

Gostolo's back was marked by the scars of the floggings and, even if the wounds on his body had healed, those on his soul were still open and bleeding. His eyes glared at the executioner.

Tosco gave in to panic, turned around, and tried to escape into the kitchen, but his way was blocked by the servants. The ax struck him on the back of the neck. He fell with a cry into the arms of those he had once oppressed.

Corrado leaned over the railing of the staircase. He had heard the uproar and, more curious than alarmed, he was about to go downstairs to check. From above he witnessed the death of Tosco and the escape of the servants from the kitchen. He didn't breathe a word.

The Count's rooms on the first floor were protected by a sturdy oak door, which gave access to the grand staircase. It was necessary to barricade ourselves and hold out as long as possible. His soldiers were on the other side of the valley, at Sant'Arduino and, in the absence of orders and communications, sooner or later the castellan would have sent someone to Pietrarubbia.

«What's this ruckus?» asked Giovanna. She slipped between the door and her brother.

«What are you doing, you wretch, get back inside immediately!» Corrado scolded her, and his voice echoed in the room below.

Zanino recognized the Count's imperious tone and, raising his eyes, saw him.

«They're up there!» he exclaimed pointing at them. Quick

as a cat, he ran up the stairs, followed by Bastiano, Martino, Agnolo and Gostolo. With a shove, Corrado made Giovanna tumble into the room and hastily returned. Martino, the seventeen-year-old son of Bernardo, slipped the handle of the scythe into the narrow gap between the door and the wall. Corrado put his feet down to resist, but gave in to the vigorous push of the villagers. He fell backward, with his stach facing up, helpless in front of the rebels. Without any mercy, they finished him off with pitchforks and axes.

Giovanna got up to run away.

«Help help!»

But who could ever help her? She took a few steps, the last before giving up.

«Have mercy!» she begged moaning.

Gostolo had no intention of being merciful and, at that moment, he didn't know what forgiveness was.

«Damned crippled humpback!»

Giovannina saw the ax rise, closed her eyes and waited for the fatal blow.

From the back room came out, screaming like madmen, two very young maids.

«Stop!»

The authoritative voice of the Domino, who in the meantime had reached them, stopped the men just in time.

«Fools, do you want to get killed?»

At the sight of the blood, the two girls cried out in horror.

«Get out of here!»

The Domino pushed them towards the exit. Terrified, they ran down the staircase.

In the bedroom, standing and leaning against the wall near the small window, Costanza was holding Roberto tenderly in her arms. The boy had the proud attitude of his father and seemed to feel no fear. He looked Zanino in the eyes, the first to enter, as if to challenge him.

The pastor pushed his way through the men.

«Nobody dare touch the Countess and her son!»

Costanza thanked him with a nod. The noblewoman wore a flowing blue linen dress, over which a long braid of brown hair fell to the side. Very beautiful, she had the languid and frightened gaze of a fawn in front of the hunter.

A miracle happened: Gostolo dropped the bloodied ax to the ground and bowed.

«My lady, as long as I live, no one will harm you!»

Everyone followed her example.

Maffiolo was only eleven years old, too big to be considered a child, but too little to take on the duties of an adult. Proud of the task received, he remained with the pitchfork in front of the scarred man and Alvisio for a few moments. Hanging by the neck like two halves of salted pork, the two seemed resigned to their fate. Intrigued by the cries coming from the keep, the boy looked out onto the courtyard and turned his back to the prisoners.

Fraudolente had strongly resisted when they had tied his wrists behind his back and the boy on guard had not noticed that he had managed to untie the knots.

When Maffiolo turned around, the scarred man, fumbling rapidly upwards, slipped his head out of the noose that tied him to the beam. He bent down and freed his ankles. Throwing away the gag with a gesture of annoyance, he pounced on the child, grabbing him from behind, covering his mouth so he wouldn't scream and violently threw him into the shadow of the stable. With one sharp movement, he broke his neck.

Alvisio was agitated, emitting an orchestra of incomprehensible moans. When he was finally free and he could move and stretch his numb limbs, the first thing he did was kick the child's corpse.

«Little village bastard!»

He added a few curses while, with a filthy hand on his stomach, he checked the extent of the wound. It was little more than a minor hole, and if it didn't get infected, it would recover. The chain mail had saved him. He sighed in relief before turning his big pale eyes to ask Fraudolente for guidance.

«And now what do we do?»

All they had was Maffiolo's pitchfork.

«Let's run away and go ask Sant'Arduino for help,» replied the scarface.

They approached the stable door and, having verified that the courtyard was deserted, they attempted to escape.

Moretto and his three fellow soldiers, perhaps because it was easy, in that situation, to pass for traitors, had not got their hands dirty with the blood from the Pietrarubbians. Once the riot was over, they left it to others to decide the fate of the survivors. The Pietrarubbians and the Montefeltros, known for their ferocity if they were to capture those responsible for the massacre, would have torn them to pieces with horrendous tortures, and publicly executed as a warning to the people and the soldiers.

After reflecting, Moretto decided, «No one should be saved. We must make sure that the Pietrarubbia lineage dies out here today!»

In that moment, he saw them flee from the castle gate.

Fraudolente ran faster, while Alvisio trudged with one hand on his stomach.

«Stop them!» ordered Moretto.

The crossbowman cocked and, taking very calm aim, fired. With incredible accuracy, he struck Fraudolente in the back of the neck. His dart, piercing his neck, came out of his throat, and the scarfaced man collapsed to the ground like an empty sack.

Alvisio stopped.

«Fraudolente! Fraudolente!»

He turned. With his right hand on his belly, he raised his left in surrender.

Moretto stepped forward and drew his sword.

«Have mercy!» pleaded Alvisio falling to his knees.

He was odd. With his big round face and wide eyes, he looked like a big child begging for forgiveness after a prank.

It wasn't easy to kill a fellow soldier in cold blood.

«Get up!»

Moretto's tone did not permit replies, and Alvisio was forced to return to the Court.

The countess tried to hide from her son the horrendous spectacle of the mangled corpses of Corrado and Giovanna.

As they crossed the room, the boy pushed his mother's hand away to prevent her from covering his eyes.

«Mother, I'm big and I'm not afraid!»

The pastor, who was following them, was amazed at the child's incredible fortitude.

Worthy son of his father, he thought silently.

Roberto's life hung by such a thin thread that Baldassarre thought it convenient not to share his considerations with the protestors. A desperate and crying child would have been much more difficult to kill than a proud young Lord of Pietrarubbia. He hoped that the blood shed was enough to quench the people's thirst for vengeance and justice.

They went down with Gasparino to the hall, and they all went out, men, women, servants and peasants, into the courtyard.

Gabriolo couldn't wait to tell his brother about the death of Tosco and the counts. Having crossed the courtyard, he entered the stable and called to him, «Maffiolo!»

It seemed to him that there was no one there anymore. The two bound and gagged soldiers had disappeared and, with them, his brother as well. He looked around, uncertain whether to raise the alarm. Then, in a corner, on the ground in the straw, he recognized Maffiolo. But what was he doing? Was he sleeping? He approached cautiously and barely touched him with his toe.

«Wake up, lazy bum!»

He didn't move. Gabriolo bent down and tried to shake

him. No sign of life. He grabbed him by the shoulders and swung more vigorously. His head of black hair moved up and down like that of the chickens hanging by their legs from the fireplace hood.

Gostolo and Gasparino ran first to his cries.

«Grandfather, grandfather, they killed him!» he exclaimed going towards them.

Gostolo knelt next to the body of his nephew and tried to revive him. Faced with the evidence, all he could do was repress the pain by trying to console his last nephew. He hugged him, caressed him and whispered useless words of comfort. He did not think, even for a moment, of revenge.

Gasparino, on the other hand, became furious, «Those two bastards, take it out on a child!»

He ran out into the courtyard, just in time to catch a glimpse of Alvisio who was sadly returning, under the watchful escort of Moretto and the soldiers, from the castle gate. He didn't explain anything to anyone. He pushed his way through the crowd brandishing his sword. Alvisio understood, and screamed before Gasparino hit him. This time the chain mail was useless. With his gut ripped open, he fell to the ground. He recognized, among the many who crowded around to witness the agony, the face of the presbyter.

«Forgiveness!» he gasped, in fear of hell, before he died.

Moretto talked at length with Gasparino. The two argued animatedly, gesticulating nervously and, in the end, Gasparino gave up.

The Domino retired to the church to pray. How to protect the rebel people from the wrath and revenge of the powerful?

Terror replaced the euphoria of victory.

Guarded by two soldiers, Constanza and her son were locked up in the great hall of the keep.

They waited for him to be in the church, but the Domino,

as soon as he noticed Moretto leave, abandoned the faithful to rush into the keep. Gasparino chased him to stop him.

«Domino, for our sakes, we can't leave any of them alive.»

Baldassarre resorted to authority, charisma and threats, «Haven't you shed enough blood already? If you kill again, how will you save yourself from the fires of hell?»

Hell was a major deterrent to simple and superstitious people. But Gasparino did not give up.

«Domino, this is the last of the Pietrarubbians.»

The poor man would have been happy to pardon the countess and her son, but the people had decided. Moretto had been very convincing and had even undertaken to complete the thankless task.

The presbyter, despite Gasparino's remonstrances, entered the hall.

The countess was seated in her chair, and her son stood beside her. The pastor noticed Costanza's desperate and pleading look. Even in that state, when all seemed lost, she was beautiful, even to a chaste and pious priest.

«My Lady, please follow me.»

Convinced in her heart that Constanza had the right, even on her deathbed, to the dignity appropriate to her rank, Moretto tried to be polite.

The only hope was Baldassarre.

Gasparino, bringing his hand to the hilt, made it clear that the attempt to save them was useless, and the Domino read the resolve in the soldier's eyes.

Roberto, very elegant, as the heir of a noble Lord should be on a feast day, wore light-colored breeches under a blue tunic and cinched at the waist with a leather belt. He was unusually calm, to the point that the pastor thought he hadn't guessed his intentions. «Mother, don't worry about me.»

After kissing her hand softly, he took leave.

Constanza steeled herself and held back the tears.

Moretto bowed and raised his arm to tell her to follow her son.

The parish priest thundered, «She's not a Pietrarubbian!»

Moretto, intimidated, looked at Gasparino to seek his support. He got it, «Domino, what if she's pregnant?»

How to find a loophole to stop them? Constanza was in the throes of anguish, while her son, only eleven years old, continued to appear more than worthy of his very noble birth.

Baldassarre approached the Countess.

«What if she isn't? Know how to wait a few months, so we will know if she is expecting a child.»

Gasparino resolved the question, «We will take her to San Lorenzo, a guest of Bonzio until we know if she has Corrado's seed in her womb!»

The name of Bonzio was a guarantee throughout Montefeltro.

The presbyter wanted to try to save Roberto too, but Gasparino admonished him, «Domino, you have to know how to be satisfied, and it is useless to try to oppose destiny, however merciless and unfair it may seem.»

Baldassarre understood the threat. No, it was impossible to save the child, too.

Before Roberto left, he blessed him with the sign of the cross on his forehead.

The boy smiled one last time at his mother in farewell.

The tension and the pain got the upper hand, and Costanza passed out, collapsing on her bench.

Even Moretto was surprised by the boy's courage. He walked in front of him, proud and determined, on the path along the stream.

Upon his return, the executioner washed the innocent blood that had smeared his hands and forever stained his conscience in the pure water of the spring.

Thanks to the knowledge of Domino Baldassarre, the assassins of the Pietrarubbia Ghibellines found asylum in the castles ruled by the Guelphs. Of the ancient family, only Count Taddeo and his two sons survived.

THE SECRET

Gasparino presented himself to the Master the day after the massacre. They saw him enter, on his customary slightly crooked horse, alongside a woman wrapped up on the back of a mule.

A tall man in a dark suit followed them on foot. When she arrived in Bonzio's presence, just before dinner time, the woman threw back her hood and uncovered her head.

Leaping to his feet, the giant profusely took a deep bow, «Lady, be welcome in my most humble abode!»

Her eyes reddened and her appearance humble, Constance was numb with grief.

«Thank you for your help,» she whispered softly.

Rosa came out of the kitchen. There were unexpected guests and, given Bonzio's bow, of notable respect. The woman was a beautiful young lady, while the priest, though elderly, had the striking appearance of a strong warrior.

«We're here to ask for asylum and refuge for Donna Costanza.»

The voice didn't have the mellifluous and false tone of the priests and, more than a plea, the words were an order.

Off to one side, Gasparino stared embarrassed at his toes.

Although Rosa, at the last moment, had tried to find a meal worthy of a Countess's table, supper did not seem welcome. Costanza ate listlessly, nibbling only a chicken leg and some vegetables.

Baldassarre, on the other hand, did honor to the kitchen, and ate with the voracity of someone who had been fasting for some time.

There were no unpleasant and inopportune conversations. In Constanza's presence, any direct question would have been irreverent. Rosa had a hot bath and bed prepared in the best room of the castle. She assigned a young servant to the exclusive service of the noblewoman.

When the Countess took leave to retire, Rosa accompanied her upstairs, and the men were left alone.

«So?» Bonzio was very curious.

Before answering, as an exception to his fleeting principles of sobriety, the Domino allowed himself a long sip of blood wine.

«The people of Pietrarubbia have rebelled and Costanza is the only survivor!»

Without neglecting or hiding details, he recounted the revolt and the end of the Pietrarubbians.

Gasparino, nodding to every detail, confirmed the story. The little man, exhausted and in need of sleep, exacerbated his tiredness by taking care of the jug of wine with diligence and gusto, until he reached the point that his head began to fall forward in repeated and painful attempts to sleep.

Bonzio dismissed him, «It's time for you to go and rest.»

Left alone, the domino confessed the secret in a low voice: «Donna Costanza is expecting a child!»

Bonzio opened his astonished eyes and the parish priest continued quoting Ezekiel, «*Patres comederunt uvam acerbam, et dentes filiorum obstupescunt?* Each will be judged according to his own actions.»

In the large, cool and quiet hall of the castle, in the quivering and comforting twilight of the candles, the two men talked for a long time, with the intention of being able to find a solution. The Domino wanted to save the mother and the unborn child at all costs, and Bonzio was tired of war, death and massacres. By mutual agreement, they agreed to keep the pregnancy a secret.

Before retiring for the night, Baldassarre said goodbye, concluding, «*Crudelis est, non fortis, qui infantem necat!* With the help of the Lord, Donna Costanza will bring her child into the world, and then we will see how to protect him from the wrath of men.»

In spite of his young age and small physique, Domino Ubertino gave the impression of being a worthy, capable and wise priest. At first, the parishioners had the notion of having an inexperienced young man. Over time, they realized how available he was towards them and how much he loved his neighbor and God. Solidarity, compassion and encouragement to confront, with the support of faith, the adversities of a miserable and very hard life, in a few months they had conquered the heart of every sheep of the small flock.

The following morning, Bonzio and Baldassarre presented themselves at the door of the parish church. The pastor received them in the communal room, where the kitchen was, and made them sit around the table next to the fireplace. The stone slab floor on the bare earth was uneven, the plaster peeling and the room was damp and dark. Despite this, Ubertino seemed anything but sad and severe.

«Dionigi!» he called to him in a ringing voice.

After a few moments, the boy appeared at the door. At ten, he was in that stage of life in which the malice of adolescence is ignored, while the purity and innocence of childhood are waning.

He recognized the gentle giant and ran towards him, «Bonzio!»

He started to jump on his knees, as he did when he was a child, but, embarrassed at not being able to express his happiness at the unexpected visit, he stood beside him. Bonzio ran a big hand over his black curls and grabbed him to suffocate him in a hug. The boy reciprocated by embracing his neck and sinking his head into the mighty chest of the warrior.

Baldassarre was amazed! The vassal had a heart. It seemed to him that Bonzio, having freed Dionigi from his grip, was a little uncomfortable, and that he was trying to salvage a more serious demeanor.

Ubertino spoke gently, like a father addressing his favorite son.

«We are hungry and thirsty.»

Dionigi ran to the back to reappear shortly after with a pitcher of spring water and a bowl filled with slices of crusty white bread. The grown-ups had important matters to discuss and, without waiting for dismissal, the boy left them to their own discussions.

Lucia was little more than a child when she was taken away from her home in Villa of Combarbio and entrusted to Maddalena as a servant in the castle. At first she missed her loved ones, but soon, comforted by the affection of the vassal's family, she began to appreciate her new condition. She ate her fill, slept on a soft bed and the chores entrusted to her were never too much. After the death of her mistress and the daughters, she was like a sister to Maria and Rosa. Lucia, daughter of a feudal serf, became a woman. She was lively and intelligent, she only had one flaw, not serious but dangerous: she was too curious.

Who was the mysterious woman? Everyone addressed her with great deference, calling her Lady, and so she was a noblewoman. The stranger was kind, and she had a habit of thanking whoever served her.

Who, before her, had ever thanked a servant?

Rosa took Lucia in private to tell her herself, «What you will see and hear in the coming months, you will have to keep to yourself. Woe to you if I find out you've been talking about it!»

Costanza spent interminable and sad days of idleness in her room. The environment was dry and clean, but in a perpetual and dismal semi-darkness. They had allowed her the luxury of changing and washing frequently. While Rosa, like most women, especially if married, usually covered her head with a cap tied under her chin, Costanza wore her hair loose on her shoulders or, at most, gathered in a braid. Lucia spent entire afternoons curling and perfuming the noblewoman's hair, but without chatting to satisfy her curiosity.

Domino Ubertino, under the vigilant control of Rosa, went to see Costanza at least a couple of times a week. On the occasion of his visits, Lucia, forced to leave the guest alone with the Lady, despite her attempts to eavesdrop, was unable to solve the mystery.

She noticed that, after her confession, the Lady would concentrate in endless prayers.

What grave sins had she committed?

Costanza spent the summer without ever leaving the disquieting darkness of her little room, and without receiving anyone but the Domino, Rosa and, much more rarely, Bonzio.

In September Lucia noticed it. She was pouring jugs of warm, scented water into the tub. Costanza, very modest, tried to protect the provocative shapes even from Lucia's innocent looks. However, one could not take a bath without undressing, and the maid glimpsed her profile against the pale light from the small window. A lady usually had plenty to eat, but Costanza had never been too plump, she had little appetite and sometimes sent the almost untouched meal back to the kitchen. Her odd belly and swollen breasts were those of a pregnant woman.

"She is pregnant!" thought Lucia stifling an exclamation.

Finally, after so many long and sad days spent in the dark and gloomy room of the Lady, Lucia obtained the coveted permission to go and visit her loved ones at the Villa of Combarbio from Rosa. At sixteen, the girl was of the right age to get married, but Bertino, her father, had warned her, «I've found you an excellent job, and you don't realize how lucky you are. With a husband, you would have been a servant, in a servant's house, to keep the family going, help in the fields, tend the animals and bring a crowd of children into the world. Instead...»

His father's gaze had been more eloquent than her words.

Lucia, however, had not resigned herself to a life of spinsterhood, and she longed for what was natural for a woman her age: love and offspring.

Mina, her favorite sister, was married to Brizio of Sant'Arduino. The husband was a young bull, the eldest son of a farmer who would bequeath the sharecropping contract of his farm. They hadn't had any children yet, even though they had consummated abundantly. Lucia, who knew little or nothing about weddings and related practices, a couple of weeks after her ceremony had made her sister confide in great detail all about that unknown and arousing matter.

Although the two girls were very close, after Mina's wedding, there were few opportunities to meet.

Both brunettes, with curly hair and big eyes, Mina was more rustic and shapely, while Lucia had learned gentle manners at the castle.

One Sunday morning at the end of September, Lucia went down to Combarbio.

«Let's hope that Mina's there», she thought.

Her fate wanted that her sister and brother-in-law be at the Villa, at Bertino's house. Setting out at the first light of dawn, they had walked briskly along the paths on the ridge. The journey was long, and they would have stopped in Combarbio just for a quick lunch.

Despite the pork stew and stale bread, it was a great feast.

As soon as possible, the two girls withdrew to their hideout. Along the path that bordered the farm, the trunk of an ancient oak had divided into four branches, which spread to form the foliage.

Careful not to trip over their skirts, they climbed barefoot to reach the nest hidden in the fronds. With legs astride, facing each other, they leaned back against the branches curving toward the sky.

Mina couldn't wait to tell her, «I'm expecting a child. It's almost sure.»

After a year of vain attempts, this was an important news.

«Oh yes? How beautiful!» Lucia congratulated.

Mina looked around her, and when she was sure there

was no one on the path, she lifted her robe to reveal herself. Among the luxuriant curves of the young bride, a slight swelling was barely noticeable.

«It doesn't look like...» Lucia doubted.

«I'm sure! Try touching.»

«Why, is it already moving?»

She placed a hand gently on her sister's belly. She didn't feel anything, but she convinced herself and scolded her, «How could you climb, in your condition? You have to be careful, take care and don't exert yourself. You were both fools to come to Combarbio...»

Mina snorted, «You too, are now giving me orders?»

Lucia became curious, «Why, is there someone else, besides your husband, who commands you?»

Annoyed, Mina grumbled her concern, «Since he learned that I'm pregnant, Domino Gaddo prevents my Brizio from doing his duty! He says it's a sin.»

Lucia consoled her, «Think of me, I've never done it and maybe I never will.»

She wanted to know about when and how she had conceived. Mina didn't need to be asked and, happy to be envied, she enjoyed magnifying the reality.

The chatter between the sisters was an overflowing river.

Mina told of the soldiers encamped at Sant'Arduino and how Brizio was worried about the men who buzzed around the women of the town.

Then, finally, she revealed the mystery.

«It seems that there has been a revolt in Pietrarubbia, that the Counts are dead, and that the castle is at the mercy of the Malatestas. There are rumors that Corrado's wife survived, and that they are keeping her in prison to find out if she is pregnant...»

Mina caught the flash in Lucia's eyes.

«You know...?»

It was useless to pretend! Lucia tried to brush it aside but, after taking a solemn oath to keep her secret, she admitted,

«The Countess is in San Lorenzo.»

Mina pressed her with a thousand questions, but, in her eagerness to know, she neglected the most important of hers. Mina did not ask if Costanza was pregnant, and Lucia, willingly, did not say so. So, at least in part, she had kept the secret.

The girls were late, and Brizio scolded his wife: «The days are short and, because of you, now we'll have to hurry!»

Lucia gave her sister an angry look. How could she, in her condition, expose herself to the risk of a long walk?

Mina laughed in amusement.

«You're a fool! Brizio walks, but I travel on the back of a mule!»

At the end of October Costanza's belly was evident, and Rosa reprimanded the girl face to face to prevent leaks of information.

«As you could not have failed to notice, the lady is pregnant, and you will have to adopt the considerations due to a woman in her state, sweetness and calm. Don't forget, make sure she doesn't give in to melancholy, and don't tell anyone about her pregnancy.»

With Costanza in a state of deep depression, Rosa feared a desperate gesture. Domino Ubertino, who harbored the same suspicion, paid a visit to the Countess's castle almost every day. A little embarrassing, the visits ended with a long string of prayers. Faith was the only comfort for Costanza, who lived in anguish over the fate of her unborn child. One November afternoon, after a long spiel in Latin, she asked softly, «Domino, what about my baby?»

The parish priest had been waiting for the question for some time. He assumed a burdensome and at the same time merciful commitment.

«Madam, I guarantee your freedom and that your child will be entrusted to the loving care of the Church.»

A smile lit up Costanza's face. She could believe him or,

perhaps, she was deluding herself. No one would have dared to touch her child.

The next day, the Domino visited her with Dionigi. The boy had been well prepared.

«Be polite and kind, don't shout and speak only if you are being questioned!»

When the parish priest entered, Costanza realized that, against the rule of morality, he was not with Rosa.

A dark curly head peeked out behind the door jamb. Costanza's eyes, long accustomed to the semi-darkness of the prison, saw the boy. Without shame or modesty, after a few moments he was standing in front of her and staring at her curiously.

The Countess held out her arms. Dionigi raised his eyes to the Domino to ask permission, and the parish priest encouraged him by stroking the back of his neck. Overcoming the uncertainty, the boy embraced the beautiful lady.

Constance squeezed him. «Roberto...» she whispered in her ear. Then, finally, she wept bitterly, as she never she had since the death of her son.

Dionigi didn't shy away, and in that sea of tears he found the memory of his distant mother.

From that day on, Domino Ubertino went to see the Countess only if accompanied by the child.

Sometimes, after having entrusted him to the loving care of Rosa and Costanza, he left him at the castle for the night.

Bonzio received him in the great hall. His face drawn, he looked Gasparino straight in the eyes. The little man, embarrassed by the clear and penetrating gaze, tried to imagine the reason for the interview. He consoled himself with the thought that he had done nothing wrong, and that his conscience was clear. When he saw domino Ubertino enter, he began to fear a delicate issue, which concerned the church and the duties of a good Christian. A shiver ran down his spine when he suspected the worst, that the devil was involved and that some woman from Combarbio had been accused of prostitution or witchcraft. The pastor began with the same tone with which he used to pray in church.

«Son, do you know the commandments that we all must abide by in order to deserve the Kingdom of Heaven?»

Gasparino would have imagined anything, except a sermon. He mentally went over the list of sins for which he had asked God's forgiveness. They were many, and some were indelible in his conscience. But what did the priest want from him?

«Domino, I'm a soldier, and my sword is at the service of God and my Master» he justified weakly.

«Have you ever used violence and killed the innocent?» insisted the implacable parish priest.

Gasparino collapsed on his knees and, in a panic, moaned, «Believe me, Domino, I fought in Piega without inflicting violence on women and children. Not me, but other soldiers raped and killed. Those from Piega were all my relatives.»

Gasparino cried. It wasn't his sin! If he could, he would have sided with the people of Piega, and would have defended the poor people, until his death, alongside Tignaccio. He felt very guilty for not doing it.

The parish priest hissed, «*Non occides*!»

It was not a commandment, but an intimidation.

«In Pietrarubbia, you murdered a boy!» he shouted.

The words shook Gasparino even more. The poor man had let Moretto kill little Roberto, and his remorse for having given in to his cousin's pressure gave him no peace. That was right, and they had done well to kill all the Pietrarubbians, cursed race, but a child is still a child. Killing an innocent person was not only a mortal sin, but also brought misfortune. It was the worst that could happen to him. Bad luck in life and hell in death.

He complained, moaning, «I tried to save the boy, but Moretto didn't want to hear it. Forgive me, Domino!»

«You must ask forgiveness not from me, but from his mother and Domineddio!»

The sentence threw Gasparino into despair. In any case... as distressed and aware of the gravity of the sin, he found a moment of clarity. The whole thing was bizarre to say the least, and he guessed that he must be up to something. What did they want of him?

Bonzio broke the pause, «And if you had the opportunity to redeem yourself?»

The parish priest could threaten eternal damnation of the soul, and the master could condemn him to corporal punishment. He was in their hands. Gasparino steeled himself and timidly offered his services, «What can I do to be forgiven?»

The presbyter, still in doubt, looked at the vassal. Was he to be trusted? Bonzio nodded, and Domino Ubertino decided, «To expiate the guilt you will have to protect the seed of your enemy!»

The man was simple, and his mind darkened by the fear of God's punishment and fear of his Master. It took him a few moments to understand the meaning. Costanza was pregnant! In amazement, he raised his head, and stared first at the Domino and then at Bonzio. Gasparino was kneeling on the bare stone, the parish priest standing beside him, and the vassal, seated high on the bench, dominated both.

«No one will ever know, and you will be responsible for the safety of Donna Costanza and her son,» thundered Bonzio.

The order did not admit replies.

When Gasparino left, the Domino commented, «I knew it. He is a good man, God-fearing, and with an innocent soul. Even if imprisoned in the body of a soldier.»

EPILOGUE

Having escaped the tragic fate of his family, Taddeo of Pietrarubbia, in command of a small army, tried to survive at the service of the powerful and depended on where the strongest wind was blowing. He fought first for the Guelph Malatestas, and then betrayed by passing over to the Ghibellines.

On 25 September 1299, he fell into a trap, and was captured by the Gaboardi of Macerata Feltria, Guelphs and faithful allies of the Malatestas.

Imprisoned in the palace of the podestà, after being cruelly tortured, he was killed.

De morte comitis Thaddaei. Millesimo CCXCIX die XXV Septembris ... filius Gaboardi de Macerata cepit, et in prisonm posuit comitem Thaddaeum Novelli de Petra-Rubea. Tandem paucis diebus finitis praedictum Thaddaeum comitem in prison crudeliter occidit.

He left two sons, Malatesta and Taddeo, who worked hard, fighting for the various Lords of central Italy, to regain possession of some of the ancient family assets. It is known that wars cost dearly and, to maintain their small army, the two brothers took on debt. Thus, little by little, they were forced to sell off all of their properties. With them the ancient and noble lineage of the Montefeltro of Pietrarubbia died out.

Gasparino continued to serve in San Lorenzo until the end of his days. He died the best death, and most unusual for a soldier. They found him in his bed, at just over sixty years old, one morning in September. The previous evening he had feasted, in a frenzy of salted wild pig meat and jugs of wine, in the company of young fellow soldiers. The memory of him remained, handed down for generations in San Lorenzo, as an example of a good, honest man, faithful to his duty and very faithful to his Masters.

Rosa remained a spinster and, like a good older sister, devoted herself to the care of her two new and very young brothers. Old, wrinkled and white-haired, she spent endless afternoons in the kitchen, in front of the fireplace, telling her grandchildren about the adventures of the vassals of Mount San Lorenzo. She died in her sleep in her grandfather Marino's old chair.

The lineage of Bonzio and Lucia prospered, and the descendants, at the beginning of the 19th century, were still owners, in the valley *della Conca,* of the land that belonged to the ancient Countship of Pietrarubbia.

But that is another story…

ACKNOWLEDGEMENTS

I would like to thank my friend Luciano Alberelli for his invaluable advice and for the information taken from his essay *Castelli Scomparsi della Valconca* (La Pieve Poligrafica Editore).

For the advice and help received, I can't help but remember all the friends from the *Forum Italiano della Commissione Internazionale per lo Studio degli Ordini Cavallereschi dell'Istituto Araldico Genealogico Italiano e di Famiglie Storiche d'Italia* and, above all, Guido Buldrini, Sergio De Mitri Valier, Pierluigi Carnesecchi, Vincenzo Delehaye and Luca Barducci.

And finally, special thanks to Professor Franco Benucci, for his wise suggestions, at the *Dipartimento di Scienze Storiche, Geografiche e dell'Antichità dell'Università degli Studi di Padova.*

Index

www.ingramcontent.com/pod-product-compliance
Ingram Content Group UK Ltd.
Pitfield, Milton Keynes, MK11 3LW, UK
UKHW041630190726
13854UKWH00006B/2406